**Praise for the Grayson Series**
**by Tracy Anne Warren**

"Few things are more fun than an enemies-to-lovers romance, and Warren delivers. . . . [She] pulls out all the stops. A truly satisfying romance."
—*The New York Times Book Review*

"Zippy yet soulful . . . deeply relatable characters and strong writing."
—*Publishers Weekly*

"A strong start to Warren's steamy new series. Will leave readers wanting . . . more."
—*Booklist*

"The feel of a fast-paced comedy made in the forties. Well written [and] witty."
—Cocktails and Books

"Well-done."
—*RT Book Reviews*

"This was such a good story. A great combination of romance [and] sex with a really good plot and characters. It was one fun read."
—Bitten By Love

Also by Tracy Anne Warren

THE GRAYSON SERIES
*The Last Man on Earth*
*The Man Plan*

THE RAKES OF CAVENDISH SQUARE
*The Bedding Proposal*

THE PRINCESS BRIDES ROMANCES
*The Princess and the Peer*
*Her Highness and the Highlander*
*The Trouble with Princesses*

TRACY ANNE WARREN

# MAD ABOUT THE MAN

SIGNET SELECT
Published by New American Library,
an imprint of Penguin Random House LLC
375 Hudson Street, New York, New York 10014

This book is an original publication of New American Library.

First Printing, October 2015



For more information about Penguin Random House, visit penguin.com.

ISBN 978-0-451-46615-0

Printed in the United States of America
10 9 8 7 6 5 4 3 2 1

# Chapter One

"Now, remember, we're here in the Hamptons for a weekend of fun, sports, and relaxation," Barrett S. Collingsworth IV said in a tone that was as smugly patronizing as his name.

*Fun, huh?* Brie Grayson wasn't going to hold her breath on that one.

Tapping the edge of her tennis racket against one trim calf, she gazed out over the refined grounds of the exclusive private club. The May air was a perfect seventy-two degrees, the sky a cloudless blue. From the courts around them came the quiet *thwack* of rackets hitting fuzzy yellow tennis balls and the low murmur of conversation mixed with an occasional grunt of frustration or shout of success.

Yet despite the undeniable benefit of spending the weekend in the Hamptons, this was a working weekend, whatever Barrett S. might say to the contrary. He wasn't called Ol' BS at the office for nothing.

It had taken her less than a day when she'd started at Marshall, McNeal and Prescott to figure out that Barrett was mostly full of crap—a sentiment shared by not only the associates but most of the partners as well. Still, for all his shortcomings, he wasn't as stupid as he looked or acted—he had earned his Juris Doctor from Harvard, after all, just as she had.

The most important thing to know about Barrett, though, was the fact that he was the nephew of one of the senior partners, and that he never hesitated to whine to his uncle about anyone or anything he didn't like. So, as irritating as Ol' BS was, she made a point of staying on his good side.

She supposed that was why she'd been flagged to come along with him for the weekend—though "punished" was probably a better description. She could have said no, but she had plans—upwardly mobile plans—and she wasn't about to screw up her fast track toward making junior partner. So if it meant putting up with Ol' BS for a couple of days, then put up she would. As for shutting up, well, she'd see how much of that she could stand.

At least the weather was truly beautiful, she reminded herself again, as were her surroundings. She tipped her fair-skinned, SPF-45-protected face up to the sunshine and drank in the rays, relishing a slight breeze that ruffled her stylishly cut, chin-length blond hair. Maybe if all went well that afternoon, she would have time for a quick dip in the pool when they got back to the hotel.

"Just play tennis and let me decide when it's time to talk business," Barrett said, interrupting her thoughts so he could continue the lecture he'd started hours ago on the drive out from Manhattan. "We've been trying to land Monroe for years, and we can't afford to let him slip away again."

She kept walking and held her tongue.

"He's a huge get." Barrett jabbed a stubby finger in

the air for emphasis. "In the past decade, he's built a line of luxury hotels here in the States and Canada that are second to none. Rumor has it he's about to go international. If we can convince him to come on board with us before he takes the business global, it'll be a massive coup. Might even earn me a promotion."

*Since I'm part of this deal, it had better earn me a promotion too.*

"And you really think playing a round of doubles with Monroe is going to change his mind?" she asked.

"The game is only a warm-up. The deal will happen afterward. Clients love attention and flattery. The trick is to get them good and relaxed. Then, when their guard's down, pounce like a tiger with a powerful business angle. *Wa-la*, deal done."

Brie kept her face as expressionless as possible, trying not to smirk at the idea of Barrett as a tiger. More like a house cat—some really annoying, overly pampered Persian maybe? Although the comparison was unkind to cats everywhere and Persians in particular.

No, Barrett might think he was James Bond smooth, but somehow she didn't believe a self-made entrepreneur like M. J. Monroe was going to be swayed by flattery and attention. If getting him to sign on the dotted line were that easy, he'd have put his Montblanc to paper a long time ago.

She tapped her racket against her leg again, the attorney in her demanding that she argue her point, however unwise. "But you said yourself that no one has been able to convince him to switch firms before, so why should he now? Surely he's already been buttered up lots of times before this."

He came to an abrupt halt and stared at her, a look of supreme arrogance on his knobby-chinned face. "Not by *me*, he hasn't. That's why Uncle Wendell sent in his big gun this time. Monroe just needs the right man to explain to him what the firm can do. Our billables alone are enough to impress even the most hardened businessmen. To say nothing of our client roster and winning track record when it comes to settlements and litigations."

*Big gun, huh?*

Brie sniffed in time to cover a snort. Not that Barrett was mistaken about the power and prestige of Marshall McNeal Prescott and what it could offer. Indisputably, MMP was one of New York City's top law firms—if not *the* top. But somehow she still didn't think that fact would sway Monroe. If he hadn't already been lured by the mystique of their one-percenter-heavy client list or their admittedly excellent reputation for winning lawsuits and making sure their clients didn't pay out a dime more than necessary for their legal transactions—except to the firm itself, of course—then he was looking for something else. Something more. Exactly what that something more might be was the key to acquiring his business.

"Besides," Barrett said, pausing only long enough to take a breath, "I went to a lot of trouble to arrange this match—"

"You mean *I* went to a lot of trouble, considering it's my sister's fiancé who has a membership here. And the fact that James is the one who very graciously accompanied us here today so we could use the amenities."

"Yes, but *I'm* the one who wrangled the court time with Monroe. I won't tell you what it cost me to bump the couple who was originally scheduled to play."

Brie managed not to roll her eyes. "I still don't see why we couldn't have just met Monroe in an office like normal people rather than resorting to all these schemes."

"Because we're not normal people. We're lawyers."

She paused, realizing that for once Ol' BS had a really good point.

Then they were courtside, the court number painted in a neat white on the carefully maintained grass.

*Showtime!*

She put on her best professional smile and followed after Barrett, only to stop dead seconds later. A shiver went through her as she stared at the man standing across the court, his head bent as he listened to whatever his curvy brunette partner was saying.

He was tall and athletically built without being overly muscled, solid without an extra ounce of fat. She guessed he was close to her own thirty-three years and in his prime. His dark brown hair was short and neatly trimmed but not in a big-city, five-hundred-dollars-a-cut kind of way. His tennis clothes were the same: good quality but not obscenely expensive.

Brie scowled, her heart racing beneath her crisp white Burberry Brit sports shirt. She gave herself a quick shake and looked away. With her eyes on her white sneakers, she trailed Barrett over to the bench that lined one side of the court and set down her bag.

*What is wrong with me? I've never met M. J. Monroe before, so why the freaky reaction?*

She'd taken a quick look at an Internet photo of him when she'd done her prep work for the weekend and it hadn't sparked any unusual reactions. He'd seemed pleasant-looking enough in a business-hardened, square-jawed kind of way, but he hadn't made her senses go on full alert, as if there'd been a breach in security at the Pentagon. But her instincts were blaring like screaming sirens now, warning her that there was something alarming about him—and something oddly familiar.

How could that be, since she didn't even know the man?

Maybe she was dehydrated and her sudden anxiety had nothing to do with Monroe at all. She just needed to drink some water and rebalance her electrolytes, even though she'd felt fine two minutes ago.

Glad for a distraction—any distraction—she pulled a bottle of water out of her gear bag, unscrewed the top, and took a long drink. From the corner of her eye, she saw Barrett lope his way over to Monroe and his companion and introduce himself with far too much enthusiasm. She stayed where she was, careful not to turn. Extra careful not to look again.

*Another minute and I will be calm, cool, and collected,* she assured herself, *all hints of weirdness gone.*

She smiled inwardly, well aware that being "weird" was the last thing anyone would ever accuse her of. Serious and intense with workaholic tendencies that her mother worried would drive her into an early grave—those were qualities usually ascribed to her. Not flaky and certainly never weird.

She took one last pull from the bottle, then sealed it and stowed it away. Picking up her racket, she turned, sure she had herself under control once more. She pasted her professional smile back on her face and strode confidently forward.

"Here she comes now," Barrett said with a toothy, well-oiled grin. "M.J.—I hope I can call you M.J.?—and Lila, his most exquisite doubles partner"—Lila the exquisite gave a throaty laugh—"let me introduce my partner of the courts—tennis courts, that is." Barrett waved a hand toward her with a flourish. "Ms. Brie Grayson."

Monroe's head turned and he looked straight at her. But instead of a handshake and a hello, he stared, running his eyes slowly over her, head to toe.

Her inner alarm shrieked again, the weirdness crawling back over her skin. She was too good a litigator, though—and Texas Hold'em player—to let any hint of reaction show on her face.

But inside . . .

She shivered.

His eyes were dark, the brown of rich teak. Under other circumstances, she might have thought them beautiful. Instead, all she could see was their shrewdness, their keen calculation and sharp understanding. It was as if he knew the punch line to some joke she hadn't heard. And if there was one thing she hated, it was realizing that someone else knew something she didn't.

Suddenly, he grinned. And not just any grin but one that was wide and shit-eating.

She was still considering that peculiar turn of events when he spoke, his voice deep and smooth. "Why, if it isn't the creamy little cheese herself. How many years has it been, Brie-Brie?"

Her mouth fell open, her mind racing backward to her childhood.

*No, it isn't possible! It cannot be him.*

She looked closer, comparing her memory of the hateful boy she'd known in junior high school with the sophisticated man who now stood before her.

*Christ Almighty, it is him!*

How could she not have seen? How could she not have known that M. J. Monroe and Maddox Monroe were one and the same? No wonder her body had been sending out warning signals. It was a miracle she hadn't broken out in hives.

Yet here he was, live and in person, her worst nightmare come back to life—the bully who'd turned seventh grade into a slice of pure hell!

* * *

Maddox stared at Brie Grayson, unable to look away.

Of all the people he'd expected to run into here at the club, it wasn't the girl who'd starred in every one of his immature, twelve-year-old male fantasies for an entire school year—and a long while after that, if he was being strictly honest.

Back in those days, he'd thought she was the cutest girl he'd ever seen.

She'd thought he was a pig.

And he probably had been; adolescent boys weren't much known for their tact or thoughtfulness.

Of course he'd noticed her the moment she'd walked onto the tennis court—how could he not have with her head of sun-bright blond hair, her gorgeous long legs, and a tight little ass that practically begged to be squeezed through her short white tennis skirt?

When she'd been a girl, he'd thought she was adorable.

But as a woman full-grown, she was a real knockout.

Still one thing that apparently hadn't changed over the years was her reaction to him. Judging by her narrow-eyed glare, she hated him every bit as much now as she had in the seventh grade. Although he supposed he was partly to blame, aware he shouldn't have renewed their acquaintance by baiting her the way he had.

Then again, that had always been the problem—she brought out the very devil in him. He hadn't been able to control his reaction to her when he was twelve, and it would appear he couldn't control it any better as a grown man.

He hid a smile, certain the afternoon was going to be a whole lot more entertaining than he'd imagined.

Brie's blowhard tennis partner looked back and forth

between him and Brie, a frown of confusion on his pale brow.

*Boyfriend?* Maddox wondered. He eyed Brie again, speculating. Surely she had better taste than to hook up with Barrett whatever-his-name-was. But you never knew with women. Taste could definitely be a subjective thing when it came to relationships.

Barrett, the blowhard, frowned harder. "So, do you two know each other?" he asked.

"No!" Brie shot back.

"Yes," Maddox said at the same moment, meeting her eyes with amused contradiction.

She stared back, her body bristling with tension and challenge.

Barrett's gaze swiveled back and forth between them again, his confusion even plainer. "Well, which is it?"

"Yes," said Lila, a tart tone in her voice. "Do you know each other or not?"

His date, who he'd forgotten was even there, crossed her arms over her chest and waited.

Maddox met Brie's gaze again and arched a single eyebrow.

"We do," Brie admitted reluctantly, "but it was a *long* time ago. I didn't even recognize him."

"I recognized *you*," Maddox said, not breaking eye contact. "Even in junior high you were the sort who was impossible to forget."

Brie scowled, her fist tightening around the handle of her racket as if she was considering using it—on him.

He nearly laughed.

His date humphed and picked up her own racket. "So are we going to play or not? We're wasting court time."

Maddox nodded without looking away from Brie.

"You're right—we should start. Would you like to serve first?" he asked Brie.

She tapped her racket edge against the palm of her hand and looked back with a barely hidden sneer. "You betcha, Monroe. Game on!"

Grinning, he moved to his side of the court.

# CHAPTER TWO

Twenty minutes later, Brie bounced the tennis ball twice on the court, caught and held it in her hand for a moment, then bounced it twice more. Studying the opposite side of the court again—the enemy court—she lined up her serve, tossed the ball high in the air, then powered through with the serve.

Her arm muscles hummed from the exertion. Her heart sang with barely suppressed glee as the ball smacked hard into the court exactly where she'd aimed it—less than an inch from Maddox Monroe.

He jogged back but couldn't set up the shot, her serve having so much topspin that it was impossible to return.

Looking across the net at her, he inclined his head.

Point to Brie.

She showed her teeth in a wide smile and bounced a fresh ball.

"What in the hell do you think you're doing?" Barrett demanded on a low hiss, sidling over from his quarter of the court.

She bounced the ball again, mildly annoyed that he'd

broken her concentration. "Serving. What does it look like?"

"Like you're trying to screw up this deal, that's what." His eyes wheeled, his usually tidy hair standing up in unlikely tufts from where he'd been yanking on it in between plays. "Whatever this is going on between you and Monroe, stop it now. We're supposed to be playing doubles, not settling some old personal vendetta of yours."

"I'm just playing the game," she defended.

"No, you're not. You're out for blood. If that racket was a gun, the court would be a crime scene by now. As for 'just playing,' you'd think you and Monroe were in a singles match for all the time you let Lila and me have a go. I don't like being made to look a fool and from the look on her face, she doesn't either."

Brie glanced across at Monroe's date and the woman's sour, thundercloud expression, pout included.

If looks could kill . . .

Still, what was she supposed to do? Just play nice with that arrogant bastard?

From the opening serve, she and Monroe had gone at each other with a vengeance. He was a good player, but so was she—collegiate women's singles champion in her division three years running. The pair of them had left their partners in the dust while they concentrated on beating each other. She'd known Barrett was going nuts as the game progressed, but she hadn't cared. All she wanted was to beat Monroe and wipe the superior smile off his face.

"Whatever he did," Barrett continued in a low hiss, "it's ancient history. You were kids last time you met, so be an adult and let it go. Or do you want revenge so much you're willing to toss away his millions and all the business that comes with them?"

"Chances are practically nil he'll come over to the firm, whatever I do," she hissed back.

"Well, he one hundred percent sure as hell won't if you keep this up. So back off and start losing. Pronto."

Brie ground her teeth and bounced the ball again. Irritating though it might be, she supposed Barrett had a point. Whatever her opinion of Monroe, it had no place interfering with business. They'd come here to sign Monroe and it was her job to help, not hinder, that objective.

Besides, even if Barrett did manage to convince Monroe to come on board, it wasn't as if she would have any face-to-face contact with him. One of the partners would want to handle his account. The most she might see of Monroe would be his name on legal briefs and documents that got dropped on her desk.

And seventh grade had been a long time ago.

So why did it still feel like yesterday?

*Shake it off,* she told herself. *He wasn't worth it then. He's not worth it now.*

"Hey, Grayson, you ever gonna serve?" Monroe called. "Or do you need a little breeze under your skirt to get you moving?"

*Breeze under my skirt . . .*

Fury flashed wildfire hot in her veins, her fingers clutched around the ball and the racket handle so hard it was a wonder they didn't explode and splinter. She'd had good intentions, but suddenly they disappeared.

"You want a serve?" she yelled back. "Here's your serve."

Tossing the ball high in the air, she brought the racket up and through, aiming straight at Monroe.

"Hey, Brie, I saw the commotion. What's going on?"

With her arms crossed over her chest, Brie turned to

look at her future brother-in-law, James Jordan, as he came to a halt beside her. She stood on the side of the tennis court closest to the gate, wishing she could bolt. But she supposed that would make her look a bit too much like a fleeing fugitive.

"There was an . . . incident," she said.

James arched one blond eyebrow. "What sort of incident? Is someone hurt?"

A physician, who had happened to be playing one court over, and a pair of security guards were huddled around a figure on the ground. A small crowd of curious onlookers was gathered as well.

Right after the "incident," Brie had sidelined herself from the action. Barrett and Lila had remained part of the fray and were even now watching over the doctor's shoulder as he tended to Monroe.

As for Monroe . . .

She cleared her throat. "I was serving and—"

"And?"

She still remembered the odd, almost wet *thwap* the ball had made when it found its target, along with the harsh grunt of pain from Monroe. His racket had clattered onto the court seconds before he'd reached a hand up to cover his injured cheek.

Just the memory made her cringe.

"Well, the ball hit kind of high," she continued, "and walloped Maddox Monroe in the face."

James gave a soft whistle. "Ouch. People don't think of tennis as a dangerous game, but put somebody in the way of a whizzing ball and smack. Looks like he's getting medical attention, though, so chances are good everything will be okay." Reaching out, he patted her shoulder consolingly. "Don't be too hard on yourself. It was an accident. Accidents happen."

Accidents did happen, only she wasn't sure this one qualified. The ball had hit where she'd aimed; she just hadn't expected it to be quite so dead-on accurate. She'd wanted to shut him up, not maim him.

She cringed again, guilt snapping at her like a sharp-toothed little terrier.

"See, he's fine," James said a moment later. "He's on his feet and ready to walk off the court under his own steam."

On a trajectory that would take him right past her.

She nearly bolted again. Instead, she stepped back and waited while Monroe and his small entourage made their way forward. Chin up, she held her ground despite wishing it would open up and swallow her first.

". . . you are not to worry in any way, Mr. Monroe," Barrett was saying in a rush, his words dripping with whining apology. "My firm will absorb the cost. It will be our pleasure—nay, our duty—to take care of everything, down to the smallest detail. If there is anything we can do, anything at all, you have only to mention it and it will be taken care of immediately."

"Come along, pookie," Lila said, one slim, tanned arm wound around Monroe's waist.

*Pookie?*

There was blood on his once clean white shirt and he was holding an ice pack up to his face.

"We'll drive straight to the hospital," Lila continued. "The doctor says you need X-rays to check for a fractured cheekbone. I still wish you'd let me call 911. What if you have a brain bleed?"

"I don't have a brain bleed, so stop worrying," Monroe said. "I'm fine."

"You are *not* fine. Your eye—"

"Is also fine. I'm just going to have one hell of a shiner, that's all."

"But—"

"But nothing. If I had my way, I'd go home. But we'll stop at the hospital first so you can quit being concerned."

Suddenly they drew abreast of Brie, pausing when they stood only an arm's length away.

Lila's eyes met hers and she bristled, practically hissing.

Brie paid her little attention, though, her own gaze fixed squarely on Maddox Monroe. Even with the ice pack in the way, she could tell that his face was swollen and discolored. As for his eye, the area around it was turning a shocking purple-black. His pupils were equal and his irises the same rich brown as before—and the expression in them as sharp and lucid as the man himself.

He stared back. "Nice shot, Grayson. Rain check on a rematch."

Then he continued past, Lila tossing her another furious glare before they exited the court. Barrett hurried after, wringing his hands in silent supplication.

Brie was about to leave as well, James with her, when Barrett suddenly stopped and spun around.

He jabbed a finger in her direction. "I have no doubt the partners will convene to discuss this disaster on Monday. Until then, you are not to come anywhere near Monroe. Is that understood?"

"Completely." It wouldn't be a hard promise to keep, since she wanted to see Maddox Monroe again about as much as she wanted to meet up with an angry skunk ready to lift tail and spray.

"You really shit the bed on this one," Barrett said. "I don't see how the firm is going to smooth things over—we'll be lucky if he doesn't sue—but I guess I have to try salvaging what I can. Pack your bags and go home,

Grayson. You've done enough damage for one weekend."

If he'd been a dragon, little puffs of smoke would have been coming out of Barrett's ears. Instead, he glared at her one last time, then moved away at a near run, presumably hoping there was still time to catch up to Monroe and his lady friend before they drove away from the country club.

For a long moment, she and James stood motionless, play from the nearby courts the only sound.

Then he slung a brotherly arm over her shoulders. "Let's go find Ivy and get a drink. You look like you could use one."

"Or five," she said, trying to keep the sharp edges of panic from taking hold.

James laughed. "Five, it is. You can tell us all about it. Or if you'd rather not, you and Ivy can talk wedding details."

She shot him a look. "That is not cheering me up."

He laughed again and tugged her after him.

An hour later, Brie sipped a glass of dry Riesling and leaned deeper into the comfortable cushions on James's sofa. She gazed around, marveling as she always did at the restrained sophistication of what James euphemistically referred to as the Cottage.

It was actually a spacious five-bedroom, three-bath house set on the beach in one of the nicest neighborhoods in the Hamptons. But considering the size of some of the multimillion-dollar mansions nearby, she supposed "cottage" was as good a description as anything.

The colors were a soothing mix of ocean hues—blues, greens, and grays—the atmosphere relaxed and comfortable, thanks in large part to Ivy, who had been steadily adding new pieces of furniture to the house as well as interesting works of art created by her own hand and by other artists.

Ivy loved to come here to paint and relax. In fact, since her engagement to James, she had been on a campaign to get him to spend his weekends unwinding rather than working. She'd even talked him into doing a digital detox routine on Saturdays and Sundays. He grumbled on occasion about being "cut off from humanity," but anyone who'd known James as long as Brie had could see how incredibly happy he was.

Her youngest sister snuggled against James on the sofa opposite, feet bare, her legs tucked up under her while she sipped on her own glass of wine.

Ivy was legal now, having turned twenty-two this past March. Some might say she was too young to get married and that James, at thirty-seven, was too old for her, but anyone who knew Ivy realized what an old soul she was and that she and James were a perfect match. Ivy was twenty-two going on forty, so for all intents and purposes she out-aged him by a couple of years.

"I'm so glad you decided to check out of your hotel and stay with us instead," Ivy said. "You should have planned on that from the start."

Brie swirled the wine in her glass and took another drink. "Yeah, well, I would have if I'd known what a clusterfuck this trip was going to turn into. I'll be lucky if I still have a job come Monday. Maybe I should spend the weekend polishing my résumé."

"Come on, you're blowing this way out of proportion," Ivy pointed out. "So you had an accident while you were playing tennis. Accidents happen. They're not going to fire you for that."

True, except for the fact that she'd let her temper get

out of control and aimed a tennis ball directly at Maddox Monroe's annoying, overstuffed head. Second-degree premeditation at the very least.

"No, they're going to fire me for single-handedly making sure that Monroe takes his business anywhere other than Marshall McNeal Prescott." She gave herself a swift mental kick, scolding herself again for letting him get under her skin. Then again, that had always been his one special talent—doing things that made her want to strangle him.

"Barrett's probably drained his cell battery twice calling everyone to tell them what happened, especially his uncle." Brie emptied her glass and held it out for more.

Silently, James poured.

"I'll be shocked if security doesn't meet me in the lobby Monday morning and hand my personal items to me in a box." Brie sighed.

"So explain what happened," James said in an encouraging tone. "You're an excellent litigator. Make your case."

*Make my case. Yeah, right.*

If this were only a court case, it might be easy. After all, the law didn't rely on guilt or innocence but on presenting the facts and making them work to one's own legal advantage.

What facts did she have?

1. Junior high bully reappears like some demon from a bad horror movie—or maybe like one of those sexy vampires, since even she had to admit he was damned fine-looking. Good outside. Bad inside.
2. Bully does what bully always does and is mean to her.

3. Courageous woman takes offense.
4. Courageous woman clocks bully with a hard serve to the face.

Game. Set. Match.

Sighing again, she sipped her wine.

If only he hadn't made that crack about needing a little breeze up her skirt, she might have withstood his baiting. But of all the things he could have said, that was the one guaranteed to light a fire, the one for which there was no forgiving.

Even now, twenty-one years later, she could still remember how it had felt. . . .

*The school bell rang, signaling the end of first-period lunch and the beginning of second. Books were slapped shut, papers rustled, backpacks were zipped, and the metallic chime of lockers being opened, then slammed closed again, echoed through the corridors. A cacophony of teenage voices ebbed and flowed, punctuated by shouts, squeaking sneakers, and Doc Martens, while somewhere within earshot, the algebra teacher, Mr. Heneke, scolded a trio of boys for roughhousing in the hall.*

*Brie did her best to ignore the mayhem, quietly hugging the neat stack of books inside her arms as she made her way out of her favorite class—English—and down the hall to her locker. Her two best friends were absent today; Becca had stayed home with a cold and Jo—who despised her real name, Josephine—had left early for an orthodontist's appointment. Rather than eat by herself in the cafeteria, she'd decided to go outside and enjoy the clear fall day and a few minutes of quiet.*

*She slid her books into her backpack in the bottom of her locker, then grabbed her lunch and a dog-eared copy of Jane Austen's* Persuasion, *which she had neatly camou-*

*flaged inside a cover made from a brown paper grocery bag. She'd decorated it with flower and rainbow stickers and written her name inside a rectangle at the top that she'd outlined in bold red marker.*

*After snapping closed her combination lock and giving the dial a good spin, she tightened her plaid hair scrunchie around her long ponytail—the accessory carefully chosen that morning to go with her blue plaid skirt and tan cardigan—and headed for the rear doors that led to a small area with trees and grass where students were permitted to sit during the lunch period. She pushed the metal hand bar. It gave a springy thunk as she let go and walked out the door.*

*Seventh and eighth graders were grouped in loose clusters, mostly self-segregated by age and gender except for a few couples who walked or sat, hip to hip, hand in hand, while they talked and laughed. One couple was coiled around each other like eels, exchanging long, slow kisses that looked like a warm-up for a porno.*

*Brie stared for a moment, then walked past. She didn't have a boyfriend. Not that she wouldn't like one, but all the boys in her classes were such immature idiots, too busy playing Tetris on their Game Boys, tossing Koosh Balls, and cracking stupid jokes to interest her.*

*The worst of the bunch was Maddox Monroe, who was in her homeroom and third-period science class. Long and lanky, with thick dark hair that he always wore too long, he spent his time doodling, passing notes to his friends, and making faces at her when the teacher wasn't looking. He stared at her too sometimes and seemed to take the most hateful pleasure in tormenting her, such as the time they'd been segmenting earthworms and he'd slipped up behind her and silently draped one over her shoulder. She could still remember her ear-piercing screams and the way the other kids had laughed as she'd frantically batted the formaldehyde-soaked annelid off her sweater. Maddox had been reprimanded by the teacher for the stunt and made to apologize, which he'd done with a smirk on his face.*

*For the most part, though, he got away with murder. Most of the teachers liked him in spite of his casually attentive attitude in class, and even the few who didn't couldn't complain, since he got straight As on all his homework and tests. The students thought he was the height of cool, revering him for his confident style and clever pranks. Brie was definitely in the minority when it came to drinking the Maddox Monroe Kool-Aid and she made no effort to hide her dislike of him to anyone interested enough to listen. She couldn't even take pleasure in trashing him to Becca and Jo, since they thought he was "dreamy." To her disgust, she knew that either one of them would have gone out with him in a split second if only he'd asked.*

*He'd actually asked her out once, though thank God no one knew. It had been during the previous summer when they'd accidentally run into each other at the country club where his parents and hers were members. They'd been pushed together, since they were the same age and were going to be starting at the same junior high in a couple of months. He'd stared at her for a while, as he always did, then cracked some ignorant joke about whether her mother had gotten knocked up in France, since she was named after their national cheese. While she'd still been fuming from that, he'd given her his patented smirk and said they should go to a movie together sometime.*

*She'd said sure, they'd do that, next time she wanted to be seen in public with a jerk.*

*And that had been that.*

*Only it hadn't been, not with him in the same classes with her every single freaking day except weekends and holidays.*

*Head lowered with her book and lunch sack clasped against her small but developing bustline, she continued through the crowd, the green space and its illusion of privacy only a few yards beyond.*

*Off to the side, Maddox Monroe and a scrum of his rowdy friends were messing around with a leaf blower that they'd obviously liberated from one of the groundskeeping crew. They were pulsing it on and off, blowing at whatever happened to be in the way, leaves whipping up into the air in mini-tornadoes, girls screaming when the forced air blew their hair and notebooks.*

*The machine was in Maddox's hands and he was revving the motor when he turned and swept it upward in an arc—straight at her.*

*The blast hit her, a noisy gust of warm air swirling around her legs and under her clothes. Up flew her skirt, flaring high and wide so that her bare legs and panties were on display like a peep show. She'd worn her favorite Mickey Mouse underwear that morning, the big-eared mouse grinning at everyone from his place on her ass. Desperately, she tried to push her skirt back down to cover herself, but it was already too late.*

*Laughter erupted, jeers and catcalls being shouted out. From the corner of her eye she saw Maddox, who looked oddly horrified. The blower cut off. But then one of his friends said something and he laughed too.*

*"Hey, those are some nice panties, Mickey," he called.*

*And they all laughed again.*

*She ran, her lunch forgotten where she'd dropped it on the ground. Her face was hot and wet with tears, her chest aching with sobs she tried to hold down.*

*She hid in an empty classroom for the next half hour, then went to the school nurse and said she wasn't feeling well. Her mother came and took her home, but she didn't tell her what had happened. The humiliation went too deep to bear repeating.*

*Brie had disliked Maddox Monroe before; now she hated him, especially once the whole school started calling her Mickey. It had been the worst year of her academic life.*

She raised her glass of wine to her lips again and took another drink, shaking off the memories. She'd come a long way from the shy girl she'd been then, gaining self-confidence and much needed poise and popularity after she transferred to an elite private school the next year.

As for Monroe, today was the first time she'd seen him since that *annus horribilis*. She'd heard his family had moved away and he'd changed schools not long after she herself left. Where he'd gone or what he'd done, she hadn't cared. She'd moved on, making a success of her life, and apparently so had he.

But she was a grown woman now—a consummate professional who was more than capable of going up against even the toughest adversaries.

So why had she let him get to her?

Why had she felt again like that embarrassed twelve-year-old girl wanting revenge?

"You're right, James," she said, setting her glass onto the coffee table with a solid click. "I will make my case. We were playing a sport and people get injured playing sports sometimes. They'll just have to understand."

*And if they don't?*

Well, she'd regroup and go on. She'd remade her life years before and she could remake it again if she had to, no matter how hard it might be.

# CHAPTER THREE

For all her supposed optimism, Brie couldn't help the tangle of nerves in her stomach as she walked into work on Monday morning. The guards at the security desk in the lobby made no move to stop her from getting on the elevator, and a pair of gossiping second years, who'd arrived even earlier than she, did nothing more than offer passing good-mornings as they made their way into the break room for a first jolt of morning caffeine.

She'd actually started to relax as she worked quietly at her desk, the office filling up with its usual hivelike hum of people and activity, when her paralegal poked her head past the doorframe.

"Mr. Prescott wants to see you in his office," Trish said.

Brie jerked, her stomach clenching in a way that made her glad she'd skipped breakfast. "Now? But it's only seven thirty."

"Yeah. Right now. A couple of the other partners are in with him too. Something big must be going down to have them all in so early on a Monday."

Brie gave her a shallow smile.

*Me,* she thought. *I'm the one going down, straight to the bottom, just like the* Titanic.

For a second, she considered making a couple of emergency calls to people she knew who could help her land at a new firm. But Ol' BS and his uncle Wendell, aka Mr. Prescott, had already had the entire weekend to poison the well, so what would another few minutes matter?

No, she might as well go face the firing squad, then come back here to her office for one last look, collect the little pink African violet she kept on the windowsill, her few personal items and family photos, and be on her way.

She stood, then smoothed a crease out of her slim-fitting pewter gray pencil skirt, straightened her pale blue, long-sleeved silk blouse and gray suit jacket, and took a deep breath. Last, she put on her pleasant poker face—the one she wore in court when she had to appear before a particularly difficult judge. No matter what happened, she would show no fear.

Prescott's large corner office was at the end of a long central hallway. She felt a bit like a dead woman walking as she put one high-heel-clad foot in front of the other.

When she reached his open doorway, she stopped, took one last breath, then knocked quietly and went inside. "Mr. Prescott, you wanted to see me?"

Wendell Prescott looked up from where he sat behind his massive antique mahogany desk. Relaxing in a pair of wide brown leather armchairs were two of the other partners—Steven McNeal and Brice Burns, an up-and-comer who everyone assumed would be added to the masthead as soon as old Mr. Marshall finally stepped down. They turned their dark heads to look at her too.

Birds of prey gathered for the kill.

She gave no reaction, careful to keep a friendly, polite

half smile on her face as she waited for Prescott to lower the boom.

"Brie, yes, do come in." He motioned with a hand toward an empty chair. "Sit and let's talk."

She walked forward to do as he asked.

So, Prescott wanted to play up the moment, did he? Well, she supposed they needed to go through their dog and pony show—appearances to keep up and all that.

Rather than perch timidly on the edge of her chair, she settled back as if she had no anxiety whatsoever. Inside, her stomach felt like she'd swallowed a bagful of glass shards.

"I might as well get right to it," Prescott said, his thin gray eyebrows creasing over his cool gray eyes. "I understand there was an incident while you were in the Hamptons on firm business this weekend. Tennis injury to one of our prospective clients."

"Yes, sir, that's correct," she said.

"Barrett Collingsworth called to apprise me of the details. He was quite concerned about Mr. Monroe's health."

*And getting me fired.*

She thought about James's comment and her earlier decision to make her case, but she would wait until they had laid out all their evidence before offering her own counterargument.

"McNeal was at home yesterday when he got a call from Monroe himself."

She froze. Monroe had called McNeal at home? She'd known Monroe couldn't be happy about getting walloped in the face, but she hadn't thought he was angry enough to track one of the partners down on a Sunday just so he could complain about her.

*Looks like he was.*

"That's right," McNeal said, entering the conversation. "Monroe and I had a very interesting talk. He assures me his injury was treated and he's already on the mend. He also told me that he wants to move his business over to our firm."

"What?" Her eyes popped wide.

"My reaction exactly, especially under the circumstances. He's certainly never expressed any desire in the past to let us represent him, quite the opposite in fact. He does have one very specific stipulation, however, before he'll agree to become a client."

*Crap, here it comes.* She braced herself, waiting for the deathblow to fall.

"Monroe will only come on board if you are the one to personally handle all his legal work. What's more, he instructed me to make you a partner, since he doesn't deal with associates."

Her mouth fell open. Quickly, she shut it.

"So, what do you think, Brie?" Prescott said, his eyes, which had looked so hard before, gleaming with a shrewd twinkle. "Shall we accept Mr. Monroe's terms and make you a partner?"

She looked at the three men, who were all watching her expectantly. Her thoughts were in a whirl; she was barely able to believe she'd heard right. Not only was she *not* being fired, but apparently a promotion was hers for the taking. And not just any promotion, a move up to partner. It was everything she'd been working so hard to achieve, everything she had dreamed of, and happening only months after her return to the legal big leagues.

She opened her mouth, wanting to say yes, but she hesitated, remembering that she would have one person to thank and that was Maddox Monroe. If she accepted, she would be forever in his debt.

Clearly, he was up to something. What was his game? What did he really want, since he had plenty of excellent legal representation without hiring her?

Talk about a devil's bargain. She'd always suspected Monroe must actually be an alias for his real name—Mephistopheles. And yet how could she pass this up? It was the opportunity of a lifetime, one that might not come her way again for years, or maybe never. Still, a woman had her pride. . . .

"Ms. Grayson?" It was Brice Burns who spoke this time, a frown on his long, square face.

So what would it be? Tell Monroe to stuff it and turn down the job—and possibly risk losing her current position? Or accept, even if it meant having to work with a man she'd hated since junior high?

Personal integrity or pragmatism? It was a lawyer's perennial dilemma. Then again, everyone was entitled to fair legal representation, even Lucifer himself. When it came to pride vs. profit, billable hours won every time.

She straightened her shoulders and looked each man square in the eye. "Whether you make me a partner is up to you, gentlemen. But MJM Enterprises is a big fish that you've been trying to reel in for years. Do you really want to toss him and all his millions back now that he's almost in the net?"

A significant silence fell. Then Prescott grinned. The other two men quickly followed suit.

"No, Ms. Grayson," Prescott said. "No, we most certainly do not."

"We knew there must be a reason Monroe would go to all this trouble just to work with you," McNeal said.

"Other than the fact that you're damned easy on the eyes. No offense," Burns added.

"None taken," she said.

"My nephew thought Monroe would want you fired after what happened on the tennis court." Prescott's eyes twinkled again. "But apparently he must like your go-for-the-jugular style."

"A quality every good lawyer needs," Burns agreed.

McNeal nodded. "Exactly."

"I can assure you, gentlemen, that I won't let you down," she said.

"From now on, it's Monroe you don't want to let down. Just consider us very interested bystanders." Burns gave her a look that was part amusement, part warning.

She swallowed, understanding that accepting this partnership meant her entire career now hinged on keeping Maddox Monroe and his millions of dollars happy.

Prescott stood and extended his hand. "Welcome, Brie, and congratulations on becoming our newest equity partner."

Standing, Brie shook hands and sealed the deal.

*Holy shit, what in the hell have I just gotten myself into?*

# Chapter Four

Maddox Monroe peeled off the bandage and stared at himself in the bathroom mirror. Reaching up, he gave the bruised, swollen area around his eye and cheekbone a tentative poke.

*Fuck, that's sore.*

Hastily, he pulled his fingers away, resisting the urge to scowl, since that would just make it hurt more.

*Brie Grayson socked me good.*

But he'd had worse beatings over the years, and according to the doctors, there was no damage to either the cheekbone, the eye, the socket, or the surrounding bone, just a lot of swollen, contused flesh. He'd been offered painkillers, which he'd refused. Instead he'd applied warm and cold compresses, tossed back a small palmful of Motrin, and gone to bed. He'd also sent Lila on her way, since a man could stand only so much fussing before he lost his temper and said something he'd regret later.

On Saturday, he'd traveled back to New York City rather than spend the rest of the weekend in the Hamptons as originally planned. Over the rest of Saturday and

Sunday, he'd read through a few work reports, spent a couple of hours ridding the world of imaginary evildoers on his Xbox, and slept.

When he'd awakened to the buzz of his Monday morning alarm, he felt almost himself again. As for how he looked, getting back to resembling an urbane businessman rather than roughed-up brawler was going to take a while longer.

A shower and a cup of coffee later, he called down to the hotel kitchen for some breakfast. As owner, he could have anything he liked, anytime he liked—a genuine perk on mornings like this one.

He'd just taken a seat on the sofa and opened a news app on his iPad to scan the day's top stories when his cell phone rang. As he checked the caller ID, his hand tightened slightly. He hit "answer."

"McNeal," he said, not bothering with the niceties; he had too many other things to do today.

"Mr. Monroe, good morning. I hope this is a good time to talk. I know it's early yet." It was eight o'clock and apparently the McNeal part of Marshall, McNeal and Prescott didn't know how to take a hint concerning conversational brevity.

"The time is fine," Maddox said. "So, did you handle the matter we discussed?"

"Indeed, I did. That is, Mr. Prescott, Mr. Burns, and I met with Ms. Grayson first thing and presented your offer to her, exactly as you asked."

"Yes?" he said, trying to contain his impatience. "And?"

"And she accepted, of course."

Maddox's shoulder muscles abruptly relaxed. Even as juicy as the bait he'd told them to dangle in front of Brie might have been, he still hadn't been entirely certain she would take it. There was a willful pride in Brie Grayson that had been part of her as a girl and was clearly still part of her as a woman. He'd half expected to hear that she'd turned them down and sent the message via grapevine that he could go fuck himself.

But ambition had a way of convincing even the most principled of people to lay aside their scruples. Then again, there was the simple pragmatism of the situation. She was smart. Smart enough to know that if she turned down this opportunity over a distaste for him, she might likely find herself out of not just a lucrative client, but out of a job as well.

And jobs like hers—especially partnerships in top New York City law firms—didn't come along every day.

She'd done the wise thing and he planned to make the most of it.

He smiled, ignoring the stab of pain in his bruised cheek. "Excellent."

"Yes, it is. And may I say that we're extremely pleased that MMP will be representing you and your company?" McNeal said. "In fact, the partners and I would enjoy showing you around the offices, then taking you to lunch. If you have the time, we could even do it today."

"Brie Grayson can do that."

There was a slight pause. "Yes, she'll be included, of course, but—"

"No, just Grayson. Tell her I'll expect her. One o'clock here at the M Hotel. My chef will prepare lunch and we can go over any necessary particulars then."

"And the tour of the offices?" McNeal sounded rather at a loss.

"I'll see them another time, I'm sure. Good doing business with you, McNeal."

"And you, Mr. Monroe."

Maddox ended the call.

The ball would be in his court this time; he couldn't wait to see how she decided to return serve.

With five minutes to spare, Brie climbed out of one of the corporate Escalades that were kept for use by the partners. It was hard to believe she was now entitled to a car and driver rather than having to schlep around on foot or by subway or cab. It was even harder to believe the reason for her sudden ascent into the upper ranks. Bringing MJM Enterprises into the Marshall, McNeal and Prescott fold was a major coup regardless of how she'd managed it.

And then there was the other perk—Ol' BS was no longer speaking to her. She'd crossed paths with him earlier in the break room and he'd practically snarled at her, his eyes wild with undisguised rage.

"From this moment forward, you are dead to me," he said, gripping his coffee mug so tightly she'd been surprised it didn't snap. "Monroe was mine and you stole him."

"Look, Barrett, I was as surprised as you when I found out he was coming here to Marshall McNeal Prescott. If you want, I can talk to him and have you added to the account, although I can't guarantee any—"

"Don't bother. I have no need of your crumbs. The only thing I want to know is how you did it, especially being offered equity partner. What did you do? Sleep with Monroe? Or was it with one of the partners?"

Her back turned rigid. "I most certainly did not. And I'd better not hear that you've been spreading malicious gossip about me around the office or I'll bring my tennis racket to work and use it on *you* this time. Apologize. Immediately."

His eyes widened. "Fine, I'm sorry. Jeez." He took a

step away from her. "Even so, you must have done something extraordinary to land the Monroe account, especially after you clobbered him with a tennis ball."

She shrugged. "Maybe he likes my adversarial style. There's no telling about clients sometimes."

"Maybe so, but Monroe would have signed with me if you hadn't been there." Barrett glared. "I wish now I'd never taken you with me to the Hamptons."

"Actually, I wish you hadn't either," she said, since Maddox Monroe was back in her life in the most improbable and unwanted of ways. Still, Barrett's assumption that Monroe's business had been there for him to pluck like a ripe plum irritated her.

"I was this close to bringing him in on my own without your interference," he grumbled.

"Oh please, Barrett, stop being delusional. We both know that Monroe was never going to come on board with you no matter what you did. So you didn't lose out on anything, because it was never yours to lose in the first place."

Barrett's face flushed again, his mouth opening and closing with the rounded gasps of a fish out of water. "From now on, you and I"—he waved a pair of fingers in the space between them—"are no longer friends."

"I didn't know we ever were." Brie crossed her arms.

After one last furious glare, he'd stomped out of the break room.

She supposed he wouldn't be the only one with ugly ideas about why she'd been the one to bring Monroe into the firm when no one else had ever before been able to manage the trick. But she'd known there would be fallout when she'd accepted her devil's bargain with Monroe. Now came the part where she got to read the fine print and find out just what he wanted in return.

And if she didn't get a move on, she realized as she gazed up at the sophisticated glass and steel exterior of Monroe's luxury New York City flagship hotel, she was going to be late for her lunch with Lucifer.

Inside the lobby, she was met by the manager. A brief greeting later, he escorted her upstairs in a private elevator that could be accessed only with a keycard. He ushered her inside a top-floor suite—obviously by prearrangement—then disappeared with a discreet efficiency.

As she surveyed the black-and-white marble entry hall, her fingers tightened around the handle of her briefcase. She'd been given the Saddleback leather case in supple chestnut brown years ago as a law school graduation present from her parents. She supposed she would be able to afford better now that she'd be earning a partner's salary—once she came up with her six-figure buy-in check, of course.

Then again, if all of this turned out to be some elaborate hoax on Monroe's part, she'd be out on her ass searching frantically for a new job, just like she'd worried she would be this morning. Whatever happened, though, she liked her trusty old bag; it had been with her through hell and back more than once—a few of those trips worse than others.

Suddenly footsteps rang out and there was Monroe, looking even taller and more powerful than she remembered. She abruptly forgot all about briefcases and buy-ins.

If she'd thought he was attractive in tennis clothes, he looked red-hot scrumptious in a bespoke navy blue three-piece suit; the tailoring was just too good for off-the-rack. She might dislike his personality, but she couldn't fault his dark good looks or his innately masculine style. He was bite-me beautiful with a capital *B*.

Of course she didn't let any of her thoughts show as he walked closer. That's when she took in the full effect of the massive shiner on his face, his left eye and cheekbone a brutal collage of swollen blues and purples that reminded her of a cross between blueberries and raw meat.

*I did that,* she thought with an inner cringe.

Which meant that he had to be getting revenge. Why else would he have made her his attorney?

She almost turned around to flee, but decided she might as well wait for the other shoe to officially drop. If she got lucky, maybe she'd get lunch out of it before she had to go back to the office to pack up her stuff.

"Brie Grayson, welcome," he said. "Pardon me for not coming downstairs to meet you, but I was on a call. I trust Oscar didn't keep you waiting."

Oscar, the manager, he meant. "Not at all. He was amazingly polite and efficient. If he weren't, he wouldn't work for you, would he?"

A smile spread over Monroe's face. "Exactly right." He gestured for her to follow him.

She fell into step behind him.

"I've asked my chef to prepare our meal," he said. "We'll wait in the living room while he gets things ready."

"You mean we'll be eating here?"

He tossed her a look, whose appeal wasn't in the least diminished by his injury. "We'll have more privacy this way. The restaurant here at the M Hotel is excellent, but I prefer not to discuss business in public when there's a better option."

Privacy and Monroe were two things she'd been hoping not to mix. She really ought to have insisted on meeting at her office.

Keeping her thoughts to herself, she followed him

into the living room. The view was spectacular, the outside wall a panorama of glass that displayed Manhattan in its glory, all the way from the lush green rectangle of Central Park to the murky gray ribbon of the Hudson River.

She turned toward him. "Before we begin, I want to apologize."

"You only just arrived. What could you possibly have done already?"

"Nothing. Well, nothing new. I just wanted to say that I'm sorry about the other day, about the tennis match and the accident with the ball."

"Was it an accident?" he asked, a knowing expression in his dark brown eyes. "I got the distinct impression at the time that your serve landed exactly where you aimed."

Unflinching, she looked back. "It did. Too bad your face got in the way."

A brief smile moved over his lips. "Careful, Ms. Grayson, or I'll be instructing you to sue yourself on my behalf."

"Then it's a good thing the law prevents me from doing so. Maybe one of the other partners could help?"

"Maybe. But we'll have to table that for another day. Now, what can I get you to drink?" Monroe asked. "Wine or a cocktail perhaps?"

Though Brie didn't let it show, she was secretly relieved that he didn't seem to be holding a grudge. Then again, she knew he was up to something. Just *what* remained to be seen. "Nothing alcoholic, thank you," she said. "I don't drink at work."

"Iced tea, then?" At her agreement, he nodded toward a waiter, whom she hadn't noticed until that very moment.

The man vanished, walking down a hallway that she presumed led to the kitchen. Listening, she thought she heard the sound of something sizzling in a pan. Then it was quiet again.

"Sit," Monroe told her, gesturing this time toward a sofa grouping upholstered in rich brown leather.

"Perhaps we could find a table? I've brought papers for you to sign." Might as well take a stab at calling his bluff.

"We can do that later," he said, "after we eat."

Well, she'd given it a shot. She wasn't taking bets, though, on walking out of there with an executed client agreement. Gritting her teeth, she sank down onto one of two armchairs in the room.

Monroe smiled as if he was fully aware she'd put as much space between them as possible, then took a seat on the sofa. He stretched a long arm across its back.

"So, Brie Grayson. What have you been up to since junior high school? Other than becoming a lawyer with a wicked tennis serve, that is."

Maddox watched her, enjoying the slight look of discomposure that crept over her face at his question. He loved the fact that he could still get a rise out of her even now. Curious how so many years could pass, years full of separate experiences and events, emotions and expectations, and yet at the heart of it, they were still the same people they'd been as kids.

She, the quiet, composed brainiac who smelled like a fresh spring rain and looked as if there were entire worlds hidden behind her eyes. He, the arrogant, leader-of-the-pack prankster who would give his left nut if she even once looked at him with anything other than disdain.

Even now, she was all buttoned up in her neat lawyer suit, her blond hair combed into carefully controlled perfection. She wore just the right shade of lipstick on her mouth—blush pink—and exactly the right shoes: feminine yet sensible two-inch navy blue heels that were professional without being dowdy.

He wished he could peel her out of the jacket and unbutton her fine silk shirt so he could see if her bra was utilitarian cotton or decadent lace. Next, he'd take off her shoes and roll down her panty hose so he could run his hands along the slim, bare curves of her thighs and calves and ankles. Then he'd tug her to him and pull her down to straddle his lap, pushing her skirt high while he kissed her deep and long and slow. Taking her mouth and caressing her body until she was trembling and wet, until she was begging him to sheath himself inside her soft, feminine heat.

But that would have to wait for later, he thought, giving himself a firm mental shake. All things in their own good time.

He supposed it would have been wiser if he'd behaved like the mature man he was when they'd met the other day. Instead, he'd shot off his mouth just like he had when he'd been a stupid moron kid. She hated his guts just as much as she had when they'd been in the seventh grade—and he had the black eye and bruised cheek to prove it. But he wasn't a quitter; never had been, never would be.

She detested him, sure, but things didn't have to stay that way. He'd find the means to push her buttons, only in a good way this time.

He studied her again, careful not to let any of his thoughts show. The question he'd asked her had been an honest one; he did want to know about her. Everything she'd done. Everyone she'd met. Where she planned to go in the future.

He knew she wasn't married; he'd ferreted out that bit of information during his phone conversation with McNeal on Sunday. He also knew she lived in a small one-bedroom apartment that was located in a safe, quiet neighborhood, and that before this past year, she'd been a lawyer for the DOJ in Washington, D.C.

Still, he wanted to hear the details from her.

Why she fascinated him, he didn't entirely understand. But he was a man who'd built an empire on gut instinct, and his instincts told him not to let her slip away for a second time. At least not until he had a chance to scratch the itch she still gave him, even after all these years.

Brie shrugged, her face unreadable. "What is there to tell? I've done the usual things. Gone to school, found a job, lived my life."

"So you're just an average young woman making her way in the big city."

"Something like that."

"What about a husband? Children?" he went on, even though he knew the answer.

"No. Neither."

"Boyfriend, then? What about that Collingsworth guy? Are you and he—"

"No!" she said, sharply enough that he knew he had nothing to trouble himself over in that regard.

"Anyone else? Live-in lover perhaps? Or do you prefer keeping your options open?"

"Whatever I prefer doing in my private life is private, Mr. Monroe, and none of your concern. You have hired me to serve as your attorney and to represent your business interests. Anything more goes beyond the scope of our association. Assuming you really are serious about having Marshall McNeal Prescott represent you, that is."

He drummed his fingers against the sofa back. "And why wouldn't I be serious?"

"Well, if I am being completely candid—"

"Most definitely. I insist on honesty in all our dealings."

She paused, studied him for an instant. "Then *honestly*, given your history, you've never before shown any interest in obtaining new counsel. That is in spite of numerous attempts by any number of well-respected firms over the years to acquire your business. Yet suddenly, out of the blue, you have decided that you want my firm to represent you."

"No."

"No, what?"

"I want *you* to represent me. Your firm doesn't matter."

"Mr. Monroe—"

"Maddox," he said, smiling. "Come on, Brie. It's no use pretending we're strangers, however much you might wish we were."

"But we are strangers." She looked him square in the eyes. "We were anything but friends as children, and we most definitely don't know each other now as adults."

"But all that is going to change, now that you're my lawyer."

"Assuming I agree to be your lawyer."

He arched a brow. "But you already have. Or was McNeal mistaken when he told me you've accepted a partnership?"

"He shouldn't have—"

"Of course he should. He works for me now too. From what I understand, you're more than qualified for the step up—highly deserving, in fact."

"I've been with Marshall McNeal Prescott less than a year."

"Yes, but you've been a practicing attorney for eight years with experience in both the public and private sectors. You graduated from Harvard and Harvard Law at the top of your class, served as an editor of the *Law Review*, and landed a position at a prestigious New York law firm straight out of college."

Her lips parted with surprise, but he continued before she could say anything. "You left corporate law to work for the Department of Justice in Washington, D.C., for a few years before returning here to the city to resume your original career track," he went on. "You're considered one of Marshall McNeal Prescott's best and brightest litigators and were already well on the way toward partnership. My . . . suggestion that you be offered partner did nothing more than move up the timetable. I'm sure you and they were already thinking along those lines well before I came along."

"You had me investigated?" she said on a sudden gasp of understanding.

He shrugged, unapologetic. "Of course. I'm a businessman, Brie. I do my homework. You don't really think I'd put the legal concerns of a company worth nearly a billion dollars in the hands of someone who doesn't know what she's doing?"

Her breasts rose and fell as she drew in several rapid breaths. "Why, you— "

"Don't worry. I told my investigator to focus on the business side of things. He left out most of the personal stuff. You're whistle clean when it comes to drugs, not even an occasional puff of a joint on the side." He made a smoking motion with one hand.

"Of course not," she shot back, her blue eyes ablaze.

"Still the incorruptible princess, aren't you, Brie-Brie? But then, I always liked that about you. You've got integrity."

The kind of integrity a man wanted to corrupt for his own personal pleasure.

He thought again about tugging her onto his lap, spearing his fingers into her hair, and kissing her until neither one of them could think straight. But she'd already decked him once. He didn't want her to have an excuse to give him a second black eye.

"Here are our drinks," he said as the waiter reappeared. "I'm sure our lunch will be ready any minute."

She accepted the iced tea, her hand tight on the glass.

For a second he wondered if she was going to toss it at him. Instead, she raised it to her lips and took a long drink.

Steadying her nerves?

He always had been able to get a rise out of her. He couldn't wait to see how long it took him to bring the banked passion he sensed in her to the fore.

Brie set her drink down with a slight click, then looked him in the eye again. "You still haven't told me why."

"Why what?"

"Why me?"

Rather than answer, he took a long swallow of his own glass of iced tea. Despite his offer of wine or a cocktail, he didn't drink alcohol. He'd been sober for more than ten years now, and he had every intention of remaining that way. He'd even refused the painkillers they'd offered him at the hospital for that reason.

"Good or not," she continued, "there are lots of excellent attorneys in the city, including the ones at your old firm. Why pick me when we never got along and when I gave you what looks like a very painful black eye the first time we ran into each other in over twenty years?"

A slow grin spread over his mouth. "Oh, that's easy. I want you in my bed. I thought we'd start with business first, then work our way up to the pleasure."

# CHAPTER FIVE

Brie stared for a long moment, then tossed back her head and laughed. The very idea of her and Monroe, it was . . . well . . . it was laughable. They despised each other for one thing. For another, she didn't hook up with men she worked with—at least not any longer. She'd more than learned her lesson a few years earlier when she'd had an affair with a fellow lawyer. To say it had ended badly was an understatement; it was a mistake she would never let herself make again.

"Are you finished?" he asked in a carefully polite tone.

"A-Almost." She held up a finger and gave way to one more belly laugh before she forced herself to sober up. Her lips twitched a couple more times before she was finally able to hold it together. Catching her breath, she wiped a tear from the corner of her eye. "I didn't know you even had a sense of humor, let alone such a good one."

He gave her a look that put her in mind of a predator. "Who says I'm joking?"

"You must be. The two of us together? It would be like a WWF match. It wouldn't be lovemaking. It would be hatemaking."

"What does love have to do with it?"

"Hey, that's an old song, isn't it?"

"Laugh if you want, but I'm going to have you, Brie Grayson."

"No, you are not. I don't sleep with clients."

"Who said anything about sleeping? I'm talking about sex."

"I don't do that with clients either."

"We'll see."

"No, we won't." She stood and reached for her leather satchel. She pulled out a folder and laid it down on the coffee table. "Here is the client agreement and letter of retainer. You can sign it and messenger it over to my office. In the meantime, I'll ask one of the other partners to handle your legal work."

"No."

"No, what?" She arched a brow.

"The understanding was that you would handle my legal work. If you refuse, then the deal is off. McNeal told me you agreed to all the terms."

"I did, but that was before you added an additional term."

"The sex, you mean? Oh, that's not a term of our arrangement. When it comes to my corporation, I'm all business, and our personal dealings will have no bearing on said business. Just consider the other a future side benefit to be enjoyed by both parties when the time is right."

"The time will never be right."

He smiled that arrogant grin of his. "We'll see. Lunch must be ready by now. Let's go into the dining room."

"Look, Monroe, this isn't going to work out between us, so we might as well put an end to our association right now."

"Why won't it work out?"

She studied him for a long moment. "Truth?"

"Always. I expect scrupulous honesty in my lawyer, at least when it comes to her dealings with me."

Brie's lips twitched upward again. "Then honestly it's because we're about as *in*compatible as two people can get. I didn't like you when I was twelve and I don't like you now. We go together about as well as peanut butter and sardines."

He took a moment to consider. "Well, you're right that they wouldn't go together on a sandwich, but in an exotic Asian dish, the combination might prove both spicy and delicious. Besides, why is likability a prerequisite to our working together? Or do you like everyone you represent?"

Tiny frown lines settled between her brows. "No, but—"

"Then I don't see the problem. Now, lunch. My chef is the temperamental sort who's been known to fling pans when he's displeased. Since he's one of a handful of Michelin three-star chefs in the city, I've learned not to piss him off."

Her eyes widened. She'd known the restaurant at the M Hotel boasted a fine-dining restaurant with one of the city's top chefs at the helm, but she had never imagined the culinary master himself would be cooking her lunch.

She scowled. Monroe really was diabolical. Did he know she was a foodie and would find a chance to sample such exquisite cuisine nearly impossible to resist, or had it just been a stroke of luck on his part? Knowing what she did of him, she guessed the former. First he tempted her with a partnership at her law firm and now a meal made by one of the best chefs in the United States and possibly the world.

*What a bastard.*

"You and I are strictly business," she said, staring him in the eye. "I am your attorney and only your attorney. Understood?"

"Completely."

"There'll be no asking me out and no more talk of sex. Ever."

His face was smooth and serious. "If you prefer." He motioned toward the dining room with a hand. "Shall we?"

She was a little surprised by his sudden, easy agreement but accepted it anyway. Letting her nose lead her toward the delicious scents of freshly baked French bread and some sort of bacon derivation she suspected might be braised pork belly, she walked on.

It was only later, after she'd eaten one of the best meals of her life, had put the signed representation agreements back into her briefcase, and had just climbed back into the company Escalade, that she realized Monroe hadn't actually promised anything when it came to not pursuing her on a personal basis.

Because, as a lawyer, she ought to have realized that the words "if you prefer" did not mean "yes."

A vacuum whined somewhere in the distance, the evening cleaning crew busy sweeping, emptying trash cans, and switching off lights as they finished their work.

Brie paid them no attention, her thoughts focused squarely on the motion she was preparing. Her fingers moved swiftly over her computer keyboard, pausing every so often to flip through her notes to locate a pertinent citation or other necessary piece of information.

She was reconsidering a section of the paragraph she'd just written when the theme music to *Mad Men* started playing on her cell phone. She didn't need to check to know that it was her older sister—the advertising executive—calling.

Smiling, she hit "answer" and put the phone up to her ear. "Hey, Madelyn."

"Hey, yourself," her sister said in a cheery voice. "What are you up to? Home having dinner, I hope."

"Nope, I'm still at work, and yes, I know it's nearly"—she paused and flicked a quick glance at the clock on her credenza—"eight. I've just got a little more to do. Then I'm shutting down for the night."

"You ought to shut down now, but you already have a mother, so I won't nag. Just promise you won't stop by the deli and take a sandwich home for dinner."

"Promise," Brie said, leaning back in her chair. "I'll order Chinese takeout instead."

Madelyn laughed and groaned.

"Hey, don't turn your nose up at Chinese takeout. The place I go is authentic Szechuan and delicious."

Brie arched her spine, only then becoming aware of the stiffness in her neck and shoulders. Maybe she should pack it in and go home. For more reasons than she wanted to think about, it had been a really long day.

"So, what's up?" Brie asked. "Or are you just calling to check on me?"

"Of course, but we'll get to that part in a minute. First, I was wondering if you'd like to have lunch with me tomorrow. It's one of my non-telecommuting days, so I'll be in the city."

"Sure. I'd love to. Let me just check my calendar." Clicking a couple of buttons on her computer, she brought up her daily planner. "I have a client meeting at eleven thirty, but it shouldn't run more than a hour. How about one?"

"One sounds great. Now, what restaurant?"

They batted around a few possibilities before settling on a trendy new Italian spot that had recently gotten a slew of rave reviews.

"How are Zack and the twins?" Brie asked.

"They're wonderful," Madelyn said, her obvious pride and contentment in being a wife and mother bubbling through every syllable. "Holly and Hannah had a stomach bug last week, but they're all better now and up to their usual antics. They tried dressing poor Millie in doll clothes yesterday, but being the self-respecting cat she is, she wiggled out of the dress and headed for high ground. You know what a sweet cat Millie is, so I'm sure she didn't mean to, but Holly got a minor scratch during the escape attempt and, oh, the tears. Thank God for Hello Kitty Band-Aids. That helped turn the sniffles into smiles. Not to be left out, of course, Hannah demanded that she be bandaged too. Zack had to apply new bandages to both girls after tonight's bath."

Brie laughed, imagining her adorable nieces wielding their considerable God-given charm.

"So, how about Zack? Has he heard any more about the chief creative director slot?"

"It's all just speculation at the moment, but supposedly the old chief at Fielding and Simmons is retiring come October. If he does, Zack is a shoo-in for the job."

"That must have you both excited."

"Cautiously optimistic, since we're trying not to count chickens and all that. But I have my fingers crossed for him."

"Of course, you do."

"If he gets it, though, you know what this will mean, don't you?"

Brie laughed again. "Are you referring to your never-ending one-upmanship and the fact that he'll outrank you again?"

"Exactly. We're both all even now as creative director for our two separate firms, but if he gets this promotion . . . well, chief jobs don't grow on trees. It could be years before I make the cut, if I ever do at all."

"You will. You're too good not to. In the meantime, the extra money will make a nice consolation prize."

"I know. Maybe to console myself we should all go on a fun family vacation. Somewhere with warm trade winds, tall, cool drinks, and a soft sand beach. Zack and the girls and I could all use a week to do nothing but relax."

"Sounds heavenly."

Brie envied her sister, wondering where Madelyn got the energy to chase after a pair of spirited three-year-old girls, hold down a high-pressure career at one of the best advertising agencies in Manhattan, and keep the romance alive in her undeniably happy marriage. Although Brie had to give some credit to Madelyn's husband, Zack, who adored his wife and children and did his half of the domestic chores and child rearing without complaint, in spite of his own high-powered position at a rival advertising firm.

Or at least he didn't complain often—the laundry the only real bone of contention between them. If it were up to Zack, Madelyn observed, they'd throw all the dirty clothes out and continually buy new—that or use a laundry service and the dry cleaner's as he'd done when he'd been a bachelor. But with two growing girls, that option was out.

There'd been one particularly memorable argument after he'd mistakenly washed one of her red silk blouses on hot with a load of white towels and underwear. The miniaturized blouse had gone straight into the trash, while the whites had turned a delicate shade of pink the twins had dubbed "princess colored." Madelyn had given up after that and agreed to do the laundry on her own. To compensate, Zack had been assigned one hundred percent of the sweeping duty. Zack loved to sweep, so it had been an easy compromise.

Otherwise, they were the most happily married couple Brie knew with the possible exception of her parents, who were already thinking up ways to celebrate their ruby wedding anniversary in a couple more years. And her older brother, P.G., and his wife, Caroline, who had a rock-solid marriage and a love that had grown even deeper since Caroline's battle with cancer and her subsequent remission.

Come to think of it, once the newest lovebirds, Ivy and James, tied the knot, she would be the only single Grayson left. The only one who couldn't seem to find the right mate and settle down. At the rate she was going, she might never find anyone.

She dated here and there, as much as her workload allowed—which admittedly wasn't much—but she'd gone out with a few guys since her return to New York City. Still, as interesting and attractive as some of them had seemed at first, their appeal had dimmed on further acquaintance. And it wasn't that they were dull or self-absorbed or lacked compatibility; it was just that she couldn't imagine spending one more day with any of them, let alone a lifetime.

She'd been in love once, and when it had ended, the aftermath had crushed her to her core. She never wanted to love that blindly again. Never wanted to feel so vulnerable and naive and, yes, gullible. She was a smart, sophisticated woman, and yet she'd let herself get used, let herself be hurt almost beyond repair. She'd built up a layer of reserve since then that no one got past. And maybe that's why she couldn't find anyone. Because her trust had been violated, she didn't trust anymore.

"So, I heard you had a rather interesting weekend in the Hamptons," Madelyn said, pulling Brie back into the conversation. "Did you really hit one of the other players in the face with a tennis ball?"

Brie flinched at the memory. "Yes, I did, but he's fine." *If you call having a face that looks like a punching bag fine.* "I see James and Ivy have been busy running their mouths."

"Oh, I didn't hear it from them. Zack told me."

"Zack? Where did he hear about it?"

"One of his clients. Apparently it's making the rounds. The local paper ran a short article and some blogger picked up on it. It's gone out to other news agencies. *Huff Post* gives it a mention and CNN actually had it on the crawl tonight."

"What!" Brie's fingers spasmed around the phone.

"Guess the guy you hit is some big-deal business hotshot and one of America's ten most eligible bachelors. After seeing his picture, I can see why."

"He isn't that good-looking."

"If you say so. Seemed pretty hot to me."

Brie gave the computer keyboard a few quick taps.

In the background, on the other side of the line, she heard a low, muffled voice. Madelyn laughed. "Of course you're hotter, Zack. Why else do you think I married you?"

There was another muffled remark; then Madelyn giggled again.

Ignoring whatever audio PDA was unfolding between her sister and her brother-in-law, she scrolled down through the links, then clicked one open.

And there he was—Maddox Monroe in all his glory. Or rather all his *gory*, since the photo was a shot of him coming out of the hospital emergency room, his face swollen and discolored, with gauze taped over his left cheek and eye. Lila, the girlfriend, was hanging on to him, her face turned away from the camera. Maddox looked far from happy, but then, why would he be when he was having his privacy invaded at such a painful, unwanted moment?

Quickly, she scanned the article, sighing with quiet relief when she saw that her name wasn't mentioned. The story stated that he'd been injured playing tennis, then gone to the hospital, where he'd been treated and released. The article went on to state that Maddox was being monitored for a possible concussion; it finished with a warning about the dangers of sports-related brain injuries. Obviously that concern for Maddox must have come and gone, since he'd seemed as sharp as a sushi knife—both mind and tongue—when she'd met him for lunch.

"What's the deal, then?" Madelyn asked. "Everything okay on your end? This Monroe guy isn't threatening to sue or anything, is he?"

"No, he actually—" Brie hesitated, wondering how much to tell Madelyn.

"Yes? He what?"

"You remember the punk kid who gave me such a hard time in junior high? I know you never met him since you were a couple years ahead, but I remember telling you about some of the crap he pulled."

Madelyn took a moment to recollect. "You mean the one who spent the year making cheese jokes about your name and got that Mickey thing started?"

"Yeah, that's the one," she said grimly.

"I do, but what does that have to do with—" Madelyn broke off suddenly as the pieces clicked into place. "No! You don't mean—it can't possibly be him?"

"It is."

"*Manhattan* magazine's 'Mogul with the Mostest' and *GQ*'s 'Hunk with the Luxury Hotels' is that slimy worm from seventh grade?" A significant pause followed. "Well, no wonder you clocked him."

"It was an accident."

"Sure, one of those accidentally on-purpose kinds of accidents."

That was the trouble with sisters—they always knew more than you wished they did.

"Look, he said something and I got mad and took aim, but I didn't mean to hit him in the face. Honestly. I was going for more of a close shave, but I guess my aim was off."

"Or his head just happened to be in the way. So? Did you know you'd be playing tennis with him? And what did he say that set you off?"

Settling back in her chair again, Brie launched into the tale—or most of it anyway. For some reason she left out the part at his penthouse where he'd told her he meant to get her in bed—which was *never* going to happen, so there really hadn't been any point mentioning it.

Over lunch, he hadn't flirted with her at all. He hadn't used so much as a single innuendo—not even when the oyster shooters with mignonette sauce had been served. He'd been a complete gentleman, surprising her with his interesting, thoughtful conversation. She wondered now whether he'd just been playing with her to see how she'd react. Besides, he had a girlfriend and was the type of man who could get any woman he wanted.

Well, almost any.

"So, you've been made partner?" Madelyn said, her voice high with excitement. "Why didn't you tell me the second I called? For that matter, why didn't you call me this morning to share the good news?"

"I was working." *And figured my head still had a good chance of being on the chopping block.*

"So was I, but I'd have found a few minutes anyway. Well, now we really have a good reason to celebrate tomorrow. Have you told anyone else?"

"No, and I don't really want to play this up."

*In case the other partners come out of their Monroe-induced haze and demote me again.*

"Why not? A partnership is a partnership."

"The circumstances in this case are rather unusual."

"Unexpected maybe, but not unusual, no more so than any other."

"But Monroe—"

"Simply hurried the process along. You deserve this, Brie. You know you do. You've worked hard, you're a fantastic lawyer, and it was only a matter of time until you were offered partner."

"I know, but—"

"No buts. Monroe might have been a grade A-one ass-hat when he was a kid, but he's a shrewd businessman now. He wouldn't put you in charge of his legal dealings if you weren't up to the job."

"That's what he said."

"And he's right. So quit kvetching and be happy. Have they given you a new office yet?"

"No, this all just happened today."

"Well, my advice is to take the one with the most windows. I took bigger when I first got bumped to director, and, boy, was I sorry."

"Thanks, I'll keep that in mind."

She and Madelyn talked for another couple of minutes, then hung up with promises to see each other the next day. After tapping "end call," Brie laid the phone down on her desk. She glanced around, thinking of Madelyn's comment about getting a new office. There would be all sorts of other new things to which she would suddenly be entitled. So why, after she'd already committed to this new course, was she still hedging and having second thoughts?

Because of the strings, she realized, the ones held by Maddox Monroe.

But as she'd known that morning when the partners made their offer, what were her options really? It was either out or up, and up was the only direction that made any sense for her to go.

*So celebrate,* as Madelyn had suggested. And who knew? Maybe Monroe wouldn't turn out to be any more of a demanding prick than any other influential client.

Right, and monkeys would shortly be flying out of her butt.

Shaking her head, she reached over and switched off her computer. Dinner and a good night's sleep would help everything make sense tomorrow.

She hoped.

# CHAPTER SIX

Three days later, Brie pushed back her new Aeron executive chair and reached into her desk drawer for her purse, unable to spare more than a few seconds to notice the view from her new office windows.

She'd hadn't been able to take Madelyn's advice about which office to select, since there'd been only one choice available. But though she didn't have the biggest or the brightest of the spaces set aside for partners, she had no complaints. She had lots of room, lots of natural light, and a stipend that would allow her to redecorate with whatever furniture, paintings, rugs, lamps, and other accessories she liked best.

She also had more responsibility, including the disposition and review of the ninety-odd boxes of documentation that had been sent over from Monroe's former law firm that morning. They'd forwarded a multitude of electronic files as well, together with a terse cover letter that might as well have been titled "We're pissed we got fired. Here's Monroe's legal work, ongoing and prior. You sort it out, bitches."

She'd set up two first years in one of the conference rooms to summarize and catalog everything that had been received. She would do her own review once they were finished. She'd also tasked her paralegal with putting together an up-to-the-minute analysis and status of all of Monroe's open legal work, including contracts for land and real estate purchases, a labor review for his mid- and upper-level employees, and tax compliance issues with a group of his West Coast holdings. She would have to pull in associates from mergers and acquisitions and tax to assist and someone with SEC experience, as well, to help with a proposed takeover of a medium-sized hospitality group that was probably headed straight for liquidation should Monroe's bid be successful. There were also a handful of lawsuits that all appeared to be of the nuisance variety. Being sued was one of the costs of doing business, and no business, however prosperous, was without them.

How she was going to fit all of Monroe's work in with her other cases she wasn't sure, but somehow she'd find the time; she always did.

Right now, though, she had a far more pressing commitment—making it across town in time for the final fitting for her bridesmaid's dress for Ivy's wedding. She'd already missed the appointment twice—once when a deposition she'd been trying to conduct for more than a year ran overtime, and next when she got bumped off an overbooked connecting flight back from a law conference in Denver; she hadn't arrived at JFK until late the following morning. If she didn't make it to this third fitting, her mother would flay her alive—probably using one of the matching hand-sewn, crystal-encrusted sashes in bridal blush pink that all the bridesmaids would be wearing.

As a highly successful professional wedding planner, Laura Grayson ran her business with drill sergeant precision and she didn't appreciate it when "uncooperative" members of the bridal party messed up her schedule—not even when the culprit was her beloved middle daughter.

For her part, Ivy had handed over most of the details to her mother, since Laura was having so much fun arranging her youngest child's nuptials. Even so, Ivy had put her foot down when Laura suggested holding the ceremony in the heart of New York City at St. Patrick's Cathedral with the reception to follow at the Four Seasons. As grand as the venues would undoubtedly have been, Ivy wanted something more natural and relaxed with an intimate feeling, despite the nearly three hundred invited guests.

Ivy had secretly confided to Brie that although she wanted a traditional wedding, she didn't want anything that would remind James of his disastrous first attempt at getting married. Years earlier, he'd been engaged to their older sister, Madelyn, and she'd left him on their wedding day only minutes before the ceremony had been scheduled to begin. Knowing the pain and embarrassment he'd suffered at the time, Ivy wanted nothing to mar the day. Her and James's wedding day, she told Brie, was going to be the happiest, most beautiful day of their lives.

So rather than in a church, Ivy had decided to be married at home in Connecticut, outdoors in the big, flower-filled garden that ranged between her parents' house and the neighboring house that just happened to belong to James's parents. He truly was the boy next door, and not only had he spent his youth running in and out of the Grayson house, but he'd known Ivy since she was an infant. It was, they had decided, the perfect place to seal their vows.

Despite the fact that the wedding was being held literally in her own backyard, Laura had a million and one things to do before the big day arrived. With fewer than three weeks to go, they were already pushing things when it came to the fitting, as her mother lost no opportunity to remind Brie.

She glanced at the time. A quarter to six. If she left now, she should just be able to make it to the couture bridal salon for her six-thirty appointment—the last of the day. She hated the thought of being packed into the crowded subway, but finding a cab at this hour would be next to impossible. If only she could take the company Escalade like she had for her lunch with Monroe. But that had been business; she was on her own time now.

She wondered if Monroe's eye was still black. Over the last three days, the only communication she'd gotten from him had been a single impersonal business e-mail. But what did she care how Maddox Monroe was feeling or what he might be doing? As she kept reminding herself, she had more important things to worry about than a former junior high school bully who through some strange twist of fate had become her client.

After powering off her computer, she grabbed her purse and cell phone and headed for the door. She made it halfway to the elevator before her paralegal, Trish, waylaid her and began asking questions. Rather than stop, she kept walking, giving rapid-fire responses, while the other woman trotted next to her, jotting frenzied notes on a long yellow pad.

The elevator dinged and the doors slid open. Brie stepped inside. "E-mail me anything else that can't wait. Otherwise, I'll see you tomorrow."

"Sure thing. Have fun playing dress-up," Trish said brightly.

"Hey, if you don't watch that mouth, I'll have to get out my Purell."

Trish laughed and was still laughing as the elevator doors slid shut.

The outside air was bathtub-water warm and just as humid, thick clouds lumbering high above the skyscrapers in patches of dull gray and muddy white. Crap, was it going to rain? This morning's weather forecast had given it only a twenty percent chance. Fingers crossed that it would hold off until she got to the bridal salon.

She hurried into the rushing just-want-to-get-the-hell-home crowd, keeping pace with a quick, confident stride. The subway station was four blocks down, an easy walk, especially on sensible yet attractive two-inch brown leather pumps. Everything was going according to schedule.

Then she got to the station entrance. A Closed sign blocked the stairwell.

"What the hell?" she said aloud to no one in particular.

Other disgruntled people came to a stop behind her, reading the same sign. "Water main break," a man said. "Happened around two, I heard. Station's gonna be closed for who knows how long."

Collective groans rose into the air.

With the resigned resilience of New Yorkers, they turned and started walking again, presumably headed toward the nearest open station listed on a sign set up next to the one that read CLOSED.

It was eight blocks away.

With sick frustration, Brie knew she was going to be late.

Again.

She supposed she should call her mother to let her

know, but even as she started to reach for her cell phone, she hesitated. She just didn't want to hear the lecture—or the disappointment. Maybe if she could find a cab, she'd still make it in time. Chances weren't good, but it was worth a try. She would head for the subway station and, when the traffic lights were against her, try flagging down a ride.

She started walking, pausing to stick out her arm every so often and wave. But the cabs all whizzed by, already occupied or off duty. She went two blocks, then three, with no luck whatsoever. She was most of the way along the fourth when a few fat raindrops splattered around her like gunshots, dampening her charcoal skirted suit and the bodice of her cream silk blouse. A cold breeze gusted along after it, sending shivers over her skin.

*Well, if this isn't the straw and the f-ing camel's back, I don't know what is.* Not only would she never get a cab now, since finding one in the rain was harder than winning the Powerball jackpot, but if the black clouds roiling overhead really opened up, she was going to be wetter than a drowned rat.

But worst, worst, worst of all, she was going to miss the fitting appointment *for the third time*.

She was walking at her briskest pace when a black Mercedes S-class sedan pulled over to the curb just ahead of her. It stopped and the rear door opened, but no one got out. Instead, as she drew even with the car, she saw Maddox Monroe leaning forward from the sleek, richly appointed leather backseat. "Hey, Grayson, need a lift?"

She stared, surprised to find him of all people riding—or should she say driving—to her rescue. But as she knew all too well, he was no white knight. His heart was black—moonless-night, stygian-mine-shaft, deep-space-where-no-one-can-hear-you-scream black.

Her brows furrowed and she shook her head. "Thanks, but I'm fine."

*Fine?* Who was she kidding? But she was off the clock now, so accepting favors from him came under the same heading as taking candy from strangers. The wind blew again and she shivered.

"This rain isn't going to hold off much longer," he told her. "Come on, get in."

As if the weather were in on their conversation, a few more doughnut-hole-sized raindrops splashed against the pavement, a low rumble of thunder reverberating afterward. The clouds were black now rather than gray, signaling that all hell was about to break loose.

As much as she wanted to refuse Monroe's offer, she knew when to put aside the pride and not be stupid. Lightning splintered the sky, making her jump.

And the sluice gates opened wide.

Sprinting forward, she ran for the car. She climbed in, then sighed with relief as she settled against the plush, heated leather seats. Monroe reached across and quickly shut the door, enclosing them inside a cocoon of comfort and warmth. Outside, the rain drummed angrily against the car's metallic shell, the world obscured by the Noah-worthy deluge.

The interior smelled of wealth and sophistication and clean, healthy male. She breathed it in, catching hints of unfragranced, fine-milled soap, high-quality wool that she guessed might be Scottish in origin, and some elusive something that could only be Monroe himself. His scent wasn't strong, but it teased her senses like a forbidden drug. She recognized it from having been with him the other day at lunch. She found his smell even more intoxicating now, enhanced as it was by the confined space of the car.

She was annoyed with herself for noticing.

Monroe regarded her out of eyes the color of bittersweet chocolate. She'd wondered about his wound and could see that he was healing, though the bruises were at the heinous yellowish green stage now. Somehow though they did not lessen his attractiveness, blending in with his dark Irish complexion.

Without a word, he reached over and brushed a few strands of wet hair off her cheek. His fingertips lingered and for a few seconds, she forgot how to breathe.

Hastily, she pulled away and settled deeper into the corner. The storm continued to pummel the car, the reason for her rapid pulse, which had absolutely nothing to do with Monroe.

He smiled, showing his teeth in a way that reminded her of a wolf—one that had just seen a nice, juicy rabbit.

"So? Where to, Ms. Grayson?"

Maddox did his best to keep his eyes off her breasts. He tried even harder to ignore the wet patches of rainwater-dampened silk that had turned her blouse into a high-class version of a wet T-shirt contest. He didn't think she realized and he certainly wasn't going to tell her and spoil the view.

His hands itched to touch, but he kept them to himself. That brief brush against her cheek had already crossed the line, the one she kept in place like police tape at a crime scene. Strictly Do Not Touch.

He knew she didn't like him—or trust him—but he sensed her personal barriers went a whole lot deeper than their old school rivalry. Someone had hurt her, someone other than him. Whoever he was, the guy was an asshole.

In that moment, Maddox decided he was going to make her forget her former lover, or any other man for that matter—anyone for whom she'd ever had feelings. Once she came to his bed, the only lover she would ever think about again would be him.

He leaned back in his seat, one hand curled on his black-suit-clad thigh. "Where are you headed? You looked like you were in a bigger hurry than usual when I had Marco pull over."

Actually he would have stopped even if it hadn't been threatening rain. Finding ways to spend time with her was quickly becoming an obsession. Luck had definitely been on his side when he'd glanced out the window and just happened to see her walking briskly along the street.

"I have to be at a fitting in exactly"—she paused to glance at her watch—"oh crap, twenty minutes. With this rain, there's no way I'll make it in time."

"Don't underestimate my driver. Marco's the best in New York. Isn't that right, Marco?"

"It certainly is, sir," said the driver with a grin from where he sat up front behind a half-open glass partition. He had black hair and eyes, with Italian features, and didn't look much older than Monroe himself. "Where are you going, miss?"

She rattled off the address of the bridal boutique on the Upper East Side.

"I'll get you there," Marco promised. He closed the partition with a soundless automatic slide of the glass and pressed his foot to the accelerator. With seamless precision, he merged the car into the dense, nose-to-tail traffic with an ease only a native New Yorker could manage.

"Marco drove a cab here in the city for eight years before I hired him. He got me to JFK in a snowstorm once in under forty-five minutes. I gave him a job on the spot."

Wild honking erupted around them, the visibility practically nonexistent as Marco muscled his way through the last millisecond of yellow left on the light in the intersection ahead. They pushed through and continued on their way. Maybe he really could get them to the bridal salon in twenty minutes.

"You said you have a fitting." Maddox raised an inquiring brow. "A fitting for what?"

"Bridesmaid's dress. My sister is getting married."

"Your older sister? What was her name? Margaret? Maggie?"

"Madelyn. And no, she's already married and has three-year-old twin girls. This is my younger sister, Ivy."

"The baby?" He smiled to himself as the years dropped away. "Your mom used to pick you up after school every once in a while with your little sister in a car seat in the back. She was just a tiny, squalling thing then, but cute."

"You remember that?" She sounded surprised.

"I remember all sorts of things about you."

And he did. Far, far too many, and in much too much detail, especially considering how long ago it had been.

Brie's mouth and jaw firmed with irritation.

"So how old is she now? Ivy?"

Brie tucked a stray piece of rain-damp blond hair behind her ear before answering. "Twenty-two."

"Kind of young to be tying the knot and settling down, isn't she?"

"If she were any other twenty-two-year-old, I'd agree. But Ivy's different, mature for her years. She knows what she wants."

"And she wants this guy she's marrying?"

"Oh, yes." Brie smiled, myriad thoughts and emotions swimming behind her blue eyes. "She's loved him her whole life. We just didn't realize exactly how much until a year or so ago. Her groom didn't either."

"So who's she marrying? Some other college kid?"

Her smile turned ironic. "No. His name is James Jordan. He's several years her senior."

Maddox ran the name through his mental files. "Jordan? You mean the financier Jordan? The billionaire with so much available cash he could invest in diamond-studded pogo sticks if he wanted to?"

"That's him. But he's far too shrewd to bother with either diamonds or pogo sticks."

Maddox frowned as a new thought popped into his head. "Tall, blond guy? He was on the court that day, wasn't he? When I was leaving after you'd KO'd me with that tennis ball."

She stiffened. "I didn't KO you. You never passed out and were lucid the whole time. And it was an accident."

A slow grin spread over his still-bruised face. "Keep telling yourself that, babe, and you just might believe it someday."

She crossed her arms over her chest, unwittingly emphasizing her breasts and still-damp silk shirt.

He let himself enjoy the view for a few mouthwatering moments before forcing his eyes up to her face again. "So, where's the wedding?"

"What?" she said blankly.

"Your younger sister and the billionaire? Where are they getting married? I suppose it's one of those destination things and they're jetting off to some French château to do the deed?"

Her blond eyebrows lifted. "No. They're getting married at our parents' home."

"In Connecticut?"

"That's right. They're still in the same house, the one

I lived in when you were busy tormenting me in junior high."

He grinned again. "How are your parents?"

He'd never actually met her mother and father, but he remembered seeing them every once in a while when he used to ride his bike past Brie's house. *Pitiful stuff really*, when he thought about it, biking block after block, more than a mile each way, in the faint hope that he'd catch a glimpse of her—not that he'd ever let her know what he was doing.

"They're good," she said. "Dad's doing well with his building company despite the ups and downs in the real estate market. And my mother is a wedding planner extraordinaire. She's waiting for me at the salon right now."

"Doing your sister's wedding, I take it?"

"Of course. Tears and blood would have been shed otherwise. But nobody does weddings better than Mom, so Ivy's happy to let her run the show—for the most part anyway. What about you? How are your folks?"

His expression turned sober. "So you don't know."

"Know what?"

"I always wondered if you'd heard, but then you transferred schools that next year, didn't you?"

"I went to a private school starting in eighth grade, yes. But what do you mean, you always wondered if I'd heard?"

"Nothing. It's not important."

"You brought it up, so it must be important. Tell me what you meant."

One corner of his mouth edged up in a wry smile. "You sound like a lawyer."

"That's good since I am a lawyer. Go on."

"Very well, counselor, if you insist. That next October, after you went off to your new school, my father was arrested for embezzling nearly a quarter of a million dollars from his investment firm. The police found several thousand dollars in cash and half a kilo of high-grade cocaine in the trunk of his BMW. The rest of the money was gone, blown on gambling and drugs.

"Every time my mother and little sister and I thought he was away on a business trip, he was really at some casino, living it up on the money he'd stolen from his clients. He cried when they caught him, said the drugs weren't his and that he'd been trying to win the money back so he could return it without anyone realizing it was missing. Because of him, we lost pretty much everything—the house, our possessions, the savings, even what my mother had earned on her own and put aside. My father died in federal prison from a heart attack after serving twelve years of his twenty-five-year sentence."

In all that time, he'd gone to see his father only once, when he'd been eighteen. He'd wanted to tell him off, to find an outlet for all the bitterness and rage he'd been carrying around. Instead, when he'd sat down across from him, he'd seen a shell of the proud, energetic man he'd once known, worn down and old before his time. When Maddox had said his good-byes that day, he'd made his peace with his father. He'd left his hatred behind as well.

Brie's eyes were soft with compassion as she reached out and laid a hand on his sleeve. "Maddox, I'm sorry. I had no idea all that had happened to you. I knew your family had moved away but not the reason for it."

He shrugged. "Why would you? You were just a kid, same as me. Plus, you'd never much liked me. That doesn't make for much interest in follow-up."

"No, I suppose it doesn't. Is your mother—"

"She's fine. Remarried and living in northern California with her detective husband and my two half brothers. I see them every so often when I travel to the West Coast."

"Your mom married a cop?"

"Yeah." His grin returned. "Beats all, doesn't it?"

She smiled back. "Life's ironic sometimes. And your sister?"

"Daphne's doing well. She owns a bed-and-breakfast in South Carolina that she runs with a college friend of hers. It was touch and go for a while, but they seem to be making a comfortable profit now."

"With some help from her big brother?"

He shrugged. "A start-up loan at the beginning that I was happy to give. But she's doing it all on her own these days." He paused. "You know, I think this is the first time we've ever had an actual conversation."

"Lunch the other day was an actual conversation."

He shook his head. "No, that was business. This was the two of us, just talking."

"I think we'd be better off sticking to business from here on out. I am your attorney, after all."

"Hmm, so you keep reminding me. I suppose you'll be billing me, now that we've discussed business?"

"I'm off the clock right now. No billable hours."

Maddox shot a quick glance out the window, seeing a street sign for East Sixty-third. Only a few blocks left to go. "Then since you're off the clock, I'm going to do something I've wanted to do for a very long time."

*For more than twenty years.*

Without giving her a second to react, he took her face between his hands, leaned forward, and kissed her.

Brie gave a muffled protest and wrapped her fingers around his wrists to push him away. He deepened the kiss, pressing her lips insistently apart so he could slide his tongue inside. Pleasure shot through him, hot and intense, desire burning like a fire in his blood. He'd always wondered how she would taste and now he knew.

Better.

Better than his fantasies.

Better than his expectations.

She was silky and sweet with a dash of spice like some exotic elixir and he wanted more. He wanted to strip her naked and drink her down, leisurely and slow as if they were on their own private island where time had no meaning.

Her long fingers tightened around his wrists, so he kissed her harder, knowing she was about to end the embrace. But then she did the most remarkable thing—one that shocked them both—she kissed him back.

# Chapter Seven

Brie knew she'd gone crazy—stark raving cuckoo, put-her-in-a-padded-cell insane—but just when she'd been ready to push Maddox Monroe away and end the kiss that he'd had no right to take, she pulled him closer instead. Even while one part of her brain was jumping up and down screaming *Stop!*, the other part was purring like a happy kitten, knowing it felt just too good to stop.

*Holy crap*, could the man ever kiss.

Even as successful as he was, his talents were being wasted in business, since he ought to have hired himself out as a gigolo instead. She couldn't remember the last time she'd locked lips with someone and been hit with such an instantaneous gut punch of lust. In fact, she wasn't sure she ever had, not even as a hormone-raging coed with a whole campus of randy guys from which to choose.

The worst thing was, she didn't even like Maddox Monroe. He was her enemy, the boy—now man—she'd sworn to hate to her dying day. Yet here she was, locking lips with him as if he were her last meal. And *sweet Jesus*, did he taste good—like seventy percent dark cacao, rich and sinful and far too delectable to resist.

Without even knowing she was doing it, she let go of his wrists and slid her fingers into his hair, tunneling them deep into the thick layers of silk. Eyes closed, she circled her tongue with his, roaming up and down and around in a warm, wet, intoxicating slide. He made a sound low in his throat and kissed her even harder.

Tingles raced over her skin, her legs shifting restlessly together beneath her skirt. She sank deeper into the passionate haze, losing herself completely in the moment.

But then, as abruptly as it had started, it was over. Maddox ended the kiss and lifted his big hands away from her overwarm cheeks.

She stared blankly, her thoughts flatlined.

"We're here," he murmured. "I don't want you to be late for your appointment."

His words took a moment to register as she looked through the car window to the street beyond. Only then did she realize that the sedan wasn't moving anymore but was parked not far from the entrance to the bridal salon, which stood only feet away.

*Holy Mary, Mother of God, the fitting!* And her mother waiting just on the other side of the tasteful brownstone's front door.

At least the rear windows of Monroe's Mercedes were tinted; otherwise who knew who might have seen the two of them playing tonsil hockey like they were trying out for the major leagues?

As for Marco, the driver, he was facing discreetly forward as if he hadn't noticed a thing. Then again, maybe he was used to Monroe kissing the brains out of women in the back of his car. For all she knew, it was a daily occurrence.

Whatever the case, she had to get away from him. *Now!*

Hurriedly, she straightened her jacket and reached for the door handle. Monroe stopped her with a hand. "Wait for Marco. He'll bring an umbrella around."

"The salon's not far. I'll make a dash for it."

"It's still pouring buckets. Wait a minute more." From the tone of his voice, Monroe was clearly used to giving commands and being obeyed.

But she'd never been the type to follow orders.

Ignoring him, she pushed the car door wide. Wind and rain gusted inside, sending a chill through her still flushed body.

But only seconds later, Marco arrived, a huge black golf umbrella spread wide to shield her from the storm.

"I'll call you later," Monroe said.

"Don't. Not unless it's business."

His brown eyes gleamed warmly. "Then I'll find some kind of business to discuss. Over dinner perhaps? I could wait for you until the fitting is finished."

"No. I'm having dinner with my mother."

"Another time, then."

*There isn't going to be another time,* she thought. *Ever!*

She didn't say anything else—she didn't trust herself to.

Climbing out of the car, she moved under the shelter of the umbrella and hurried with Marco up to the salon, where he saw her safely inside.

Once he was gone, she forced herself not to look back through the shop window. She didn't want to know if Monroe was still there.

Watching.

Waiting.

It was only then, as her mother and one of the salon assistants approached her, that she finally remembered to breathe.

To Brie's relief, Monroe didn't call the next day or the following Monday. In fact, her phone and e-mail remained a Monroe-free zone for several days more, much to her surprise. As for what had happened in the back of his sedan, otherwise known as her What-the-Hell-Was-That moment, she'd been too busy to think about it. Or at least she'd been too busy to dwell on it, shoving the memory aside each time it sprang to mind—which was only about two or three hundred times a day.

When she'd walked into the office that first morning after the kiss, she'd been prepared to hand off Monroe's account to one of the other partners no matter the fallout. But then one emergency after another had cropped up, including a hysterical visit from a client who'd just been served notice of a company-wide audit by the IRS. By the time she'd worked him down from DEFCON five and gotten the rest of the day's fires under control, it had been too late to bring up Monroe.

The following Monday hadn't been any better—hectic from the first morning cup of Starbucks that Trish had stuck in Brie's hand the moment she'd walked off the elevator to the last bite of take-out pappardelle with Bolognese sauce that she'd eaten at her desk while reading through a headache-inducing stack of discovery materials. When she'd arrived home that night, she'd taken a hot shower and gone straight to bed.

By Tuesday she'd decided it was pointless to try passing off Monroe's account. What reason was she going to give for jettisoning such a plum client from her roster? If she brought up the fact that he'd kissed her half-blind—not to mention her own enthusiastic response—she would just make trouble, for herself and the firm.

Better to stay quiet.

Nothing further was going to happen between her and Monroe anyway, so it was a moot point. It was in the past and best forgotten. Which was probably what Monroe had already done.

Forgotten.

Their torrid lip-lock just one of dozens of carnal encounters in which he likely indulged on a regular basis.

Finally another weekend arrived.

She slept until ten thirty on Saturday morning, got dressed, then made herself a cheese and mushroom omelet with toast and a cup of hot tea. After she ate and put the dirty dishes in the dishwasher, she did two loads of laundry, then went out to the market for bread, milk, fresh fruit, and other essentials. Once that was all put away in her cupboards, it was time to get ready for her date.

To be honest, if the reminder hadn't been on her smartphone calendar, she would probably have forgotten all about having agreed to take in a Broadway play with a guy she'd met at a party last month. He'd been pestering her to go out ever since, and when he'd dangled tickets in front of her for one of the hottest shows in town, she'd finally said yes.

Stifling a yawn, she wished now that she hadn't. Streaming a movie or reading a book on her couch sounded a whole lot better. But maybe an evening out would be fun. That's what she'd tell herself anyway.

Three hours later she was dreaming again about that book and her couch. Jeff, the insurance actuary, was every bit as dull as his profession, though apparently he found it fascinating. In between mouthfuls of blood-rare New York strip and smashed potatoes at the Theater District steak house he'd chosen, he regaled her with story after story about the world of statistical analysis and insurance claim forecasting.

Long before they had to refuse dessert because there wasn't enough time to eat it and still make the curtain, she was deciding where the evening ranked on her list of dates from hell. Hopefully the play would help move it out of the top-ten-all-time worst.

The theater was one of the small, older ones with narrow, velvet-covered seats and a kind of nostalgic intimacy that harkened back to bygone days. She leafed through her *Playbill* and did her best to nod occasionally as if she were actually listening to Jeff's rambling monologue.

After his initial greeting at her door, he'd barely let her get a word in edgewise. He had the most annoying habit of asking a question, then cutting her off midway through her answer. Half an hour into the date and she'd mostly gone silent, which he seem to find quite satisfactory.

Had he been this annoying when she'd met him at her friend's party? Must have been the wine she'd drunk that night that had caused a case of temporary deafness. If not for the play, she would already have found a way to ditch him. But she figured she was due some kind of compensation in light of all her obvious pain and suffering.

With an inner sigh, she waited for the play to begin. As she did, she took a few moments to look at the other people in the audience. And that's when she saw Maddox Monroe walk down the aisle and make his way to a seat two rows ahead and to the left. He was with a curvaceous redhead, whom he took solicitous care to show to her seat.

Obviously, Lila, from the tennis game, was yesterday's news.

Poor Lila.

Brie had suspected that Monroe was a player, but now she had the proof. Her jaw tightened as she remembered the mind-blowing kiss he'd stolen from her only a week or so ago. Her teeth ground together as she thought of the way she'd kissed him back. He was probably congratulating himself even now for his hat trick, bagging a brunette, a blonde, and a redhead, all within a few days of one another.

But he hadn't really "bagged" her, since all they'd done was kiss. As far as she was concerned, the fact that she'd temporarily lost her mind there in the back of his sedan didn't count. Neither did his having been the one with enough functioning brain cells to call a halt to their snog-in-progress. If he hadn't, who knows how many bases she might have let him run.

Crossing her arms over her chest, she looked away. He was welcome to enjoy his date. No doubt he and the redhead deserved each other.

She checked her wristwatch. Nearly time for the play to start. She picked a minuscule dot of lint off her skirt and nodded absently at Jeff's latest remark. Unable to resist the temptation, she snuck another look in Monroe's direction.

And looked straight into his coffee brown eyes.

A little jolt went through her as if she'd stuck her finger into an electrical socket.

The corners of his mouth turned up and he lifted a hand in greeting.

She thought of a curse not suitable for work—or a public theater—then gave a short wave back.

"Someone you know?"

It was Jeff, whom she'd forgotten all about. "Yes. He's a client."

Luckily the houselights began to dim, the curtain going up. Without turning her head, she looked at Monroe again. But he was facing forward, his own head bent toward his date as they exchanged some bit of conversation.

One of the actors stepped onstage and said his first line and the play began.

But hard as Brie tried to focus, her attention was scattered, her awareness of Monroe as annoying as a scratchy clothing tag you couldn't reach to cut out. Still she managed not to look his way again. As for the play, she only heard about half of it. Count on Maddox Monroe to ruin the only good part of the evening.

Finally intermission arrived.

The houselights came up and people began shuffling out of their seats. Brie stood to let several individuals in her row squeeze past.

"Wanna drink?" Jeff asked.

"Sure. Why not?" She moved back to let him slip by her as well.

She was about to sit down again when she heard her name.

And there stood Monroe, tall and dynamic in a well-made dark gray suit but no tie. His collar was open, showing his strong, masculine throat. The bruises on his face looked better; only a slight tinge of yellow remained under one eye.

"Enjoying the play?" he asked.

"Yes. It's excellent." What little of it she'd been able to concentrate on, that was. "You?"

"It's fine. Broadway's not usually my thing. Daphne wanted to come."

Daphne. His date, she presumed, who wasn't with him at the moment.

"Ladies' room," he volunteered, as if reading her mind. "And your . . . companion?"

"Getting drinks."

He nodded and moved closer as a couple in the aisle tried to walk past. "So? How was the fitting?"

She stared for a few seconds before his question clicked. "Oh, the fitting. For the bridesmaid's dress. It went fine. Really well actually, especially since it got me off my mom's PITA list."

He arched a brow. "PITA list?"

"Pain in the ass. Or PIHA, pain in her ass, depending on how you want to think about it."

Monroe laughed. "And dinner out with your mother? How did that go?"

"Great. We tried a new Indian place that was really good."

"You'll have to give me the name. I love anything spicy. The hotter, the better."

She'd just bet he did.

He slid a hand into his pants pocket. "So? Have you thought about my invitation? When are you going to let me take you out to dinner?"

*Ah, and the real Monroe returns.* Obviously it was "out of sight, out of mind" with his date. Her mouth tightened. "I'd have to say *never* given the circumstances."

"What circumstances? Or are you still carrying a grudge from the old days?"

"I'm referring to your date," she said tartly. "Or do you always hit on one woman while another is off reapplying her lipstick?"

"You mean Daphne? Actually, she's my—"

"Did I hear my name?" the redhead under discussion said as she trotted up to them on a pair of stiletto heels so high most women would have landed on their asses at anything faster than a careful walk. "What did I miss? Maddox isn't telling stories about me again, is he? By the way, I'm Daphne. And you are?"

Daphne thrust out a hand.

Brie hesitated a fraction of a second, then took the offered hand. They shook. "Brie Grayson."

"Nice grip. You box?"

"No. At least not in the physical sense."

Daphne frowned.

"She's a lawyer," Monroe explained. "My lawyer, as it happens."

Daphne's blue-gray eyes lit up. "Sue anybody interesting lately?"

Brie couldn't help but smile. "There's usually somebody who needs suing. But no one for Mr. Monroe, at least not yet."

"Ooh, *Mr. Monroe*. So formal. Tell her she can call you Maddox, Maddox."

Monroe met Brie's eyes. "She can call me anything she likes."

"Careful," Brie murmured. "I just might take you up on that."

Monroe grinned. "I look forward to it, Brie-Brie."

Daphne glanced between the two of them, a speculative look in her eyes.

Brie ignored his use of her old nickname. "Yes, well, I ought to let you get back to your date."

"Date?" Daphne's red eyebrows arched high and she giggled. "We're not on a date."

"You aren't?" Brie said.

"Not unless you call badgering your big brother into

taking you to the theater a date. I practically had to hog-tie him and drag him out the door to get him here tonight."

*The redhead is his sister?*

As if to confirm that fact, Monroe shot Daphne a look of pure brotherly exasperation. "I don't think I was quite that reluctant."

"Of course you were. You hate the theater. And if it weren't for the fact that I'm visiting from out of town, and you agreed that we could do whatever I liked this weekend, we'd be at a Yankees game right now watching grown men make outrageous sums of money hurling balls at each other."

"She's a sports fan; can you tell?" He jerked a thumb in his sister's direction.

Daphne puffed out her not-insubstantial cleavage. "I'm a shopping fan, especially for clothes and shoes. And clearly I enjoy taking in a Broadway show whenever I get the chance."

"She means when I can get tickets at the last minute."

Daphne grinned. "That too."

If Brie hadn't realized they were siblings before, she certainly did now. No one could sling gibes like a sibling, and she ought to know, since she had three of her own.

"Actually, *I'm* a Mets fan," Brie said.

"Then you clearly thrive on losing." Monroe rolled his eyes. "Maybe I should rethink my decision to make you my chief legal counsel," he teased.

Brie shrugged. "You're the client, so it's up to you. But anyone who knows me knows that I'm loyal through and through. When I believe in something, I never give up, not even when others might see it as a lost cause."

"I happen to like lost causes and long shots," he said. "If I didn't, it's doubtful I'd be where I am today."

"It's true," Daphne interjected. "He was a broke-ass kid when he got into the hotel biz at the tender age of seventeen. Started as a desk clerk and worked his way up while earning his business degree in only three years. He lined up investors and owned his first hotel by the time he was twenty-five. Now he's got first-class, boutique hotels all over the U.S. and Canada with plans to go international when the time is right."

"Quit boring Brie, Daph. She hears enough about my business at work already." He gave his sister a quick hug, then winked. "Daphne moonlights as my PR rep when she isn't busy running her own very successful B and B on the South Carolina shore. She comes to the city periodically to run her mouth to anyone who will listen."

Daphne mock elbowed him in the side. "Only because it's the truth. He's the brilliant one in the family and we're all so proud of him we could bust. As for running my mouth, he's got me there. It's one of my particular specialties, that and saying whatever comes to mind no matter how inappropriate it might be."

Brie couldn't help but laugh.

Daphne joined her. "Everyone says it's the red hair. Brings out the wild."

"Not to mention the cray-cray," Monroe said, straight-faced.

Daphne elbowed him again, harder this time. He groaned comically and clutched his side.

Just then, a man came to a halt next to Brie. She looked at him for a long blank moment before she realized who he was.

Jeff. Her date. Whom she'd forgotten all about—again.

"Sorry it took so long," he said. "The line was a killer." In both hands, he held tall, lidded cups with the logo and graphic of the play printed on the outside. "Wasn't sure what you wanted, so I got two different kinds. One's Coke and the other's Sprite. Your choice."

She wished one was an iced tea, since she wasn't much of a soda drinker. But when in Rome . . . "Coke."

Jeff started to hold one out to her, then changed his mind and held out the other. Then he pulled them both back. "Shit . . . I mean crap . . . I had it all straight in my head until I got here. Now I can't remember. Is the right one Coke or Sprite?"

"Either's fine." Brie extended her hand again. As she did, she saw the look Monroe gave her out of the corner of her eye.

*Really?* he said with perfect nonverbal derision. *He's the best you can round up for a date?*

*At least I'm not out with my sister,* she eyeballed back.

He smirked.

"No, no." It was Jeff, gibbering again. "Let me figure this out. I can figure this out."

"Why don't you just take a sip from one of the straws?" Daphne suggested.

Jeff shook his head, looking repulsed. "And share germs? In case you missed the news report, there's a gnarly late-season cold going around. I wouldn't want to give anything to Brie."

"Or vice versa, right?" Daphne's eyes danced.

"Well, yeah, right."

"I'm Daphne by the way."

"Jeff."

Brie realized that she hadn't made introductions. "Jeff, this is Maddox Monroe and his sister. They're . . ."

"Friends of Brie's," Monroe supplied. Rather than shake—since Jeff had no free hands—he nodded, then stuck his own hands into his pants pockets. Clearly he was enjoying the Jeff show a lot more than he apparently had the first half of the play.

"Hey." Jeff nodded back. Glancing at the drinks, whose outsides were beginning to turn slick with condensation, Jeff stuck one cup in the crook of his arm. "Quick peek should do it."

He reached to carefully twist off the spill-proof top.

Suddenly, the lights flashed, signaling everyone to return to their seats. Jeff had just lifted the top off for his "quick peek" when a big man bumped him from behind.

Ice and soda flew out in an arc—and hit Brie square in the chest. She sucked in a gasp as sticky cold soaked straight through her thin, pink silk dress and seeped into her bra underneath before leaking downward in rivulets.

Of course, it would have to be the Coke. The stain would never come out.

But Brie wasn't much concerned about the stain at the moment, too wet and shocked and pissed to say a word.

"Oh, Christ," Jeff moaned. "Brie, I'm so sorry. That guy, he knocked into me. Bastard didn't even stop. Ah, crap, just look at you."

*Yeah, look at me.* She'd rather not.

"Here." Monroe held out a handkerchief to her.

Numbly, she took it and began to blot—for all the good that would do.

"Daph, why don't you go to the ladies' room with Brie to clean up?"

"Sure," Daphne agreed.

"No, really, that's sweet, but there isn't any point in us both missing the second act," Brie said, finally recovering her ability to speak. "Go back to your seat. I'll get cleaned up on my own."

As if her words were a signal, the lights went down

and music began to play. People were staring at them, a few making hushing noises as the actors came back out onto the stage.

"Is there a problem?" It was one of the ushers. She scowled as she took in the scene, which included the wet carpet, the dripping "spill-proof" cup, and Brie.

"Just a little accident," Monroe said in a low, reassuring murmur. "We're taking care of it."

The usher scowled harder. "Yes, well, you need to retake your seats. I'll see to this lady."

"Go on," Brie whispered to Monroe and his sister. "There's nothing you can do. Enjoy the play."

As for Jeff, he just stood there, a cup in each hand, one empty, one full.

Brie barely spared him a glance as she moved out into the aisle.

The usher left her in the ladies' room, where she used handfuls of wet paper towels to blot at the sticky disaster. But it was pretty much useless and after a couple of minutes she gave up. The wet silk clung to her. She held it away from her body and used some more paper towels to absorb enough of the wetness so she didn't look indecent. After carefully washing her hands and scrubbing the sticky off her neck and chest, she decided things were as good as they were going to get.

With a sigh, she turned and walked out into the corridor.

There stood Monroe. He was leaning against the opposite wall.

"Why aren't you in watching the play?" she asked.

"Because I'm waiting for you. Thought I'd give you a ride home. I figured you wouldn't want to sit next to Jeffie boy for another hour and a half. Am I right?"

He was most definitely right. As far as she was concerned, her date with Jeff was over. "I can get a cab. You don't have to take me."

"My driver's already here. It's no trouble."

"What about your sister?"

"She's enjoying the show. I'll swing back around to pick her up after I see to you. She says to tell you how sorry she is about your dress and that she enjoyed meeting you."

"Tell her I enjoyed meeting her too. But really, go watch the rest of the play. I'm fine getting home on my own."

"I'm sure you are, but I can use a break. All that dialogue is hurting my brain. Besides, the trip will give Marco something to do. He gets bored waiting."

Brie considered refusing, but finding a cab on a Saturday night in the Theater District would be a total pain. And in her damp, ruined dress, she didn't much relish the idea of riding the subway. She could only imagine the pervy comments that might come her way.

"Why is it lately that you're always around to offer me a ride?" she said.

" 'Cause you're lucky, sweetheart. Maybe we should swing by a convenience store along the way and buy some lottery tickets." Grinning, he caught her hand up in his and led her toward the entrance.

She tried to pull free, but he held on, letting go only when they reached his now familiar, polished black sedan idling at the curb. She remembered the last time she'd ridden in that car—and everything that had happened.

"Good evening, Ms. Grayson. A pleasure to see you again," Marco said, giving her a polite smile. He didn't so much as blink twice at her disaster of a dress before he held open the rear door.

"Hello, Marco."

"Nice weather tonight. No rain."

"Small mercies, huh?"

"Exactly."

The driver waited and she hesitated, Monroe standing silent at her back.

With an internal shrug, she climbed inside. Monroe would kiss her only if she let him. And that one hundred percent wasn't going to happen.

She relaxed back into the comfortable leather seat as Marco shut the door. Monroe joined her from the opposite side while Marco took his seat behind the steering wheel. She leaned forward, intending to give Marco her address.

"He knows where we're going."

She looked at Monroe. "How could that be?"

"Because I gave him your address. I make it a point to know where my attorneys live."

Where *she* lived, he meant. Somehow she doubted he'd bothered to memorize the home addresses of any of the other partners. But what did it really matter? He could have found out anytime with nothing more than a quick phone call.

The car set off into the night, leaving her alone once again with Maddox Monroe.

# Chapter Eight

Maddox watched her, enjoying the play of expressions that seemed to move constantly over her face. The city lights flashed past as the car merged into the pulse of the traffic, but he paid no attention, his thoughts fixed squarely on Brie.

He'd read her hesitation about getting into the car. No doubt she was remembering the kisses they'd shared. God knew he was; he couldn't get those moments or the sensations out of his head.

They'd haunted him ever since that day, popping up at some of the most inconvenient times, such as in the middle of a board meeting when his focus should have been on projections and analyses rather than on the lush softness of Brie's pink lips. Or the way the silky curves of her cheeks had felt against his palms and how the sweet, clean fragrance of her hair had teased his senses until he'd gone half-mad.

He was always hovering on the brink of arousal whenever she was near, and it wouldn't take much to push him over the edge. A tiny, come-on crook of her finger was all that would be necessary. But tonight wasn't the night, much as he wished otherwise. He'd promised his sister a late supper out and after the evening Brie had endured, he suspected that all she really wanted was a hot shower and a good night's sleep.

He would be patient—for a little while longer anyway.

"How is the Newport acquisition coming?" He settled deeper into his seat and tried to ignore thoughts of her standing wet and naked in the shower, soapsuds sluicing down her body.

She angled her head. "You want to talk business?"

*I'd better,* he thought. Otherwise, he wasn't sure he could trust himself not to initiate another backseat make-out session. His hands curled into fists. "No time like the present."

She drew a breath. "We've filed all the required papers. I should have something for you by early next week."

"Good. What about the labor review?"

"In process. I've set up a conference call that will bring all the pertinent players to the table. I can give you the time, if you want to sit in."

"No. A postmortem of the salient points should be sufficient." He fired off another trio of questions, which she did her best to answer.

She withdrew her cell phone from her purse and typed in a few quick notations. "If I'd known we were going to have a meeting tonight, I would have brought along my laptop. Do you always put your lawyers on the spot?"

"Frequently." Though generally not in the backseat of his car and as a means of keeping his libido under control. Considering the simmering arousal still riding him, he wasn't altogether sure his efforts were having the desired effect.

He'd need a cold shower for that.

The car slowed a few minutes later, then pulled up to the curb. The building was a modern, well-maintained high-rise with a doorman who stood at the ready. Maddox got out after Brie and walked her to the entrance.

"Thank you for the lift," she told him. "Sad to say but it was actually the best part of the evening."

"Glad I was there to help. Why don't we go in? I'll see you to your door."

"I can see myself. This is a great building with round-the-clock security and Joe here doesn't let in oddballs or strangers, do you, Joe?" She nodded to the doorman, a forty-something man with graying black hair and a burly build that more than filled out his uniform.

"Sure don't, Ms. Grayson," he said with his Brooklyn accent. "I'll make sure she gets inside safe."

"Undoubtedly." Maddox looked at Brie. "Thing is, I promised Daphne that I'd walk you to your apartment. You wouldn't want me to tell her I just left you standing outside your building."

"Daphne is very thoughtful, but it's not necessary."

"Necessary or not, I'm escorting you." He took hold of her elbow.

Her eyes narrowed.

"Only to your front door, counselor," he said. "It'll put Daphne's mind at ease."

After a moment, she gave a wry laugh and shook her head. "Well, if it will let your sister sleep tonight, then who am I to refuse? Joe, if he's not back down here in fifteen minutes, send up the cavalry."

"Sure thing, Ms. Grayson." A grinning Joe held open the door. "Sir."

"Joe."

Maddox had to stop briefly and sign in at the security

desk as a visitor. Together, he and Brie walked to the small bank of elevators.

After punching the button, they rode up.

"Your sister didn't really say anything about you walking me up, did she?" Brie gave him a knowing look.

"Not in so many words, but she would have if she'd thought of it. She really will be relieved. Worrying is another one of her specialties. She checks up on me far more often than I might wish."

Brie smiled. "Ah, the blessing and curse of families. It's wonderful being loved, but murder putting up with all the well-meaning butting in."

"Exactly."

Far too quickly for his liking, the elevator arrived on her floor. He walked beside her down the hallway.

She stopped in front of a door that read 10-G. "Here I am."

"*G* for Grayson?" He tapped a finger against the letter on the door.

"No. *G* for weird coincidence, since this was the only one-bedroom available in the building when I was looking for an apartment."

"Must have been meant to be."

She tipped her head to the side. "I wouldn't have pegged you for the fatalistic type."

"I'm not, not usually. Still, I like to keep an open mind. What else could account for the two of us meeting again so unexpectedly after all these years?"

"Really bad luck?"

"Or really good, depending on your way of thinking." He gave her a slow smile, pleased when her eyes got a slightly glazed look that meant she wasn't nearly as immune to him as she wanted him to think.

She blinked twice and turned to fit her key in the lock.

The door opened with a soft click. "Well, thank you again for the ride home. You seem to be coming to my rescue a lot these days."

"That's me. Your white knight."

"I think you've got the color wrong. Black's more your style."

"If that were true, I'd have left you back at the theater with Jeff."

"Not even you would be that cruel."

"I'm not cruel."

"You were when we were kids." She met his eyes, her own blue as a summer lake. "You made my life a living hell that year and you know it. Why would I think anything good about you now?"

"Because we're not twelve years old anymore." Reaching out, he stroked the edge of one finger along her cheek, then caught her chin in his hand. "Besides, don't you know that little boys are only mean to the little girls they like the best? Think about that, Brie, while you're lying in your bed tonight."

"I'll be too busy sleeping," she told him in an arrogant tone as she shook off his hand.

He laughed. "My fifteen minutes must nearly be up. I'd better leave before the cavalry gets here. Go inside, Brie. I'll see you again soon."

Her mouth opened as if she wanted to say something—maybe a whole lot of somethings—then closed it again. After one final look, she went into her apartment.

Whistling softly under his breath, he headed for the elevators.

Brie leaned back against her door, hands splayed flat against the painted wood, her heart beating hard beneath her ribs.

*Ooh, that man. He drives me crazy.*

Just like he had when they were kids.

But as he'd reminded her, they weren't kids anymore.

So why did she always feel like a six-year-old who'd just gotten her pigtail yanked whenever he was around? And why did she suspect that tonight when she crawled between the sheets, he would be on her mind—and not in a childish kind of way?

*Well, he won't. I'll kick him straight out of my head,* she promised herself as she engaged the dead-bolt lock, then went to switch off the hall light she'd turned on before she'd gone out for the evening.

Going to her bedroom, she peeled off her ruined dress and tossed it on top of the laundry hamper. Even though it was probably a lost cause, she'd take it to the dry cleaner's tomorrow and give them a crack at removing the stain.

In the bathroom, she stripped off her bra and panties and stepped under the warm shower spray. Temporarily, she lost herself in a cloud of gently scented steam.

But later, as she settled into bed with her clean, blow-dried hair and fresh nightgown, his words popped into her mind.

*Don't you know that little boys are only mean to the little girls they like the best?*

And big boys?

They were even worse, using sweet words and even sweeter kisses to get precisely what they wanted—and having the power to make women forget exactly why they were so dangerous.

"Yum," Daphne said, laying her spoon neatly across her plate.

After Maddox had picked her up from the show—

which she told him had been fabulous and a shame he'd missed—they'd gone to an excellent but hideously expensive restaurant. Taking advantage of the culinary adventure, she'd ordered a seven-course tasting menu, which featured everything from appetizer to dessert with amuse-bouches, bread, and palate cleansers in between. And wine, of course. She hadn't stinted on wine. Maddox didn't mind, however, content with good dark-roast, French press coffee—black, one sugar.

He'd ordered seven courses as well, enjoying the meal, but not as much as he enjoyed watching his sister ooh and aah over each subsequent offering. With seven years between them, it always pleased him to make his baby sis happy.

After their father went to prison, Maddox had assumed the role of more than big brother, acting at times as a kind of surrogate father. Always there to lend a strong shoulder, always available for protection and support. Even their mother had taken to leaning on him, especially during those first few terrible years. She'd looked to him to be the man of the house when he'd still been nothing more than an immature kid. But he'd grown up fast. When he'd left home at eighteen, he'd been an adult, full-grown.

So Daphne's visits were always an occasion for indulgence. And she deserved the pampering. Particularly after the heartbreak she'd suffered in the wake of a brief but disastrous marriage, which had brought her east, then left her abandoned and alone.

But she hadn't been alone. She'd had him and she always would.

She ate one of the tiny chocolate entremets that had been served at the end of dessert, closing her eyes as the sweet melted against her tongue.

Curiously, it put him in mind of his lunch with Brie. She'd had that same expression of wonder and delight as she'd eaten his chef's three-star cuisine—although in her case the look had been tempered with a wary reserve, through which he was still trying to break.

He wished now that he'd kissed her again. But he hadn't trusted himself not to try taking things further and Brie wasn't ready yet. Not for all the things he wanted.

And he definitely wanted them all.

"You thinking about Brie Grayson?"

He blinked, his eyes going to his sister. "Why would you say that?"

Her lips curved in a knowing half smile. "Just the way you looked at her tonight and the way you were just looking again. You really like her, don't you?"

His fingers wrapped around his coffee cup. "Maybe."

Daphne laughed. "Right. And maybe I only kind of liked this meal. So have you asked her out?"

"Yes."

"And she said no?"

"She says we shouldn't see each other because she's my attorney. Ethical concerns."

"Well, what does that have to do with anything? It's not like she's a psychiatrist trying to do inappropriate things to you on her couch. Not that you'd probably mind."

"Now why would you say that?"

She laughed.

"We've also got a history," he told her.

"What kind of history?" Tiny lines creased her brow.

"We knew each other as kids. Back when you were just a drooling rug rat working hard on graduating to curtain climber."

Daphne made a face; she hated it when he made references to her baby days.

"She didn't like me," he admitted.

"Probably with good reason."

"Definitely. I was a regular little shit."

"Well, grade-school history or not, you've got a clear field, especially if that date of hers tonight was any example of the kind of guys she's been seeing."

"He was rather pathetic."

"He was. But cute. I'm having dinner with him tomorrow night."

"What?"

"I invited him to sit with me after you left. He looked like a kicked puppy. I couldn't just leave him there all alone."

"Christ, Daphne. Tomorrow's your last night in town. What are you doing going out with some random guy?"

"He's not a random guy. He was Brie's date tonight. Now he's mine. Considering how they left things, I don't think she'll mind. But let's put all that aside, since we were talking about you."

"Not because I volunteered. I don't usually discuss my love life with my little sister."

"Maybe you should from now on. I saw the way Brie was looking at you."

"Oh, and how was that?"

"All sultry-eyed and interested in spite of what she might say." Daphne sipped from her own cup of coffee—hers a light, sweet beige. "Anyway it'd be nice to actually like someone you were seeing for a change, not that any of your women stay around long."

"My women?" He smirked. "You make it sound like I keep a harem."

"You could if you wanted to, you know, what with

your looks, influence, and money. What was the last one's name?"

"You mean Lila?"

"That's right. Li-*lah*," she said, stretching out the name. "How long did it last with her?"

He thought for a moment. "About six weeks. It wasn't anything serious."

Especially not after he'd run into Brie again. He'd broken it off with Lila after his lunch with Brie and was glad he had, considering the nasty rant Lila had started when she'd figured out she was being dumped. But he'd warned her from the start that he didn't do commitment and that they were just having fun. Guess she hadn't been ready yet to find someone new to keep her amused.

"I think six months is the longest you've ever been with anybody." Daphne drank the last of her coffee. "If you don't count Ellen, that is."

"I don't." His voice was hard, the subject a closed one.

"And you're sure you have no interest in ever getting married again?"

"Zero point zero percent."

"But what if you meet someone and really fall in love?"

He shrugged. "Even if I did, it still doesn't mean I'd want to get married. Been there, done that, end of story. Anyway, considering what you've been through, I'd think you'd be the last person out there waving her pompoms and cheering on the institution of marriage. Surely you don't have an interest in going there again?"

Their waiter approached and refilled his and Daphne's cups with fresh hot coffee. Daphne waited until he'd gone, taking an extra minute to stir in cream and sugar.

"I might," she said slowly. "If I met the right person. In the meantime, the business is doing great, I love living on the shore, and I'm having way too much fun being single to worry about serious things like whether I'll ever tie the knot again."

"That's right. You're having fun. I'm having fun. Let's agree we're both happy exactly the way we are." He flipped open the leather holder containing the bill and did a quick scan before signing the slip inside. "You finished?"

She drank another swallow of coffee, then reached for the last sugarcoated square of passion fruit gelée that sat on the ultramodern entremets plate. "Seems a shame to waste it." She popped the confection in her mouth and smiled.

Maddox shook his head and smiled back.

# CHAPTER NINE

It was Thursday afternoon nearly a week later when Brie's office phone buzzed. With her mind squarely focused on a corporate spreadsheet analysis she was reviewing, she pushed the speaker button with only partial attention.

"Yes? What is it, Gina?" she asked her administrative assistant. She didn't take her eyes off the screen, typing in a couple of notations.

"Sorry to interrupt, Brie, but there is a client here to see you."

"A client? I don't have any appointments today. Tell them I'm sorry but they'll have to come back."

"I did, but he says he needs to see you now. It's Mr. Monroe." Her admin added the last part in a kind of stage whisper.

*Monroe? Here? Now?*

What did he want?

Whatever it was, she supposed she would have to see him. He was a significant new client and however much she wished she could tell him to schedule an appointment and come back another day, she worried about the blowback, and the reaction of the other partners, if she did.

She swallowed a sigh. "All right. Give me two minutes, then send him in."

After typing in a final comment and marking her place, she clicked the electronic file closed, then enabled a sleep corner that brought up a screen saver of the law firm's blue and gold logo. She shoved a handful of stray pens into a caddy, retaining one, which she set atop a bright yellow ruled legal pad.

Gina's quiet tap came at the open door, and there stood Maddox Monroe, waiting just behind her administrative assistant. He towered over the diminutive brunette, looking undeniably attractive in a gray three-piece suit with a white pocket square and a dark eggplant-colored tie. He'd gotten his hair trimmed recently, yet a stray piece lay tumbled over his forehead; it practically begged to be brushed back.

She ignored the impulse, curling her hands into relaxed fists as she stood and came around from behind her desk. "Mr. Monroe, what a pleasant surprise."

He quirked a brow, plainly amused by her carefully polite greeting.

"Come in and have a seat." She gestured toward a comfortable corner grouping of sofa, chairs, and coffee table. "What can I get you to drink? Water? Soda? Coffee?"

"Nothing, thank you." Monroe went to take a seat on the sofa.

Brie followed, perching on one of the chairs. She waited until Gina left before she dropped the customer service routine. "So, why are you here? Is this business or personal? And I hope you're going to say business."

"Is that any way to speak to your newest, most important client?"

"No, but it's how I'm speaking to you. What's up, Monroe?"

"Maddox." He met her eyes. "You used to call me Maddox."

"I used to call you a whole lot of things, including Mad Bastard and Ox Breath—oh, and Creepface—but I never had the nerve to use any of them to your face and it was a long time ago. 'Monroe' seems preferable now and far more politically correct under the circumstances."

He gave her a crooked half smile. "I suppose I deserve that, Brie-Brie, considering some of the taunts I used to make about you."

"Hmm, such as calling me a creamy little cheese?"

"Well, you did look smooth and luscious, even to a smart-ass seventh grader. But I apologize now for any hurt I may have caused."

She sat, surprised not only by his apology but by his apparent sincerity as well. Did he really mean it? Was he sorry for the way he'd once treated her? Even if he wasn't, it seemed shallow and immature to continue nursing a grudge over things they'd done when they'd been children. Time to move on. Time to act like adults.

"Apology accepted. Maddox."

"Good." He relaxed back, laying an arm along the back of the sofa. "Ox Breath? Really?"

She smirked. "Ox Brains too; and *that* was *very* accurate, since you got As in every damned class without studying."

"I had to crack the books hard in college, so don't feel bad. And I didn't graduate from Harvard and Harvard Law."

She saw his gaze move across to her diplomas displayed on the east-facing wall. They were arranged near a large, attractive landscape painting of Connecticut in the fall, the setting not far from where she'd grown up.

And he had as well.

"So, is this just a personal visit? Did Daphne get back home okay?"

He looked at her again. "She did. She's back at the B and B making blueberry scones and homemade jams, scrubbing toilets and putting fresh sheets on guest room beds."

"You probably shouldn't let her hear you talk about her work that way."

"She'd be the first to say she's the goddess of all things domestic. I'm very proud of her. Her business is small but thriving. As for your question, I did have another reason for dropping in on you." Pausing, he reached into his interior jacket pocket and withdrew a folded sheath of papers. He held it out to her. "This was delivered to me yesterday."

Brie accepted it, then leaned back to peruse the contents. She said nothing as she scanned the document, taking note of the name of the rival law firm, whose reputation was nearly as good as MMP's. For them to take a case like this, they must smell blood in the water, or at least the potential for a hefty payout.

"You're being sued for fifty million dollars." Her surprise didn't show on her face or in her voice; she'd learned long ago how to hide her reactions, especially in front of a client. "This man . . . this"—she glanced down to locate the plaintiff's name—"Roger Mergenfeld. He says he was a partner in your company and that he was driven out. He claims he is entitled to half of your business but will accept fifty million dollars in exchange for his waiving any current or future interest in the corporation."

"He's a greedy little weasel, that's what he is. He isn't entitled to a penny."

"I can see you have strong feelings on the subject. I have to ask, though, does his complaint have any merit? Was he your partner?"

Maddox's jaw clenched, teeth grinding. "He was, but it was a long time ago when he and I were both starting out. We opened the first M Hotel together in Santa Barbara, California. Roger put up most of the money, an inheritance he'd gotten from his aunt. When the hotel took off and I wanted to expand, he said it was too much work and trouble and that he wanted out. He'd rather surf and write music.

"He's always been a wannabe rocker. So, I paid him back his initial investment plus a fair cut of the profits to that point. He seemed happy and I was glad to be on my own, free to make my own decisions without any one else's say-so. I assumed that was the end of the matter."

"Is this lawsuit the first time you've heard from him since then?"

Maddox shook his head. "No. He started writing and calling me about six months ago. He sold a couple songs, but his solo music career isn't going well apparently, and, from what my investigators discovered, he's burned through all but a few thousand dollars of his money."

She jotted down a few notes on the legal pad. "How much was the original payout you gave him?"

"Seven hundred and fifty thousand. Five hundred for the initial investment and two fifty for his share of the business. I had everything valued at the time, so it was more than fair."

"Did you put everything in writing including the dissolution of the partnership?"

"I did. We used a lawyer, not one of your caliber, but he seemed legitimate."

She nodded. "I'll need to see all that paperwork. The contracts, valuations, separation agreements, everything you have from that time, even notes. From the sound of it, he's just casting out lures, hoping he'll get a bite. But I can't say for sure whether there's any merit to his claim until I've started a review."

"He doesn't have a claim. I paid him what he was entitled to."

She met his eyes. "Yes. But the firm he's hired is a good one and I doubt they'd have taken his case unless they think there's a chance of a settlement at the very least."

He scowled.

"Don't worry. Send over everything you have and I'll get on it right away. Hopefully all I'll have to do is send a cease and desist letter and maybe threaten to countersue and they'll decide to drop the whole thing."

"Good. I'm relying on you to take care of it, Brie."

"That's why you hired me."

She stood.

He did as well, tucking his hands into his pockets. "Now, back to the personal."

"We have nothing personal to discuss." She went behind her desk.

"Of course we do." He smiled. "You still owe me dinner. How about tonight?"

"I never promised to go to dinner with you. Besides, you just added a huge amount of work to my already full schedule. I don't have time for dinner."

"Of course you do." He flattened his hands on her desk and leaned forward. "You've got to eat. Why not with me?"

"I'll order something in and eat here." She looked into his rich brown eyes. "Go away, Monroe."

"Maddox," he reminded, his voice low and dangerously appealing.

"Go away, Maddox."

"I'm a client. Surely you wine and dine clients?"

"The firm does. Would we be discussing more firm business, then? Maybe I should invite a couple of the other partners. I'm sure they'd love to tag along."

"Do you always aim for the jugular, counselor?"

A genuine smile broke over her face. "Every chance I get. Now I really do need to get back to work. Surely you have business to attend to, or do you let your subordinates do all the heavy lifting these days?"

"Like I said, straight for the jugular."

She laughed and waved him out.

To her surprise, he went, looking far too tempting for words.

With an inward sigh, she watched until he disappeared into the hallway, and wondered when he'd gone from detestable to *GQ* delicious.

Frowning, she sank into her Aeron chair and clicked her computer back on. With a focus she'd cultivated in law school, she put Maddox firmly out of her mind.

# Chapter Ten

Brie took the train up to Connecticut the following Thursday, leaving the office in time to snag a seat with a table so she could spread out while she did some work along the way.

Ivy and James's wedding was that Saturday afternoon and family and friends were arriving from all corners of the globe. James's parents had flown in from Bora-Bora, arriving only two nights before, and an aunt from the Grayson side of the family had come all the way from Tierra del Fuego, where she was studying migratory birds.

Tomorrow would be a busy day with the rehearsal at five, followed by the rehearsal dinner, which was being held at a fine-dining restaurant in a lovely old historic mansion.

Since Brie didn't have a car, her brother had volunteered to pick her up at the train station. P.G. was waiting on the platform. His russet hair glinted red-brown in the bright June sunlight, his strong, intelligent features seeming to grow more attractive with each year. His blue eyes were full of patient good humor, which was a good thing considering the pair of children who were practically jigging at his side with pent-up excitement. The kids screamed, "Auntie Brie, Auntie Brie" the moment they saw her step off the train, racing like a pair of lunatics to grab her for hugs and kisses.

She laughed and caught them both to her for a hard squeeze, ruffling nine-year-old Brian's brown hair, then bending low to give six-year-old Heather a smacking kiss on the cheek. Heather giggled, her auburn curls dancing around her fair-skinned cheeks, while Brian launched into a story about a new video game he'd just gotten that was "super gnarly," and how soon did she think they could play?

"I doubt your grandmother is going to cut either one of us enough slack for video games right now."

Brian let out a loud, deeply put-upon sigh. "I know. Grammy caught me 'idling' yesterday and made me fill about a bazillion little white bags with lavender seeds. My hands smelled like a girl when I was done."

"That would be the worst ever, huh?" Brie said, hiding a sarcastic smile.

"Yeah."

"I like smelling like a girl," Heather piped with a proud smile.

"You would, twerp, 'cause you are one." Brian smirked.

Heather's face fell.

"Brian, what did I say about not calling your sister names?"

P.G. sent his son a stern look.

"Sorry, Dad." Brian scuffed a tennis shoe against the concrete and looked down. "Sorry, hair ball."

*"Brian."*

"Sorry, Heather."

Brie hid another smile. "You know, Heather, I'm a girl. I like smelling girlie too sometimes."

Heather beamed and tucked her small hand inside Brie's.

Brie looked up again and met P.G.'s eyes. "Hey."

"Hey, yourself." P.G. stepped forward to give her a hug and a kiss on the cheek. "How are you doing?"

"Good. Better obviously than you."

P.G. rolled his eyes. "The house is a zoo; you wouldn't believe. This wedding prep is driving everyone crazy."

"Of course it is. It wouldn't be a wedding otherwise."

He laughed and relaxed, then leaned over to take her bag. He extended the handle as far as it would go, then angled it to roll on a pair of small, built-in wheels.

"Can I pull it, Dad?" Brian gave P.G. a hopeful look.

"I don't know. Can you?"

"*May* I pull it?" Brian said, correcting his grammar. "I'm strong. Please. Please let me do it."

"Famous last words," Brie murmured softly to her brother. "In a couple more years, you'll be begging him to do stuff like this."

P.G. met her eyes and grinned. Then he looked down again at his eager young son. "Sure, why not? Here you go, kiddo. All yours."

With Brian and the suitcase leading the way, the four of them walked along the platform and out through the station to the parking lot beyond.

"Caroline decided not to come?" Brie said after they reached P.G.'s SUV and popped the trunk to stow her bag.

"She's back at the house, napping."

"She's okay, right?"

Caroline, P.G.'s wife, was a cancer survivor. Diagnosed with uterine cancer roughly two years earlier, she'd undergone a series of grueling treatments, including a couple of experimental ones. Everyone had feared the worst, along with Caroline herself, who'd been quietly preparing those she loved best for the day she would no longer be with them. But then, to everyone's joy and relief, she'd started getting better.

She'd looked so healthy and happy the last time Brie had seen her that it was hard to believe she'd ever been sick at all. Surely the cancer wasn't back.

P.G. laid a reassuring hand on Brie's arm, obviously reading her alarm. "Hey, she's great. Really."

He waited while Heather and Brian clambered into the backseat of the car and shut the door; then he continued. "She just saw the doc three weeks ago and got a clean bill of health. She's still in remission and everything looks good."

"Then why is she tired?"

"'Cause she's been doing too much and running on too little sleep. Heather had some twenty-four-hour bug a couple days ago, which kept both of us up most of the night. Then Caro offered to help Mom and Ivy out with last-minute details and didn't get to bed until nearly two this morning. I made her stay home and nap."

His face took on a fierce expression. "I told her if she didn't get some rest, I'd get out a hammer and nails and some boards and seal her in the bedroom. Since I'm an architect and know my way around a jobsite, I could do it."

Brie smiled. "You're a good husband."

He shrugged. "Caro makes it easy. She's my anchor and I can't imagine life without her. Every day we have together is a blessing. I know it now, more than ever. I cherish each and every moment we have."

P.G. blinked and looked away, then reached up to slam the trunk closed.

Brie said nothing as she walked around to the passenger side of the car, thinking how lucky he and Caroline were to have each other in spite of the problems they faced.

What must it be like to love and trust someone with that kind of depth? To know that the person you loved more than life would never desert you, would never deceive you, and would always be there no matter what dark storms appeared on the horizon.

She'd loved someone once and he'd left her heart a wasteland. Yet for all her adoration, she realized that she hadn't known a fraction of the devotion P.G. and Caroline shared together each and every day. She'd never experienced that kind of deep mutual respect and affection. Or a desire that went far beyond the flesh and into the very spirit itself.

Ah, to love and be loved like that.

What a joy.

What a sorrow should it ever be lost.

She worried that real love was never going to happen for her. That she would always be alone, taking more comfort and satisfaction from her work than she ever did from a relationship.

She'd been burned and emotionally held men at arm's length. She wanted someone strong enough to tear down those invisible walls. A man who would love her enough to fight for her—for them. And she wanted to feel the same way in return.

Foolishly, perhaps, she wanted it all.

She wondered what Maddox Monroe would think of her sentimental yearning. He'd probably laugh and make one of his patented smart-assed remarks. Except his remarks hadn't been so smart-assed lately. In fact, he'd said a few things that were so nice, so tempting, that he'd made her downright tingle.

But what the hell was she doing thinking about Ol' Mad Ox?

She was here in Connecticut with her family, gathered to celebrate her little sister's special day of happiness as she and one of her oldest friends joined their lives in marriage. She was going to enjoy herself and not let annoying thoughts, and even more annoying people like Maddox Monroe, ruin the occasion. This wedding was a Maddox-free zone and she was going to make the most of his absence.

The Grayson house was brimming with noise and activity when P.G. parked in the long driveway, which was filled with a dozen other vehicles.

Off to the side in the vast green backyard, Brie could see a huge white tent that was being set up for the wedding reception, workers moving busily about their labors. She'd heard enough about the wedding plans to know that a romantic wooden arbor was also being built in a lush portion of the garden where roses and peonies and daylilies flourished in abundance. The arbor itself would be covered in freshly cut white and pink flowers in time for the ceremony.

Ahead in the driveway, a trio of men were off-loading chairs and tables from the back of a white van. More fresh flowers, china, crystal, and linens were scheduled for delivery in the morning. Brie knew the day would be long and eventful and she planned to assist her mother and Ivy in whatever way she could.

The homey scents of lemons and roasting chickens greeted her as she walked through a side door that led directly to the kitchen. P.G. and the kids had gone in the front and were busy taking her suitcase up to her old childhood bedroom, where she would be staying through the weekend.

Her mother stood in front of the stove, stirring something in a large saucepan. Two pies, not long out of the oven—peach and cherry from the look of them—waited on cooling racks on the big center island. A tall coconut layer cake stood on a delicate pink Fostoria glass cake stand that had been handed down from her maternal great-grandmother. Brie's mouth watered at the delectable sight.

"Hi, Mom."

Her mother turned her head, her eyes lighting with pleasure. "Brie! You're here!" Setting down the long-handled wooden spoon, she hurried over to envelop Brie in a warm hug, which Brie returned with enthusiasm.

"How was your trip?" her mother asked.

"Good. The train was crowded, but I found a seat without too much trouble."

"And worked the whole way up, no doubt. Well, there'll be no legal work this weekend."

"Just wedding work, huh?" Brie teased.

"Exactly!" Her mother laughed. "My assistant, Edyth, is outside now keeping track of the crew while I get things together in here. I don't know what I'd do without her. She's twenty-five and has more energy than a lightning storm."

"Kind of like you, Mom."

Laura waved a hand. "Oh, not the way I used to. Even I'm beginning to slow down."

"Well, if you are, I haven't seen any signs."

Her mother chuckled, then went to the refrigerator. She took out a tall pitcher of fresh lemonade, poured a glass, and handed it to Brie.

Brie thanked her and took a long drink, the taste deliciously tart, sweet, and cool on her tongue.

"Assuming you aren't the one who's too tired," Laura said, "I could use help with dinner."

"Sure thing."

Crossing to the large farmhouse sink, Brie soaped and rinsed her hands, then dried them on a bright yellow kitchen towel.

Meanwhile, Laura reached into a basket on the far counter, then gathered several thick, emerald green zucchini, a plump, shiny purple eggplant, a pair of large golden onions, a clove of garlic that crinkled in its papery skin, and several ruby and yellow heirloom tomatoes. She rinsed the vegetables in the sink, then passed them to Brie, who had already gone to get a cutting board and a knife.

"Ratatouille?" Brie confirmed.

"Of course. What goes better with roast chicken and buttered mashed potatoes than a big bowl of ratatouille?"

"Just-picked asparagus?"

"We're having that too."

Brie set to work while Laura returned to the stove, where it looked and smelled like she was making soup. Wedding soup appropriately enough, the rich, fragrant chicken stock simmering with onions and escarole. Tiny meatballs waited in a bowl nearby. They would be added at the end, along with beaten egg and extra salt and pepper to taste. Summer or winter, Laura always liked to start a meal with soup, and this was another family favorite.

"P.G. said he'd take my bag upstairs," Brie remarked. "Then he and the kids are heading out again to pick up Caroline from their house. So, when is everyone else rolling in?"

"Madelyn and Zack and the girls should be here any minute—they called from the road about half an hour ago," Laura told her. "As for your father, he and your uncle Owen and several of your cousins went out to pick up a few last-minute things. Beer, of course. Apparently I didn't buy enough of the right kind."

Laura tapped the spoon on the side of the pot. "Your aunt Constance is upstairs sleeping. Jet lag. Or at least she's supposed to be sleeping. She brought a new male friend with her, of course. Ricardo. He's a marine biologist. Very dashing and very Latin."

Laura's younger sister was a notorious free spirit who believed in the sanctity of marriage—for everyone other than herself. Confirmed single though she might be, she never went without male companionship and seemed to have a new lover with her every time she came for a visit.

Laura went to the kitchen window for some herbs that grew there in small pots. "I told Constance if she breaks the guest room bed, she's paying for it."

"Mom!"

"What?" Laura's eyes twinkled. "Her driver's license may say she's fifty-two, but she acts like she's your age. You haven't brought a male friend with you, have you?"

Brie resisted the urge to sigh. "No. I think you'd have noticed him by now if I had."

"A mother can always hope."

Brie sliced the eggplant with extra force. "So where are the bride and groom? Off stealing a few moments alone?"

"No, they're next door with the Jordans. James's parents are giving Ivy some heirloom crystal and china that has apparently been passed down for generations. Oh, and the keys to a seaside villa in the south of France. Apparently, that's Donald and Sylvia's wedding present to Ivy and James. And one of the places they're going for their honeymoon. James is keeping the other location a secret. He won't even tell me."

Brie smiled to herself over her mother's hurt feelings at James's keeping secrets from her. "His parents are giving them a trip to France? Wow, that's generous."

"No, the present is the *villa*. They're getting an entire house. Mansion probably, knowing them."

Before Brie had a chance to reply, footsteps echoed in the doorway.

"Did I just hear you say that Ivy and James are getting a villa in France as a wedding present? The Jordans didn't offer to give me a villa when I was engaged to marry James. I always knew they liked Ivy better."

"Madelyn!" Brie set down her knife and went forward to embrace her sister.

When Zack and the twins appeared moments later, she did the same with them. More kisses and hugs were exchanged with Laura, including ones that made Hannah and Holly squeal with delight. Visits to see Grammy and Grampa were always a big hit, especially when she led the girls over to the sink and gave each of them a big red strawberry.

"You have any wine, Laura?" Zack asked.

"Of course, dear. It's there in the rack. Choose whichever one looks good." Laura pointed with a hand. "Long trip?"

Madelyn sent her husband a sympathetic look over the girls' heads. "Like you wouldn't believe. Terrible traffic and a chorus of are-we-there-yets every five minutes."

"Told you we should have gotten the optional DVD player for the rear passenger seats." Zack went across to study the wine selection, deciding quickly on a bottle of something red. He went to find a corkscrew.

"We agreed that the girls don't need to watch TV in the car. They're much better off reading books, coloring, and playing road games."

"Which would be wonderful if we could get either of them to actually do any of those things." Zack popped the cork, found a glass, and poured himself a healthy draft. "Ah, sweet manna from heaven. You want a glass of red, Red?"

Madelyn sighed. "God, yes."

The adults in the room laughed, while Zack got out more glasses.

Over the next hour the kitchen filled to bursting with family and conversation. P.G. and Caroline and their kids arrived. Brian and Heather joined several under-thirteen cousins who banded together in a kind of roving pack—the Grayson family dogs trailing from room to room with them. The cats, always wise, chose to retire upstairs. Hannah and Holly were taken upstairs too for a predinner nap, so they wouldn't be cranky later on.

Philip Grayson shouldered his way inside not long after, his red hair glinting in the last of the evening sunshine, his arms laden with beer. He stopped to give Brie a huge bear hug and a kiss on the cheek that made her laugh and smile. The uncles twisted open bottles of Irish beer and kicked back while Aunt Constance introduced Ricardo around. Laura was right that he was very Latin and very charming, flirting in a way that left all the women in the room blushing. Even so, he made it plain that he and Constance were together—he was constantly touching her—and for the first time, Brie wondered if there might be more wedding bells on the horizon.

The meal came together while everyone talked and caught up on their lives and plans. James and Ivy appeared, along with his parents, who, despite their long years of acquaintance, never looked completely at ease in the company of the noisy, gregarious Grayson clan.

Brie embraced James, who grinned and laughed, his

eyes brimming with love every time he looked at Ivy. He was even happy to see Madelyn and Zack, the old hurts dead and buried, truly a thing of the past.

Then she turned to Ivy. "Hey, soon-to-be-a-Mrs. How are you doing?"

"Wonderful. Excited."

"Nervous?"

"No." Ivy smiled. "I've wanted this since I was fifteen years old. How could I be anything but jazzed to the max? As for James"—she shot a glance from under her blond lashes at her fiancé, where he stood talking to P.G.—"I think he's nervous."

"He doesn't look nervous."

"He's good at hiding it. Still I know he can't help but remember the last time he was a groom."

"Well, you're not going to ditch him at the altar. You're more likely to lasso him and drag him up to the officiant."

"True dat."

*"True dat?"*

"Neil's been instructing me on the finer points of rap culture."

"Neil would."

Neil Jones was one of Ivy's best friends and the only male member of her bridal party. He would be wearing a tailored suit rather than a bridesmaid's gown.

Brie chuckled. "Only tomorrow to go. And then it'll be your wedding day!"

"I know."

They grinned at each other, Brie happy to see her sister so happy.

"Okay, everybody," Laura said, raising her voice. "Dinner is served."

Amid laughter and conversation, they all filed into the dining room.

# Chapter Eleven

Brie took her place in front of the wide bridal arch, which burst candy-sweet with masses of white and pink flowers—delphiniums, viburnums, ranunculus, white lilacs, and sweet peas, all woven together with an abundance of leafy greenery.

The day was sunny and comfortably warm with a light breeze that sent her tea-length, blush pink organza bridesmaid's dress billowing delicately around her calves. A string quartet played soothing strains of music while the multitude of guests seated on white wooden chairs murmured quietly to one another in anticipation of the bride's arrival.

To Brie's left stood Neil Jones, Ivy's man of honor, looking dapper in a charcoal gray three-piece suit with a pink rose boutonniere that matched the flowers in the bridesmaids' bouquets. He took a moment to wave surreptitiously to his partner, Josh, who sat in the second row, next to their friend Fred, and Fred's new girlfriend.

To her right was Caroline, looking pretty and well rested; Ivy's leggy dancer friend and former neighbor,

Lulu Lancaster; and, next to her, Kayla Cardwell, Ivy's old college roommate, who'd flown in all the way from Colorado just for the wedding.

Ivy had asked Madelyn to be one of her attendants, but Madelyn had declined. This was Ivy and James's day, Madelyn had told her, and even if they'd all put the past behind them, she didn't want any awkwardness or bad memories that might cast a shadow over their happy celebration to crop up. So Madelyn had cheerfully opted to be just a guest.

Madelyn smiled at Brie from where she sat next to Zack in the second row behind their mother and aunts and uncles. Beside them were Hannah and Holly, looking cute as buttons in their pink wedding finery. The girls had already done their walk down the aisle, scattering pink rose petals with surprising aplomb, before hurrying into their seats next to their parents.

Young Brian stood with obvious pride next to P.G., who was one of James's five groomsmen. The others, including James's best man, were all friends of James whom Brie barely knew. Then there was James himself.

As Ivy had predicted, he looked nervous. He waited, tall and dashingly urbane in his elegantly tailored gray vested suit, his thick, short blond hair gleaming as vibrant as gold under the June sun. Every minute or so, he would cast a glance toward the house, an almost imperceptible frown riding his handsome brow.

Was he remembering the last time he'd stood at the altar, waiting for his bride? One who had decided to call off the wedding at the last moment.

But, as Brie knew, having been with a euphorically grinning Ivy less than two minutes before, he had nothing to worry about. Unlike the last time, his bride wasn't about to desert him.

Then the "Wedding March" began to play.

Heather, the eldest flower girl, walked out onto the petal-strewn runner, looking sweet and pretty in her frilly dress. She held a small petal-filled basket over one arm. With a solemnity that brought smiles to everyone's faces, she moved forward, scattering additional white rose petals as she went.

Less than a minute later, Ivy appeared.

The entire company drew a collective inhalation of pleasure; Ivy was just that beautiful. Her dress was timeless and elegant, pure white with a sleeveless illusion neckline and a soft lace-overlay bodice. The full tulle skirt was as light and frothy as a confection with an airiness that made it seem as if she were floating rather than walking down the aisle, their father at her side. Her blond hair was coiled high and pinned in soft waves that framed her face, a long sheer veil completing the look, which was nothing short of heaven.

Clearly, James agreed, his expression one of reverence and soul-deep love. A slow smile spread over his face as he waited for Ivy to join him, his anxiety replaced with confident joy.

The ceremony began, the judge, who was also a family friend, having the honor of officiating.

Brie watched and listened, blinking back tears when Ivy and James began to recite their unique vows. As part of his, James read the E. E. Cummings poem "I Carry Your Heart with Me," his voice ringing out with such sincere emotion that there wasn't a dry eye left. Even the judge had to blink a time or two before he began speaking again.

Then the rings were exchanged, the final vows spoken, and they were pronounced husband and wife.

"You may kiss your bride," the judge told James.

Grinning, James pulled Ivy into his arms for a passionate kiss that sent titters of indulgent amusement through the crowd. He was laughing when he let her come up for air, and so was she, her cheeks stained as pink as the roses in her bouquet. Her eyes glowed with a happiness that seemed to know no bounds.

The string quartet burst into life once more, music filling the air as the happy couple started back down the aisle.

As they did, Brie's gaze moved idly out across the multitude of assembled guests. Suddenly a tall, dark-haired man in the back got to his feet. She looked hard, then harder still, her eyes popping like a cartoon character's as recognition set in.

*What in the hell?*

Her fingers tightened around her bouquet, nails digging into the satin-wrapped stems. Of all the places she might expect to bump into Maddox Monroe, this was the very last one.

"Brie," hissed a voice near her ear.

She turned her head to see who had spoken.

It was Lulu.

"Time to go," Lulu said. "You're holding everybody up."

Looking to her left, she saw that one of James's groomsmen—Evan, if she remembered right—was indeed waiting for her to join him as part of the processional back down the aisle.

"Oh, sorry." Gathering herself, she took his arm and walked forward.

But all the way down the aisle, she was aware of only one guest, one man, the tall, dark thorn in her side who seemed to pop up wherever she went these days. As she passed his row, she met Maddox's twinkling brown eyes. He grinned at her and waggled his brows.

She looked straight ahead and continued on.

"Christ, I need a drink," she said the moment she and her groomsman escort were clear of the crowd.

"Me too. Wanna go with me and find the bar before we have to line up for photos?" Evan waited, his attractive features and pale blue eyes clearly hopeful.

"Yeah, you're on. My mother set up this shindig, so I know exactly where it is. Follow me."

Smiling, Evan followed.

One flute of champagne and a half hour of photographs later, Brie slipped into the huge reception tent, all the sides wide-open to let in the sunlight and the mild, cooling breeze.

She scanned the milling guests, checking for Maddox, but didn't see him. Maybe he'd thought better of crashing the wedding and had left. But she rather doubted it. He was probably off hitting on one of the other bridesmaids.

Lulu most likely.

What was he doing here? And how had he known when and where the wedding was being held anyway? Surely Trish hadn't told him? She was always very tight-lipped about personal information concerning the employees, partners, and associates of the firm.

Then the truth dawned on her. She herself had been the one to tell him about the wedding, that day he'd dropped her off for the fitting. Obviously he'd figured out the rest of the particulars on his own.

But why bother coming to her sister's wedding? Surely there were other ways of tracking her down, if that's the only reason he was here. Then again, she was easy to find and easy to corner and she couldn't buzz for security the way she could have at her office. Bottom line, he was trouble.

Irritated, she considered going on the hunt for him just to get whatever-was-coming over with. But then Ivy and James arrived and made their big entrance as the new Mr. and Mrs. James Jordan and the opportunity passed.

She was standing off to one side, watching the bride and groom's first dance, when a large hand curved around her shoulder from behind. A masculine thumb skimmed down the back of her neck, his touch making hot shivers chase over her skin.

"Hey, Brie-Brie, fancy meeting you here."

She swung around and shook off his hand. "Monroe."

"Ah-ah." He metronomed a finger side to side. "Maddox, remember?"

Studying him, she was annoyed to discover that he looked absolutely scrumptious in a tailored brown suit, pale lavender shirt, and dark purple tie that would have looked ludicrous on any other man but did spectacular things for him.

"What are you doing here?"

He arched an eyebrow. "Attending a wedding, obviously."

"Crashing it, you mean. You've always had a lot of nerve, but this goes way beyond."

"I'm not crashing. I was invited."

"By who?"

"Whom," he corrected. "And your mother asked me to come."

Her lips parted. "Why would my mother invite you to Ivy's wedding? And how do you even know my mother anyway?"

"Business, as it happens. I ran into her at the hotel one afternoon. She's planning a wedding at the M for one of her clients and we got to talking. Seems she's been having trouble with her usual caterer and had another wedding that was in free fall because she couldn't find anyone to provide the food. I made some arrangements with my kitchen and we were able to help her out last minute.

"When I happened to mention that I know you, that you're my lawyer and that we went to school together as kids, well, she insisted I come up today to enjoy the festivities."

Brie crossed her arms. "She never said anything to me about it."

"Is she in the habit of consulting with you about everything she does?"

"Of course not, but that's beside the point. You finagled this—I know you did. You live to get under my skin."

"I'd like to get under lots of things when it comes to you, Brie-Brie, but you ought to remember that sometimes things aren't about you. Your mother invited me, so I came to be nice."

"Ha. You and nice don't even belong in the same sentence."

He shrugged. "I suppose you've got me there. But we're here to have a good time, so why don't you sheath your claws for now and dance with me?" He took her arm. "You can have at me again once we're finished."

"Maybe I don't want to dance." She followed him out onto the floor.

"And maybe I'm not giving you a choice."

With that, he tugged her into his arms and swung her out into the mass of couples who were circling to the rhythm of a half-tempo slow dance.

She refused to put her arms around his neck, placing

one palm on his wide shoulder and allowing him to keep the other tucked inside his own.

It ticked her off to admit it, but he was an excellent dancer. He led with a confident ease that made her feel as if they were gliding on a cloud. To her additional annoyance, she realized that she was enjoying herself, but only the teensy-tiniest little bit. This was Maddox Monroe after all.

"So where did you learn to dance?" she asked, trying to make conversation.

He looked her in the eye. "*Dancing with the Stars*, of course."

"Be serious. You don't watch *Dancing with the Stars*."

"How do you know? Maybe I'm a big fan."

"Right. And you never miss an episode of *Say Yes to the Dress* either."

"What's that?"

She laughed. "My point exactly. I'm surprised you've even heard of *Dancing with the Stars*, not that I watch it either. But fess up. Admit that you've never seen a single episode."

"I watched ten minutes once, I think. But you're right, it's not on my regular DVR lineup. My entire housekeeping staff is crazy about it, though, so I can't help but hear things. I even know who won this year's Mirror Ball trophy."

He repeated the name of the celebrity winner.

"Yes, but can you remember the name of his dance partner?"

He paused for a moment, then took a guess. "Is that right?"

"How would I know? I told you, I don't watch it either."

A grin spread across his face; then he laughed.

She joined in, tossing her head back as he spun her in a quick, smooth circle that made her dress billow around her calves.

Then the dance was over, the band putting down their instruments as it was announced that guests should take their seats so that dinner could begin.

"I'm at the head table," Brie explained.

"I'm not."

Oddly, she wished that she weren't either so they could sit together at one of the multitude of guest tables and continue their conversation.

Inwardly, she gave herself a hard shake. *What am I thinking?*

Must be the wine, she decided. She'd have to remember to go easy on the booze for the rest of the evening.

"I'll find you for another dance when the music starts up again." Maddox took her hand and gave it a gentle squeeze.

She didn't immediately pull away. She really must be more inebriated than she'd thought. "Okay."

He smiled, his thumb drawing a line along the center of her palm, setting off an explosion of tingles.

"See ya." Then he winked and was gone.

It took a minute before she got her legs moving. Her palm was still tingling when she reached the long, beautifully decorated table and found her place among the bridal party.

# CHAPTER TWELVE

The five-course meal was excellent, the surroundings sublime, and the company pleasantly entertaining, but Maddox paid only passing attention, his eyes all for Brie.

He'd watched her as the evening progressed, enjoying the way she talked and smiled, the graceful movements of her head and shoulders and hands as she ate her dinner in full view of the entire room. And he took particular pleasure in her obvious delight as she stood and raised her glass to toast the newlyweds, wishing them a long and happy life together.

Her love for her sister and new brother-in-law was plain, radiating from her like a golden sun.

What must it be like to have even a small measure of that affection? To have her passion for his own, and maybe more besides?

He danced with a couple of different women when the music began again, the band playing a wild, thumping brand of rock that had everyone gyrating to the beat. Even Jordan was out there with his bride, his suit jacket forgotten over the back of his chair as he let his high-class hair down for some well-deserved fun. As for the bride, she glowed with youth and beauty and an over-the-top zest for life.

But to his way of thinking, as pretty as she was, Ivy Grayson Jordan couldn't hold a candle to her sister. Brie was a knockout in her floaty pink dress, her fair cheeks flushed with becoming color, her blue eyes soft and bright.

Even while he danced, he kept track of Brie, noting her location and whom she was with. He'd decided not to appear too eager by immediately racing over for their promised dance. He hoped that if he let her wait a short while, her guard would be down, as it had been at the end of their first dance. Because when he found her again, he didn't intend to let her go.

The band paused so the bride and groom could cut the cake. He watched as Brie went with them.

Brie stood among the guests gathered to watch the cake-cutting ceremony. The cake itself was a masterpiece, an exquisitely decorated, seven-tiered confection iced in pale ivory buttercream and festooned with a virtual garden of pastillage flowers—cascading roses, lilacs, and poppies.

Ivy chortled, visibly nervous as she picked up the long knife that she and James would use to slice the first piece of wedding cake. James grinned and slid his hand over hers.

Brie stood next to Madelyn and their mother. Laura beamed with pleasure, happy not only because of the occasion, but because her plan for the wedding was proceeding with an orchestrated precision that made it all look easy.

"You can't say anything to Ivy," her mother told her in a low voice, "but James told me where he's taking her on their honeymoon."

Brie looked at her mother. "I thought it was top secret and that wild dingoes couldn't drag it out of him."

James had used the dingo reference more than once, leading to hushed speculation that the destination might be Australia or New Zealand.

"It still is a secret, but he decided he'd better clue me in since they don't get cell reception there. He didn't want me worrying, sweet boy that he is."

"So? Is it Down Under? Or are they doing the rest of Europe once they get tired of France?"

"Neither. He bought her a private island in the Caribbean."

"He what!"

Laura waved a hand, motioning for her to lower her voice.

Luckily Ivy was too busy having James feed her cake to notice the sidebar conversation going on nearby.

"She gets a whole island?" Brie repeated in a near whisper.

"I know. So extravagant. But for James, I'm sure it was no great hardship. He says it has a lovely two-story colonial house with a pink sand beach, tennis court, and a boat dock deep enough for a yacht. Plus, he's put the deed in Ivy's name. He really does love her."

"He sure does. He didn't even ask for a prenup."

As a lawyer, she'd been interested in that particular detail. Through the family grapevine, she'd found out that his parents had floated the prenup idea, but that he'd squashed it immediately. Whatever he'd said had been harsh enough that the older Jordans had never mentioned it again.

"Here I thought the house in France was impressive," Brie said.

"Well, when you marry one of the richest men on the

planet, you get primo gifts," Madelyn said, finally joining the conversation. "But knowing Ivy, she wouldn't mind if he hadn't gotten her anything at all, just so long as they're together. To Ivy, marrying James *is* the gift."

From the expression on Ivy's face as she and James shared a sticky-lipped kiss, she knew Madelyn was right. Arms looped around each other's waist, the bride and groom moved away as the catering team swooped in to start cutting and passing out slices of cake, guests' choice of orange blossom white or chocolate cherry.

Beside her, Madelyn scanned the crowd. A sweet smile curved her lips when she found Zack, who was talking to P.G. and one of the other groomsmen on the other side of the room.

"Zack is my gift," Madelyn said. "He might not be able to buy me an island, but I don't mind. He and our babies are all I need to be happy."

"You guys are lucky."

Madelyn looked at her again. Clearly, she'd caught the note of longing in Brie's voice.

"We are lucky," Madelyn said. "And you will be too someday."

Brie shook her head. "Smart money disagrees. But lightning could always strike, right?"

"Maybe it just did." Madelyn's gaze moved past her to someone in the crowd beyond. "Hmm-hmm, who's that slice of tall, dark deliciousness?"

"What were you just saying about Zack being the love of your life?"

"He is. One hundred percent. Doesn't mean a girl can't appreciate a bit of eye candy every once in a while. Weird, but Mr. Tall, Dark, and Delicious looks oddly familiar. And I think he's coming this way. Brie, he's looking at you."

"Me? Who is—?" Brie started to turn around.

But she didn't need to ask who, as her mother's face lit up like a firework. Laura rushed forward, arms outstretched. "Mr. Monroe! I'm so glad you're here. I hope you're having a good time. Forgive me for not being able to do more than wish you a quick hello when we bumped into each other earlier."

"You've had a lot on your plate." He gave her one of his patented charming smiles. "Mother of the bride and wedding planner, that's enough to exhaust anyone, even a gorgeous whirlwind like you."

Laura laughed—more like giggled actually—then exchanged a friendly hug with him.

Behind their backs, Madelyn met Brie's eyes and mouthed a silent "O-M-G."

"And it's Maddox, Laura," he said. "I thought we got all the formality out of the way the other afternoon at the M."

Her mother's smile widened even farther, if that was anatomically possible. "Of course, Maddox. Let me introduce you to my daughters. This is Madelyn, my eldest."

"Nice to meet you." Madelyn extended her hand, her expression carefully rearranged. "Though Mom here could have done without the birth-order commentary."

They shook hands.

"Oh, and here is my Ivy. The bride." Laura motioned to her youngest, who hadn't made it far, waylaid by talkative guests. Ivy murmured what was obviously an excuse to an older white-haired lady and came forward. She towed James in her wake.

"Ivy, James, I'd like you to meet Maddox Monroe. He did me a great favor recently, so I didn't think you'd mind if he came to celebrate with us today."

"Of course not. You're very welcome." Ivy smiled.

"Thank you for including me. And may I wish you every happiness in your marriage."

"Thank you." Ivy's face softened, her smile spreading gently across her face.

He turned to James. "Congratulations. You're very lucky to have such a beautiful bride."

"I am." The men shook hands. James studied him for a moment. "Hotels, right?"

"Yup, that's me. International finance?"

"Guilty as charged. I hear you may be broadening your reach soon."

"It's under consideration. You offering funding?"

"I'm always open to a profitable business opportunity. Give me a call. We'll talk."

"I will."

"He will. *When* he gets back from his honeymoon." Laura waggled a chiding finger at the two of them. "No business talk. It's your wedding day, James."

"Sorry, Laura. I mean, Mom."

She'd insisted that James start calling her Mom now that he and Ivy were married. Of course, Laura had treated him like one of her own kids since he'd been a teenager. But she wanted to make it official.

James looped his arm around Ivy again and pulled her close. "Sorry, love."

Ivy met his gaze. "That's okay."

"My apologies as well," Maddox said.

Ivy nodded. "No worries. Oh, listen. The band's playing again." She looked at James. "Let's go dance."

James sent them all an apologetic look. "If you'll excuse us, my wife wants to dance. Hey, I like the sound of that. *Wife.*"

Ivy chuckled. "Come on, *Husband.*"

Taking his hand, Ivy pulled James out onto the crowded dance floor.

"Nice couple." Maddox tucked his hands into his suit pockets.

"Aren't they, though?" Laura smiled again. "Forgive me, Maddox, I would have introduced you to Brie, but you two already know each other." She looked at her middle daughter. "You should have told me you're his lawyer."

"Sorry, but it never crossed my mind. It's not like I'm in the habit of sharing my client list with you."

"Well, no, but Maddox is a special case. He says you were in school together."

"He's a special case, all right," Brie muttered.

Maddox choked back a laugh.

"Was it sixth grade, you said?" Laura asked. "I'm sorry I don't remember you. I usually remember all of Brie's school friends."

"It was seventh grade, Mom. And you don't remember him because he and I weren't friends."

"Really? But Maddox is so nice."

"What he is, is a— "

"What Brie means to say," Maddox interrupted, "is that we were young and I might have given her a bit of a hard time then."

Madelyn crossed her arms. "By 'hard time,' you mean you were a real little shit."

"Madelyn!" Laura looked shocked.

"Well, he was. I won't go into specifics, but believe me, whatever he was then, it wasn't nice."

"She's right, Laura," Maddox said, looking uncharacteristically contrite. "I was a smart-assed twelve-year-old. But times and people change."

"Exactly. Now he's a smart-assed thirty-three-year-old." Brie grinned, showing her teeth.

Laura darted a glance at Maddox, clearly waiting to see whether he was going to get angry.

Instead, he laughed again and met Brie's eyes. "I believe you promised this smart-ass a dance."

Brie stopped grinning. "My feet hurt."

"Then take off the heels. I won't tell anyone you're barefootin' it, if you don't."

"Really, I can't. Ivy will probably be wanting to change into her traveling clothes soon and I need to be available to help her."

"Don't worry about that, dear." Laura sent her an encouraging smile. "I'll help her change and get ready."

"But I don't want to miss her and James's departure."

"You won't. We'll come find you so you can wave them off. Won't we, Madelyn?"

Madelyn gave Brie a you-might-as-well-give-in-'cause-you'll-never-wiggle-out-of-this-one look. "Sure will."

*Traitor.* Brie glared back.

Maddox squatted down and grabbed one of her ankles to slip off her shoe. He had them both off before she could do more than let out a strangled gasp of protest. He stood and held out the shoes to her mother. "Laura, if you wouldn't mind?"

Eyes twinkling, Laura accepted the dress shoes.

"Ladies." Maddox looked at Laura and Madelyn. "It's been a pleasure."

He grabbed Brie's hand and tugged her forward. "Come on, you. Let's dance."

Brie trotted along beside him, twisting her hand free once they reached the dance floor. "One dance, then we're done."

"Are you always in such a bad mood at weddings?" he asked as they both started moving in time to a fast-paced rock song.

"Only when I'm at one with you."

"Nah, it can't be me. Probably just your feet. How are they feeling by the way?"

Actually, her feet felt great. Absent the confining high heels, her toes and arches felt light and free. The ache, which hadn't completely been a lie, was quickly fading as she bumped and shimmied to the music.

"Better," she admitted.

He sure could dance, she thought as she watched his body move with a fluid, almost catlike grace. He'd taken off his jacket and tie, leaving him in his shirt and trousers. The muscles of his arms and chest shifted subtly beneath the fabric of his shirt, hinting at toned male perfection beneath.

She almost sighed. Whether she liked to admit it or not, he was a damned sexy man.

A few of the young women dancing nearby clearly agreed, their eyes shifting away from their own partners to sneak increasingly long looks at Maddox, their gazes filled with interest and sexual hunger.

But Maddox seemed oblivious, his eyes never straying from Brie.

One song ended and a new one began with no break in between. She'd said only one dance, but when she paused for a moment as if to leave, he grabbed her hands and pulled her toward him again, silently compelling her to continue.

She ought to have turned away then regardless. Instead, she kept dancing, the beat that pumped from the band's instruments almost visceral, each note lush and heavy with a raw, evocative sensuality.

The rhythm settled inside her and some inner restraint unwound like a ribbon pulled loose from a bow. She wasn't sure when or how or even why she allowed it, but suddenly Maddox had his hands on her hips, his own hips swaying and circling as he guided her even deeper into the movement and the music.

She put her hands on his chest, his body warm, firm. Without her shoes, he seemed taller, her head coming only to his shoulders, so she had to angle her neck back to meet his eyes. They glowed, those eyes, with a dark inner heat that ignited a spark inside her as well.

He inched her closer, his hands large and strong against her pliant flesh. He spread his legs so she fit in between, his feet on either side of hers, as if the two of them were moving closer and closer to another kind of dance entirely.

His head bent.

Her hands slid upward to clasp his shoulders.

His black pupils dilated with desire.

Her lips parted, breath coming in soundless gasps.

The music faded and the crowd disappeared.

His hands slid over her butt and pulled her even closer, his mouth only millimeters away.

Suddenly someone knocked into her, shoving her hard from behind. She stumbled in spite of Maddox's grip on her, then cried out as a splash of cold liquid whooshed down her back and along her side, drenching the fabric of her gown.

A man blinked dumbly at her, two empty glasses in his hands. Whatever had been inside them was now all over her, which from the smell of it must have contained fruit and booze—whiskey specifically, if her nose was working right.

Clearly, he was hammered. So much so that she wasn't sure if he even realized what he'd just done.

"I don't believe it." She threw up her hands, her stocking feet wet now too from where she'd stepped in the residual cocktail puddle. “Not again! *Jesus Christ on a crutch*, what are the chances?”

Maddox looked as if he couldn’t quite believe it either. He swept his eyes over her, then glared at the drunk.

The drunk gulped, looking like he might be sick.

With her luck, he would be—all over her.

Rather than wait around to see if things really could get worse, she walked away, leaving Maddox behind to sort matters out however he preferred.

Her dress clung to her skin; she could only imagine what a sight she must be. And she was miserable, wet and sticky, her pretty bridesmaid’s gown a complete mess.

Rather than take the time to let any of her family know what had happened, she went out into the yard and started toward the house.

The night was dark, trees casting shadows where small yard lanterns helped to light the way. In the driveway beyond, she saw a long black limousine waiting, streamers and old shoes tied to the back bumper, a *Just Married* sign affixed in the rear window.

When James and Ivy were ready to leave, they would be heading straight to the airport, where James’s private jet was fueled and waiting on the tarmac, prepared for departure.

She walked faster, knowing she needed to get changed so she could make it back in time to tell them good-bye.

The house was cool and quiet when she let herself inside the side door; everyone was still out enjoying the reception. Padding through the shadowed space, she went upstairs to her bedroom.

One of the cats, Tobias, leapt down from her bed when she came inside. She bent to pet him, his green eyes shining with clear pleasure as she stroked his long black fur.

He purred and took a moment to weave around her legs.

Then he was off, disappearing out into the hallway at a quick trot, no doubt off to find the bowl of dry food left for him and the other cats on a high spot in the mudroom where the dogs couldn't reach.

The wet organza of her dress felt clammy now, chilly in the air-conditioned space. Reaching up, she found the first button on the back of her dress and slipped it free. She managed two more before she realized that unfastening the rest was going to be a problem. Twisting, she tried to work the cloth higher up her shoulders.

She sensed, more than heard, someone step into the room behind her.

A long shadow fell in the low lamplight and then he spoke. "Hey, you need some help with that?"

# CHAPTER THIRTEEN

Maddox leaned against the wall, arms crossed.

He had a hard-on from just watching her shimmy around in her blush dress as she struggled to find the next button. The wet, booze-stained material clung to her butt and legs in the most amazing ways, the pale color making the dress seem almost invisible.

Brie's head whipped around at his question, her blue eyes widening slightly. "What are you doing in here? How did you even find me?"

Her arms dropped to her sides and she turned to face him.

"I followed you at a distance. I'm surprised you didn't notice me before. Thought I'd come to make sure you're okay."

Shrugging away from the wall, he walked deeper into the room. He took a moment to look around, noticing the girlie green and pink decor, the long, lacy white curtains at the windows, and the big fluffy cream flokati rug laid out on the right side of the double bed with its rosebud comforter. Two tall bookcases took up most of the east-facing wall. They were crammed with old textbooks and ragged-edged paperbacks that were obviously well read. On the top shelf were trophies and ribbons that appeared to be a mix of awards for tennis and swimming wins and academic achievements. Her high school diploma hung on the far wall next to a wooden desk with an old study light on it and more books. A few stuffed animals were scattered here and there, including a Snoopy, whose worn-out neck hung at a precarious angle under his cracked leather collar.

"I've always wanted to get a peek inside your bedroom." He studied the titles on some of her books. "It's haunted my imagination for years. Though I didn't expect to still find the room so youthfully decorated."

"Mom keeps talking about packing up my old stuff and updating everything, but somehow she never gets around to it." Brie crossed her arms. "Well, you've had the tour now, your imagination satisfied, so you can leave."

He turned to face her. "When it comes to you, my imagination is never satisfied." He walked a step closer. "What about your dress? It didn't look like you were having much luck with the rest of those buttons."

"Don't worry about it. I'll manage."

"Right," he said with drawn-out sarcasm. "Turn around and let me help."

"I don't need your—"

He closed his hands over her shoulders and gently but firmly spun her around. She stiffened as his fingers moved to the first unfastened button. "I said hold still."

"God, you're overbearing."

"And you're mouthy and temperamental."

"I am not."

"Yes, you are, counselor. I'm surprised you're not regularly held in contempt of court." He slipped another button loose.

"You are the most—"

"Most what?" He slid another small, cloth-covered button free. "Most fascinating? Most attractive? Most tempting man you've ever known?"

"Most annoying and infuriating man I've ever known. Are you finished?" She laid a hand over her loosened bodice to hold it in place.

He took a moment to let his eyes slide down the long ivory length of her bare back, exposed now to his view. Her bra was the same pale pink as her dress, a mouthwatering combination of lace and silk. She was wearing matching silk panties with a frothy band of lace at the top, and, if he wasn't mistaken, a garter belt.

He bit his lip so he didn't groan out loud.

"There." His voice was husky. "All done."

She took a step away, then turned around. "Thank you."

"You're welcome."

Her eyes were deeply blue even in the low light, her lips the color of roses. And she smelled just as sweet. He'd been viscerally aware of the light, floral fragrance of her skin when he'd been unfastening her dress. And earlier when they'd been dancing. Even now, if he inhaled deeply, he could pick up hints of her scent, a fragrance that was natural to her and not due to something artificial.

He wanted to breathe her in, up close and personal again.

"Well, I'd better get changed." She shifted slightly, almost nervously, on her stocking feet. "Are you going back to the reception?"

"That depends."

"On what?"

"On how you feel about this."

Reaching out, he pulled her to him and fit his lips to hers, muffling the faint gasp that rose in her throat.

She put her hands out, flat against his shoulders, with the clear intent of pushing him away. But even as the energy gathered in her muscles to shove, she paused, her fingers curling into the fabric of his shirt.

That brief flash of hesitation was all he needed in order to press his advantage. Angling his head, he deepened the kiss, his touch harder and more demanding. He pressed her mouth open and slid his tongue inside. But he used only the tip, dipping in a subtle tease that implored her to accept more.

To want more.

She gasped again softly and relaxed her jaw, her lips turning pliant as she opened for him, inviting him in. Her hands clutched again at his shoulders, to draw him nearer this time.

Smiling, he delved deeper into her mouth, pushing his tongue fully inside to circle around her own, entwining, enticing, seducing them both.

His hands eased inside the opening at the back of her dress. A shudder went through him at the first touch. She felt like silk and smelled like heaven.

He wanted more.

He wanted everything.

Closing his eyes, he let his fingers play, stroking the length of her spine in a slow sweep that made her arch against him. He edged her legs apart and pressed himself into the soft V she made, making no effort to conceal the heavy ache riding him.

She pulled slightly away and blinked, shaking her head a little as if she were trying to shake off a drug.

He felt drugged as well, intoxicated by her in a way no alcohol or narcotic could ever match.

Burying his lips against her throat, he kissed her there, openmouthed, drawing on her skin in a way that would surely leave marks.

He liked the idea. He wanted to mark her. He wanted to leave something behind that would claim her as his, a visible sign to warn other men away.

Needing more, he slipped his palms under the silk of her panties and cupped her naked ass. He squeezed lightly and pulled her even tighter against his stiff cock.

If it weren't for the clothing between them, he suspected he might already have been inside her. Usually he had no trouble controlling himself, taking matters one step at a time so his partner enjoyed herself as much as he did. But with Brie, it was like tossing a match on a pool of gasoline, one spark and the whole world went boom.

Even so, he had to have more.

Now.

His hand moved lower, searching for feminine heat and softness. He found it and more, found her where she was slippery with wetness and swollen with need.

"Open your legs," he told her, holding her securely as he nuzzled her earlobe, then gave it a nip.

She shuddered and tried to do as he asked, her thighs quivering against his fist.

Realizing that she needed some help, he did the adjusting for her, sliding his feet sideways against hers to part her thighs. The moment he did, he opened her and pressed two fingers deep.

She moaned, then moaned again when he transferred his mouth to the other side of her neck and began to suckle the tender spot just above her collarbone.

A full-body tremor went through her.

"Like that, do you?" he murmured, lapping at her damp skin.

"Yes." The word sounded forced, as if she wanted to conceal her pleasure but couldn't keep it hidden.

He bounced her a little on his palm, lodging his fingers even farther inside. "How about this?"

"Ah-ah-ah," she cried, unable to even form a coherent word.

He thrust, rubbing and sliding in ways that were designed to make her go wild.

And she did, grabbing his head and forcing it up so she could ravish his mouth. Little humming sounds of desire purred from her lips. She thrust her fingers into his hair and her tongue deep into his mouth.

And then she broke, her climax shuddering through her with such force that he felt her muscles quiver around him as her tender flesh clenched inside.

He picked her up and carried her over to the bed. He laid her back, stripped off her dress, and tossed it to the floor. Next, he reached down and pulled off her panties, taking a moment to enjoy the sight of the pale triangle of nether curls that proved she was a real blonde. As for the lacy pink garter belt and sheer panty hose, he'd decided to leave them be, since they were a total turn-on.

He shucked off his shirt, popping a button on the way, then reached for his belt buckle and zipper.

"Wait," she said.

"Wait?"

After what they'd started?

No way.

Being with her, especially in this room, where he'd once fantasized about being, was a dream come true. Stopping now would surely kill him.

He worked the buckle free.

"No. The door." She pointed with a hand. "It's open," she whispered. "Shut it."

So she wasn't trying to toss him out. The knowledge relieved and pleased him more than he cared to admit.

Still, it was an effort making the short trip there and back, especially given the state of his raging erection.

Door closed—and locked—he came back and reached for her, curving his hands around her knees and soft thighs before gliding upward over her hips and flat stomach.

She sucked in an audible breath, then a second one, when he covered her breasts with his hands, cradling her through her bra as if to test their weight and shape. Her breasts were ample but not overly large, exactly as he liked. He squeezed her rounded flesh, then massaged the tips to straining peaks. He pinched at one, but it slipped away beneath the slippery silk.

Instead of removing her bra, he reached inside the cups and eased her breasts free. He slid the straps down so that her arms were trapped ever so gently at her sides.

"Maddox, what are we doing?" She watched him, doubt suddenly mixing with the dazed passion in her eyes.

"What we should have done a long time ago." He laid his palms over her naked breasts and fondled her again, flicking the pink tips with his thumbs in a way that made her moan and her eyes roll back in her head.

"God, I must either be drunk or crazy," she muttered, almost to herself.

"You aren't. You're just being honest for a change."

"Is that what I'm being?"

"You want me as much as I want you. Say it."

She shook her head, her eyes a vivid blue.

"Say it. Why are you always so stubborn?"

"If I am, it's only with you."

"I guess we bring out all sorts of uncharacteristic emotions in each other."

He set a knee on the bed and lowered himself down beside her. He kissed her long and slow, pressing her mouth open to take his tongue, imitating the thrust and retreat action he planned to initiate quite soon in a far more intimate part of her body.

She tried to wrap her arms around him but couldn't because of the bra straps. He realized that he rather liked having her at his mercy for a change.

The thought made him smile.

She made a sound of frustration and arched toward him, kissing him harder.

On a wicked laugh that trembled against both their lips, he cupped his hand behind one of her knees and slid her leg up and open. He teased his fingers through the V of curls there, making her arch again with longing.

She was wet and very ready.

He was just reaching for the condom in his pocket when a knock sounded at the door.

"Brie, are you in there?"

Both of them froze.

The doorknob rattled. "Why's the door locked? Brie?"

It was her sister Madelyn.

He met Brie's wide eyes, then shook his head, telling her to keep quiet.

A scowl creased her forehead, indecision written all over her passion-flushed face.

"What?" Brie called, her voice unnaturally high.

He bit back a curse, keeping silent.

"You okay? You sound funny."

Their eyes met again. He arched a brow.

"I . . . um . . . I'm fine. Just changing. What's up?"

"I wanted to let you know that Ivy and James are getting ready to leave. Another ten or fifteen minutes maybe, then they're going to take off. You'd better get downstairs if you don't want to miss them."

Maddox shook his head.

She looked away. "Okay. Thanks. I'll be down in a couple."

"Okay," Madelyn called.

Neither of them moved until they heard her sister's footsteps fade away.

He groaned and rolled away, cursing under his breath.

*Of all the colossally shitty timing, this had to be the shittiest.*

Here he was, hard as a jackhammer, and now he was supposed to stop. For a minute he considered trying to convince her to pick up where they'd left off, but he could see from the look on her face that it wasn't going to happen.

His mood suddenly black, he watched as she sat up. She wiggled her breasts back inside the silken cups of her bra, then hooked the straps up over her shoulders.

Really, it was a crime, he thought, seeing her tuck her goodies away. Like watching Christmas presents being put back inside their boxes and returned to the store.

She ran her fingers through her hair and jumped off the bed, bending over to scoop up her underwear in a way that exposed everything.

*Jesus Christ. She's trying to kill me.*

He bit his lower lip, his cock throbbing in fresh complaint.

With quick jerking motions, she rolled off the garter belt and hose and kicked them aside. She put her panties on and pulled them into place, then leaned over for his shirt.

She flung it at him. “Put that on. My mother and Ivy are just down the hall, not to mention Madelyn.”

“Yeah. So what?” he said, laying the shirt beside him on the bed. “Or aren’t you allowed to have a man in your bedroom? You’re not sixteen, you know.”

She stared wide-eyed for a few seconds. “No, but I don’t . . . that is, I’ve never . . . I don’t boink men in my parents’ house.”

“Not ever?” That surprised him. “No secret hookups with high school or college boyfriends? No lovers you’ve brought here for a holiday weekend?”

“No.”

She padded quickly across to her closet and yanked jeans and a white shirt off a pair of hangers. They sang out as the metal clinked together.

“You’ll have to wait here until I go down,” she told him. “Then you can leave.”

He stood up and went to her, taking her hips in his hands and pressing her ass against his heavy erection. “I’d rather stay here so we can get busy again once the newlyweds are on their way.” He kissed her neck and rocked himself against her.

A shudder went through her body, her hands clenching on the clothing in her hands.

Then she visibly got control of herself again and twisted out of his grip. “Forget it, Monroe. The moment has passed.”

Pulling away, she stepped into her jeans and zipped them up. She worked the shirt over her head next, tugged it into place. Almost like she was donning armor.

“I never took you for a coward.”

Her pale eyebrows went up. “What’s that supposed to mean?”

“You’re running. But as the saying goes, you can run, but you can’t hide. Both of us know this is far from over.”

She shot him a quick glance. "It is for me. Sorry about the . . ." Her hand motioned toward the very obvious arousal straining against his trousers.

He swallowed a groan. If she'd wanted to get revenge for his past misdeeds, she'd more than managed. He was going to be in agony for the rest of the night. But he was a grown man and no matter the provocation, he could deal with the consequences.

As for her claim that she didn't want him anymore, she was a liar. It wasn't arrogance on his part to know that he could have her begging for it again with just a few skillful touches.

If he were a different sort of man, he could push the issue right here and now, slip his hand inside her jeans, and make her forget about everything but her passion, about her need for him.

But he didn't operate like that, and if he maneuvered her now, she would hate him for it later.

Hate herself.

Returning to the bed, he scooped up his shirt and slid his arms inside the sleeves. "When do you get back to the city?"

Surprise flashed in her eyes. "Tomorrow afternoon."

"Good. I'll come by your place. Tomorrow. Early evening. Don't bother making dinner. I'll bring something with me."

"Maddox, I told you. Whatever tonight was, it's over."

"Expect me by five. Now, you'd better hurry." He started buttoning his shirt. "You don't want to miss saying good-bye to the happy couple."

She scowled, clearly aware that he was right about the rapidly elapsing time.

"God, you're aggravating."

He grinned, showing his white teeth.

Finding a pair of flats, she shoved her feet into them, then went to the door. She flipped the lock open.

"Brie."

Her head came up. "What?"

"Sleep well tonight."

"I usually do."

"Good." He tucked his shirt into his waistband. "'Cause you won't be getting a whole lot of shut-eye tomorrow."

Her lips parted, words gathering on her tongue. But rather than speak, she huffed out a breath and disappeared out into the hall.

Taking a deep breath of his own, he willed his body to calm down. Only then did he follow after.

# CHAPTER FOURTEEN

Brie checked the time on her smartphone and wondered if there was still a chance for her to duck out before Maddox came knocking at her apartment door.

She should never have let him strong-arm her into a date tonight. Although *date* was a rather placid term for what she figured he had in mind, especially considering his parting words about her not getting much sleep tonight.

God, what had come over her last night? Letting him kiss and touch her the way he had? One minute she'd been telling him to get lost; the next she'd been wrapped around him as tightly as a glove, sucking face and a whole lot more.

If not for Madelyn's interruption, she and Maddox would have done the nasty right there in her childhood bedroom, with her mother and sisters, and Lord only knew who else, just down the hall. What if they'd heard, even with her door locked?

Aunt Constance was the one most likely to get caught fornicating in the house. But everyone kind of expected that from her, and to give Constance her due, she had very little shame. She would just have laughed it off and gone to open a fresh bottle of wine.

But though Brie wouldn't put herself in the uptight prude category, she wasn't as casual and free-spirited about S-E-X as her notorious aunt.

She wished she could blame her rogue behavior on too much wine. Or maybe a roofie somebody had slipped into her drink when she wasn't looking. But neither of those options applied.

Maddox had kissed her and she'd liked it.

Then he'd touched her and she'd liked it even more.

Like gasoline poured on a drought-ridden forest and set ablaze, the passion between her and Maddox had exploded, out of control.

Of course it had been a while since she'd been with somebody—well over a year. She was busy with her career and didn't care for casual sexual encounters with guys she barely knew. She supposed that offered her some slim margin of excuse for last night.

Yet even that wasn't true.

She'd never lost her mind like she had with Maddox. Never lowered her inhibitions and just let herself go wild. Not even with Stephen, the man she'd once loved with a heartbreaking intensity, had she been able to lower all her barriers.

But with Maddox, there hadn't been any barriers at all. One touch from him and her brain cells had turned to mush, her usual sense of caution and logic gone straight out the door.

So where did that leave her?

Clearly, Maddox wanted to pick up where they'd left off last night.

As for her, she knew what she ought to tell him and that was a big fat *no*.

Getting involved with him—well, to be honest, even more involved—would be a mistake of monumental proportions. They had a history of animosity between them. Plus, he was her client and therefore off-limits.

Really, the answer was obvious.

So why was she sitting here on her couch, dithering over what to say when he showed up at her door?

She glanced again at the time.

Five o'clock.

The doorbell rang.

She stood and ran a quick hand over her beige linen slacks to check for nonexistent lint, then straightened the tail of her green and yellow long-sleeved cotton shirt. Less exposed flesh to tempt him, she'd told herself when she'd picked the outfit from her closet.

Taking a deep breath, she went to the door.

Maddox was in black.

Black trousers. Black polo shirt that hugged the contours of his amazingly well-sculpted chest. As she now had reason to know, his torso looked even better without the shirt. He could have been a model if he'd had any interest.

"Hi," he said.

He swept his eyes over her in a way that didn't make her feel very covered up after all. Maybe he was busy remembering her shirtless too.

She swallowed and looked up at him again. Had he always been so tall?

"Hi," she answered back.

Holding the door open, she waited for him to come inside.

"What's all that?" She nodded toward the large cloth shopping bag he held in one hand.

"Our dinner. I told you I'd bring the food."

"So you did."

Without waiting for further invitation, he walked into the kitchen. It was easy to find, since her apartment had an open-plan format where everything except the bedroom and bathroom flowed into one large space without the necessity of walls or doors.

"Kudos for not ditching on me," he said. "I half expected to find out that you'd taken off and left me literally holding the bag."

He set the groceries on top of the cooking island.

"I thought about it," she said honestly. "But what's the point? You'd have tracked me down regardless."

His dark eyes glinted. "You're right. I would have. Plus, you'd have had to have come home sometime."

"I could have gone to a hotel."

He shook his head. "Nah. You're too frugal. Besides, a hotel would only have made you easier to find."

"Is that some secret insider hotel mojo? What? Can you track people if you want?"

"I'll never tell." He winked. "You like spaghetti?"

"Of course. Who doesn't like spaghetti?"

"My point exactly."

Still, he looked pleased as he began to unload the groceries. On the counter he laid onions, plump red tomatoes, crisp green peppers, garlic, and small bunches of fresh oregano, marjoram, and thyme. Two brown-paper-wrapped butcher's packages containing some sort of ground meats came next. There was also tomato paste, red pepper flakes, olive oil, vinegar, and other fixings for a salad, and a loaf of heavenly smelling Italian bread. And last, a box of dry pasta noodles, also Italian.

"I take it that's what we're having. I didn't know you could cook."

"I can't. Well, not much, but I do make a mean red sauce. That and grilled steaks are my two specialties."

When he'd said he was stopping by with dinner, she'd never expected this. She'd assumed he would have his chef at the hotel whip something up. But here he was cooking for her.

How was she going to kick him out now? He really was diabolical.

"You have a stockpot?" he asked, as he washed and dried his hands, then found the cutting board and knife that were on her countertop.

"Underneath in the far cabinet. I'll get it."

"It's no trouble. You sit." He walked in the direction she'd pointed. "In here?"

"Yes."

He reached inside and found the big, bright blue Le Creuset pot her mother had bought her one year for Christmas. He set it on the stove and turned on the heat, then poured in a golden green stream of olive oil, enough to thinly coat the bottom.

"Want some help?" she asked.

He shook his head as he began slicing onions and mincing garlic. "I've got it. Like I said, sit, relax."

"Would you like something to drink?" As soon as she asked, she remembered that he didn't drink alcohol. "I have sparkling water or I could make us some iced tea. It shouldn't take too long."

Without waiting, she went over to put on the kettle, then rummaged through a nearby cupboard for the tea.

"Sparkling water is fine," he told her.

The garlic, onions, and green peppers hissed as he added them one after the other to the pot, stirring in between.

She got down a large glass pitcher, then a pair of glasses. "I'll make both."

The room was filling with rich, aromatic scents by the time she passed him his water. "That smells fantastic," she said.

"Good." He smiled and stirred the meat—ground beef and sausage—so it would brown. He took a long drink of water, then went back to chopping.

Once the tea was steeped and chilling in the fridge, she took a seat on one of the high barstools on the far side of the island.

"Did Jordan and your sister get off on their trip okay?"

"Yes, as far as we know. My mom got a call from James at the dock in the BVIs. Then that's the last we've heard. No cell service."

He added the tomatoes and tomato paste, then the chopped herbs, red pepper flakes, and finally salt and freshly ground black pepper. "Must be nice. My managers would all have meltdowns if they couldn't get in regular touch with me."

"I know the feeling. I'm electronically tethered to my law firm. You never know when the next emergency will spring up and demand immediate attention."

"Even on Sundays?"

She took a swallow of her water. "Sometimes especially on Sundays."

He tapped the spoon, then adjusted the heat on the stove so the sauce would simmer. Her mouth watered; the rich red concoction looked and smelled delicious.

"There. We'll let that cook."

He returned to the sink and finished prepping the salad, putting torn lettuce and sliced orange carrots in the salad bowl she pointed out to him.

She sat and watched, aware that they'd just passed the

most normal forty minutes they'd ever spent together in their entire lives. It was almost like they were a regular couple, cooking and chatting and relaxing together on a quiet evening at home.

The thought disturbed her.

She set down her glass. "Maddox, this is really nice of you, cooking me dinner and all, but you know nothing's going to come of it."

"Oh?" He rinsed his hands, then dried them slowly on a towel.

"What happened last night . . . it was . . . unexpected. We were both out of our element, what with all the excitement of the wedding. Neither of us was thinking straight and things just got out of hand. It didn't mean anything."

He didn't speak. Just leaned back against the counter.

"What I'm trying to say is that nothing between us has changed. Not in any measurable way. We still have a lawyer-client relationship that ethically precludes us from acting on . . . well, from moving any further along that particular path."

Quickly, she met his eyes, which were dark and frustratingly enigmatic, then glanced away again.

"As for anything more," she went on, "we've never gotten along, so a friendship seems rather unlikely at this point. We don't like each other and I understand that."

"Who said I don't like you?"

Her eyes flashed up.

"I like you just fine, Brie. I even liked you when we were kids."

Her mouth twisted up at one corner. "You certainly had a strange way of showing it."

"I already told you—boys do stupid things around the girls they like best." He pushed away from the counter and crossed to her. "Are you finished with your little speech?"

Lines creased her forehead. "I wouldn't characterize it quite like that. I just want to get things straight between us."

"Oh, I think things are totally straight when it comes to the two of us."

Leaning down, he slipped one arm under her legs, the other around her back, and hoisted her over his shoulder into a fireman's carry.

She let out a cry. "Maddox! What do you think you're doing?"

"You're a smart woman. Surely I don't have to explain it." Playfully, he smacked her bottom and walked toward her bedroom.

"Put me down. I didn't say you could manhandle me like this."

"That's true, you didn't."

He laid her onto her back across her big, king-sized bed. If there was one thing she loved when she slept, it was space and luxury. Her bed had both, including five-hundred-count cotton sheets and a baby-soft, down-filled duvet in a soothing sea green.

Before she had time to sit up and scramble off the bed, he hooked a leg over hers and took her hands inside one of his own, pulling her arms over her head.

He smiled with obvious satisfaction. "Good. We're back where we left off last night."

She wiggled against him. For her trouble, she felt his shaft swell up hard inside his pants.

"Now we're *really* back where we left off," he said, dropping a kiss on her neck.

"Cut it out, Maddox. This isn't funny."

"It isn't meant to be funny." His mouth slid slowly

along the underside of her jaw, then up the other side of her neck.

"I told you to stop."

His head came up and he met her eyes. "Okay. Then we'll stop."

"Let me go."

She stared back. His eyes were deeply brown; the late afternoon sunlight glinted off his thick, dark hair.

He shook his head. "Not yet. Not until you admit that you want me."

"I don't. Last night was just . . ."

"Just what? Amazing? Great? Something to be repeated as often as possible?"

"No. It was a mistake. I had too much to drink."

"You hardly had anything to drink. Don't try blaming your behavior on inebriation."

"Insanity, then. What other reason could I have for wanting to be with you?"

"Lust maybe?" He laid a palm over her breast.

To her immense irritation, her nipple came to attention like a soldier giving a crisp salute.

"See?" he murmured, fondling her delicately. "Your body knows what it wants."

"Well, my body isn't in charge."

"Maybe that's your problem, Brie. Maybe you ought to shut off that superior brain of yours every once in a while and let yourself go. You did last night and I know you liked it."

"Whatever I did last night is in the past. Done. Over."

He stroked the traitorous peak of her breast again, making her ache, then kissed her temple and her cheek and the corner of her mouth. "Why are you fighting so hard, Brie-Brie? Why won't you just let me make you feel good?"

And there he had it, the crux of the problem.

She was afraid.

She'd given her heart once and ended up with it smashed to pieces. She'd made a promise to herself then that never again would she let herself be so weak, so vulnerable. So foolishly trusting.

When she thought about it in those terms, she really didn't know why she was worried about Maddox Monroe.

He wanted sex and only sex.

No promises.

No commitments.

Frankly, he didn't strike her as a commitment kind of guy.

As for love, that wasn't even part of the equation. Of all the men she knew, he was the last one she would end up falling for.

No, whatever might happen between them, love would be the last thing involved.

So was he right? Was she being stupid resisting him? Resisting herself? Was she being a stubborn idiot not to give in and just let herself enjoy?

God knew that's what her aunt Constance did. She had short, hot, passionately intense love affairs that lasted until the flames went out and turned to embers. Then she and her lover of the moment would move on. Amazingly, she even managed to stay friends with most of them.

*Not that Maddox and I will ever be friends.*

But what the hell? Maybe she ought to live on the wild side for a change and take her pleasure where she could find it. What's the worst that could happen?

Something inside her began to unwind, her willpower failing.

"There are still the ethical barriers of our association to consider."

His lips nuzzled behind her ear, making her nerve endings sizzle and spark. "Your warning is duly noted. If you'd like, I'll sign a waiver, acknowledging my understanding of possible ethical conflicts in your representation of me and absolving you of any and all liability. You can draft it up whenever you'd like for my signature."

"Even if I did, it would never hold up in court." She sighed as he feathered kisses along her collarbone. "Any good lawyer could argue that it was signed while under mental duress."

He unbuttoned the top three buttons of her shirt and slid his hand inside. "But we'd both know different. I'm fully cogent. What about you?" His fingers tunneled under her bra and started playing on her naked flesh.

A sigh of pure pleasure escaped her throat.

"So? Do you still want me to stop?"

Her eyelashes fluttered, her breath coming fast. He rolled the aching tip of her breast between his thumb and forefinger, then pinched just hard enough to make her shudder. Need gathered between her legs, a needful ache that begged to be filled.

Casting all caution aside, she shook her head. "Christ, no. Don't stop."

He laughed low in his throat and pinched her again until her hips arched.

Then he kissed her.

# Chapter Fifteen

"Let me go," she implored as he slipped the rest of her buttons free and spread her shirt open.

"Not yet." His hand went to her waistband and unfastened her pants as well, sliding the zipper down to its base. "I rather like having you at my mercy."

"Maddox," she said with a warning growl, shifting against his hold.

"Shh, you'll like it." His breath whispered over her skin, her stomach muscles tightening as he wet the tip of his little finger and dipped it into her belly button.

Her toes curled inside her shoes.

Kissing her there first, he began journeying upward, licking and nibbling on his way. Every so often he would pause to suckle on a particularly tender bit of skin, leaving more marks than she already had from last night.

As before, he didn't unhook her bra. Instead, he eased her breasts free, first one, then the other, so the two mounds were supported by the elastic and silk, yet plumped together.

He buried his face between and started kissing and suckling again.

Her back arched, her arms straining against the big hand he had gripped around her wrists. He didn't hurt her, though, careful to restrain but not injure her in any way.

His teeth grazed against her, raking her nipples, one, then the other, before he started the whole kiss-lick-suckle routine again.

She bit her lip, wondering if she might go mad from the heated torment.

Then his free hand started sliding low, teasing its way across her bare skin, caressing and exploring with sinful intent. His fingers stopped when they reached the lacy waistband of her panties, sliding sideways back and forth, but going no farther.

"You're wearing red today," he said, lifting his head from her round, throbbing breasts to slide his gaze along her body. "Did you do it for me?"

"No."

But maybe that was a lie? Maybe subconsciously she had.

"Either way, I like them. Red suits you, kitty cat."

"I'm not a cat," she said, meeting his eyes and seeing the desire burning in them.

"Oh, I think you are. A sweet, pretty little cat. Shall I make you purr?"

"Maddox."

He slipped his hand inside her pants and covered her mound, threading his fingers into the short, soft nest of curls he found there.

Of its own volition, her body pressed toward him.

He smiled. "I loved the way you came for me last night. I'm going to enjoy watching you do it again."

Instantly, she turned wet.

"You're a beast," she told him.

"And you love it."

To her shame, he was right.

She did.

Her restrained breasts trembled, her wrists flexing within his hold.

He locked his eyes with hers, then slid a finger, inserting it deep, up past his knuckle.

She moaned.

"You're so hot and wet," he said. "It's like touching heaven. I wish you could feel yourself as I do."

"I'll have to take your"—her breath hitched in her chest as he massaged her—"word for it."

Pulling back, he eased out, then slipped in two fingers this time, filling her.

Slowly, he began his massage again, varying his strokes as he paused to scissor his fingers wide in a way that sent shivers coursing through her frame. In and out, again and again, he increased the speed and intensity as if another part of him were involved in the action.

And he never looked away, his eyes holding her own as he swept her high, then higher still, but never quite enough to send her over the edge.

"Maddox," she sighed, her voice pleading.

"Maddox what?" he taunted.

"You know what. Finish this."

"Oh, I will. I'm just getting started. But if you want to come right now, all you need to do is ask."

"What?"

His fingers circled deep and thick again, tormenting her. "Just say the words. 'Please' will do."

"You expect me to beg?" she panted.

"No, just ask."

She let out an infuriated breath. "You're a bastard."

"Never said I wasn't. Come on, Brie. Say it."

She wanted to tell him to get lost, leave him as high and dry and unsatisfied as she had last night. But he finger-thrust inside her again, increasing the ache to an almost savage edge.

She looked into his eyes and realized he knew exactly what he was doing. "I'll get you back for this," she said.

His mouth curved up. "I look forward to it." He teased her inside again, heightening the ache.

"Please." The word burst from her lips. "Please make me come."

"Well, since you asked so nicely."

He pressed her with his thumb and pumped his fingers, using a touch that must surely be outlawed in every red state in the nation.

And suddenly she couldn't think at all, pleasure breaking through her like a tidal wave.

"Ah, God," she cried.

Still, he didn't let her go, holding her in his dual grip, above and below, while her body quaked and shuddered from the force of her climax.

She was still soaring when he leaned down and kissed her, taking her mouth with a wild, ravenous demand. She kissed him back, extra little cries reverberating against his lips.

Then suddenly he released her and sat up in the bed.

She lay there, drifting as if on a cloud, her bones feeling as loose and malleable as warmed wax. Dimly, she felt and heard her shoes fall to the floor, her pants and underwear stripped from her body.

Brie expected him to take her, part her legs and sheath himself inside. She presumed he'd brought protection, but still she knew she ought to say something to make sure.

But before the words could even form, he grabbed her hips and slid her forward, positioning her near the edge of the bed, his palms under her bare butt.

Glancing down the length of her body, she watched him drop to his knees between her spread thighs. Then to her surprise, he buried his face against her tenderest flesh.

A ragged gasp filled the air. *Her* gasp, she realized, as his lips and tongue set her ablaze. She shifted her hips, not sure if she was trying to get closer to him or get away.

But he held her tight, his touch inescapable, inexorable, as he built her passion high, then higher. His every move seemed designed to inflame her, to push her to the very brink of madness, driving her to new, ever increasing heights.

She whimpered and moaned, her fingers clutching at the comforter, her breath coming in harsh, labored pants.

And she was beyond shame, beyond inhibition, as he took her where she hadn't known it was possible to go.

She let out a sharp little scream when the climax hit her, merciless and mesmerizing. Her whole body quaked, heat and light and ecstatic pleasure sweeping over her in a warm, dark rush. Head to toe to pelvis and back again.

But before she even had time to catch her breath or gather a single coherent thought, he began once more, forcing her hunger to rage again, making her yearn for what seemed an impossible pleasure.

She wept this time, the delight so intense it was nearly unbearable. Yet he didn't slow or slacken in his efforts, silently demanding that she follow his lead to race one more time to the abyss and dive inside.

Just when she was on the verge of another mind-blowing climax, he stopped. She cried out, reaching for him blindly.

Surely he wasn't going to leave her like this? Even he couldn't be that cruel.

Then he was back, leaning over her, completely and gloriously naked, to strip off the rest of her clothes. But she scarcely had time to admire his beautiful masculine form before he was there, rolling her into the middle of the big bed and parting her thighs with his knees.

She heard the sound of a condom package being opened and then he was over her, in her, his large shaft filling her almost to completion. Her inner muscles tightened around him, too stretched for comfort yet inexplicably craving more.

He eased back, then thrust, hard and fast.

And again, lodging himself deep, deeper still.

His mouth found hers, claiming her in a series of wild, wet, rapacious kisses, his tongue thrusting in time to the movements of his hips and cock below.

She kissed him back, needy and avaricious, strangely excited to find her own flavor like sweet and salt on his tongue. Her fingers tunneled into his hair, massaging his scalp and neck. Her legs wrapped around his hips to urge him on, one heel digging into his ass as he plunged in and out.

Heavier, deeper, quicker.

She ached with need, her blood and body on fire, her mind dark and enslaved, empty of everything but him. Everything but the yearning to be his in all ways.

His hands glided over her in hot, sweeping circles, shoulders, arms, breasts, hips, and thighs, pausing to angle her up so he could find even more purchase inside her wet, silken depths.

She cried out, gasping against his mouth. And again,

as he grazed his teeth over her earlobe and neck and down to her breasts.

He drew upon her again, using tongue and teeth, so that she was left dazed and dizzy. He reached between them, his fingers like a magical flame.

And up she went, body and mind turning instantaneously to ash. Pleasure roared through her, engulfing her in a firestorm of bliss.

He pumped inside her again. Faster, harder, his face beautiful in his need. Suddenly he stiffened, his large body caught in a storm that looked as fearsome as the one that had shaken her.

Together, they collapsed, arms and legs tangled, bodies still joined. He didn't move and she didn't either, even though he was heavy where he lay on top of her.

As if realizing, he rolled them over, leaving her draped limp and drowsing over him. With one large hand, he stroked her lazily from shoulder to thigh, then back up again.

Smiling, she curled into him like a kitten, burying her face against his damp neck. She inhaled, liking the way he smelled. His hand curved against her bare bottom.

"You hungry?" he said after a minute.

"Hmm, I don't know. I can't even think yet."

He chuckled. "The sauce is probably ready. I suppose I ought to check it."

Until that moment, she'd forgotten all about the spaghetti sauce simmering on the stove while things had been more than simmering between them there in her bedroom.

"You probably should go give it a stir."

Rather than let him up, she shimmied against him, searching for the most comfortable spot on his sculpted body.

His shaft flexed inside her.

Was he already getting hard again?

She looked at him, met his passion-filled eyes.

He squeezed her ass in his hand and sent her squirming again.

Now he really was hard. She could feel him stretching inside her.

"I've got another condom," he said.

"I'm kind of tired."

"I'm not."

Rolling her over, he leaned down to get his pants.

Then he was back, protection in hand.

Looking down at his impressive display, she inexplicably felt desire curl inside her again.

Maybe she wasn't so tired after all.

"Surely, the sauce can wait a little longer," she whispered, running her hand over him from chest to thigh to cock. She played her fingers over him there, enjoying the sensation as he throbbed inside her grasp.

Pushing her back against the tangled comforter, he rose over her and kissed her. "The sauce'll have to wait," he murmured against her lips. "Because I can't."

When she and Maddox finally got around to eating dinner, the sun had set. It was dark in the main part of the apartment and his famous red sauce was on the verge of burning.

Somehow, he managed to salvage enough sauce for a meal.

While he was busy putting water on the boil for the spaghetti and assembling the salad, Brie set the table with her everyday china. She poured tall glasses of cold iced tea—luckily neither she nor Maddox was sensitive to caffeine—then lit a quartet of squat beeswax candles;

their fragrance filled the room with a warming sweetness.

She switched on a couple of lamps, leaving the apartment mostly in shadow. Then, she started some classical music on her sound system, beginning with Chopin, one of her favorites.

Earlier, after she'd climbed out of bed, loose-limbed and thoroughly satisfied in a way she hadn't been in a long time—if ever—she'd slipped into her panties and a long Metropolitan Museum of Art T-shirt that hit her midthigh.

As for Maddox, he hadn't bothered putting on anything other than his black boxer-briefs.

"If I get dressed, I'll just have to take my clothes off again once we finish eating," he'd explained when she'd raised an eyebrow at his solo garment choice.

She'd offered no further complaint. Not about his lack of attire or his assumption that they would be having sex again, soon.

Warm shivers ran through her at the thought.

She wondered if he planned to spend the entire night. If he did, would they be sharing breakfast too? She wasn't sure how she felt about that.

Dinner, when it was finally served, was delicious. In spite of its near scorching, his "mean" red sauce tasted as good as advertised. The crisp salad with its slightly tart dressing and the fresh bread smeared with creamy yellow butter were perfect accompaniments.

To her surprise, Maddox kept her laughing throughout the meal, amusing her with stories about the hotel staff and a few of the more flamboyant guests. He was careful not to name names, but she had her suspicions about a couple of them, one being an incredibly famous movie star who had a list of more than twenty specific room requirements whenever he stayed at the M Hotel.

These included keeping six bottles of Dom Pérignon on hand at all times, chilled to an exact forty-five degrees; vases filled with long-stemmed organic white roses, one for each room of the suite; brand-new pairs of Haflinger boiled wool slippers set out each day in both the bedroom and the bath; and, most amusing of all, four packs of new Hello Kitty playing cards and a box of sharpened Ticonderoga number two pencils.

"I know the M has a rep for great customer service, but do you really go to such extremes to please your guests?" Brie asked as she set down her fork and leaned back in her chair.

"Sure." Maddox ate a last bite of spaghetti and bread. "So long as they're willing to pay, we'll honor any request short of kidnapping or murder."

She laughed. "I should hope not."

But Maddox just smiled and drank his iced tea.

One of her brows went up. "*Have* you ever received a request for either of those?"

"I'm not at liberty to say, but you'd be amazed what people will ask you to do, or turn a blind eye to at least."

"And I think my work has its unusual moments."

"You have no idea." He set down his glass. "You ready for dessert?"

"No." She laid a hand on her stomach. "I don't have the room."

"Not even for cream-filled profiteroles?"

She glanced toward the small bakery box on the kitchen island, which she'd only recently noticed. "Hmm, that does sound delectable. But I won't be able to waddle if I have them now."

"Dishes first, then. Dessert later."

"You helping?"

"Of course. What kind of date would I be if I cooked, then left you to clean up the mess by yourself?"

"A typical one?"

A roguish smile spread across his face. "You've been seeing the wrong kind of guy. You'll find that I'm anything but typical."

Glancing down, she carefully folded her napkin. "So are we seeing each other?"

He waited until she looked up again and met his eyes. "I don't know. Are we? Despite what you may think, I'm not much for one-night stands."

Her heart thumped under her ribs. "So after tonight . . ."

"I'm looking forward to another night. And another after that. I could even be talked into a few days too."

"Maddox, I . . . I'm just not sure."

"You don't have to be sure. We're just having fun, Brie. We'll take things one day—or rather one night—at a time."

Getting to his feet, he stacked their plates and carried them over to the sink. She gathered up the salad bowl and the drinking glasses and followed.

To the strains of Mozart, they loaded the dishwasher, wiped down the counters, and put leftovers away in the refrigerator. He talked about easy, inconsequential things while they worked; she followed his lead.

All the while an inner debate raged in her head. What was she doing getting involved with Maddox Monroe? He was the last man she wanted in her life.

Or her bed.

He drove her crazy. And the two of them barely even tolerated each other. So why was she considering seeing him again after tonight?

For more of the best mind-blowing, lick-your-lips-good sex ever, maybe?

Her vag muscles tightened just at the thought, anticipating the next time he stripped her naked and buried himself inside her.

God, she really needed her head examined.

If she was smart, she would hand him his clothes and the box of profiteroles and shove him out the door. They'd go on as they had before—childhood adversaries who now had a polite but distant professional association. Tonight's encounter, for lack of a better word, would be filed under mistakes not to be repeated and never spoken of again.

Yet, as she watched him give the countertops one final wipe, his beautiful, long-limbed muscles shifting and flexing, his pale golden skin gleaming with warmth and vitality in the low light, she couldn't find the willpower to do it.

He neatly folded and placed the dishcloth on the edge of the sink, then rinsed his hands.

Finished with cleanup duty, he glanced over at her and into her eyes. "Time yet for dessert?"

She shook her head. "No, not yet."

A spark flickered in the depths of his gaze. "Maybe another sort of sweet treat, then?"

At first she didn't know what he meant. Then, before she could stop him, he reached out and laid his still-wet hands over her breasts.

She pulled in a surprised breath. "Maddox."

Droplets of moisture seeped into her cotton T-shirt.

He gazed down critically. "Not enough."

Flicking on the tap, he filled one cupped palm with water and splashed her.

Then he splashed her again.

"Maddox! What on earth? Stop that!"

But he just grinned, reminding her of the devilish little boy she'd once known.

He turned off the faucet, his eyes glued to her front.

She looked down and saw why.

Her shirt was drenched, the thin white material clinging to her breasts like a second skin. Her nipples drew into hard points. Her mouth grew suddenly dry.

"You've gotten me all wet," she said.

"Yes, I have."

Reaching out, he took one peak between his thumb and forefinger and massaged.

A moan sighed from her throat.

"Ready for me to get you even wetter?"

The space between her legs turned instantly slick, desire curling in the base of her belly.

He played with her other nipple as well, then slid his palm under one breast and bent to take the hard nubbin into his mouth. He sucked deeply, pulling on her through the wet material.

Her fingers wove into his hair and urged him closer.

"Yes," she cried, letting her head tip back as he wrapped an arm around her waist and arched her into his body. "Oh. Hell. Yes."

With a low, throaty chuckle, Maddox lifted her onto the just cleaned countertop and proceeded to give her exactly what she asked for.

# Chapter Sixteen

"And as you can see, Mr. Monroe," explained the first of the three architects in the conference room, "the projected redesign will add an additional twenty-four thousand square feet to the new M London. By using your plan to combine the three properties on the block and build up by two stories, we will be able to offer twelve more guest rooms than originally planned as well as two extra luxury penthouse suites with excellent views of the park."

Maddox studied the scale model set up in the middle of the long table, then the 3-D computer renderings projected on the screen, analyzing each with an eye for detail. Overall, he liked what he saw.

"And the cost to break ground? You have those figures? Along with the projected timetables and completion dates?"

The oldest of the three men nodded. Reaching for a heavy binder, he thumbed through to find the information requested. He was just opening his mouth to answer when Maddox's cell phone vibrated.

Maddox gave the phone a quick glance, recognizing the number. "Sorry, if you'll excuse me for a minute, I need to take this."

"Of course," the older architect said.

Maddox hit "answer" and put the phone to his ear. Getting to his feet, he crossed the room for some privacy. "Hey."

It was Brie.

"Hey, yourself," she said. "Am I calling at a bad time?"

He slipped a hand in one trouser pocket, blood humming in his veins from nothing more than the sound of her voice. "It's never a bad time when you call."

He could almost hear her melt on the other end of the line. She cleared her throat. "What I ought to have asked is, are you busy right now?"

"I'm in a morning meeting."

"And I'm just on my way to one. But I wanted to let you know we got a response on our motion to have the Mergenfeld suit dismissed."

"And?"

"It's been denied. The judge has ruled that it can move forward. Do you want to discuss a settlement?"

Maddox's hand tightened around the phone. "With that double-crossing, moneygrubbing little p-tard?"

"I take it that's a no."

"It's most definitely a no. Anything else on the business front?"

"Nothing that can't wait until we both have more time."

He played with a button in his pocket, rubbing it between his fingers. It was small and green and had popped off one of Brie's shirts last week when he'd surprised her at her office for lunch.

He'd stopped in to sign some papers and had ended

up taking her in a frantic coupling in her private bathroom. He could still remember the way she'd felt. Her legs had been wrapped around his waist, her fingers in his hair, her mouth on his as she kissed him with crazy abandon from where she balanced on the granite countertop next to the sink. He'd thrust into her over and over, one hand on her ass while his other hand tunneled inside her shirt to play with her breasts.

Somewhere along the line, he'd popped one of her buttons loose. He'd found it on the floor while he'd been tidying himself up afterward and had secreted it inside his pocket rather than returning it to her.

He'd taken to carrying it with him ever since.

As for Brie, she'd warned him not to drop in on her for "lunch" ever again. His visit had completely messed with her day, since she'd barely been able to think about anything else and had lost her train of thought that afternoon during a presentation attended by all the partners.

"I was mortified," she told him later.

He'd laughed and apologized, then proceeded to fuck her blind seated on one of her dining room chairs.

"So, what time should I come over tonight?" he asked, staring out the window with an idle gaze while the architects waited patiently on the other side of the room for him to return.

"I'll be working late. I have a client dinner that'll probably go until ten or eleven."

"Male or female?"

"Male or female what?"

"Client. I don't like the idea of you out late with some other man."

"If it's a client, then it doesn't matter what sex they happen to be. But if it makes you feel better, it's a woman and her husband."

"Need a plus one?"

She laughed. "No. And *definitely* not you. You're much too high profile and I don't need everyone speculating about things that are none of their business. Besides, one of the other partners and an associate are coming along too. You'd just be bored."

"I believe I could keep up."

"No doubt about it. But still you don't need to waste your time. So rain check on tonight. We both could use some sleep."

"Maybe, but I'll be there anyway. Let's say midnight. Unless you'd rather just come over to the hotel. I could send Marco with the car."

"No, I . . . it'll be easier if I see you at my place."

So far, whenever he'd suggested she come to his penthouse at the M, she'd declined. He supposed it was too public for her taste. But as he'd explained, no one needed to know if she visited him overnight; he could easily bring her in through the private back entrance, which he usually used himself.

"Look, I've really got to run," she said.

"Me too. See you at midnight."

"Bye."

He ended the call but didn't immediately return to the conference table; his mind was still too full of Brie.

In the weeks since they'd first slept together, they'd spent only three nights apart. He'd needed to oversee some work at one of his other properties in Miami. Originally the trip had been scheduled for four nights, but he'd pushed everyone hard and finished a day early.

It had been late Friday night when he'd arrived back at JFK. He'd considered going to his penthouse at the M, but had ended up knocking on Brie's door instead. Sleepy-eyed, her hair mussed, she'd let him in despite the late hour.

She'd welcomed him into her bed and her body as well, her guard down in those dark, quiet hours while the world slept around them.

As close as they now were physically, there was a barrier she worked hard to keep between them. He sensed it didn't have anything to do with him, but with someone from her past. She didn't talk about the men she'd been involved with, and truthfully, he didn't want to know. But someone had hurt her; he couldn't help but wonder who.

He found himself wishing occasionally that he knew so he could track the bastard down and punch his lights out. But then he reminded himself that if that man had treated Brie better, she might still be with him. They might even be married.

*She wouldn't belong to me now,* Maddox thought.

And she did.

Exclusively.

He didn't know how long the fire would burn between them, but while it did, he planned for them both to enjoy themselves to the max.

Turning, he went back to the conference table. "All right, gentlemen. Where were we?"

"Sorry, I'm late." Brie slipped into a seat across the table from Madelyn. "Got held up in a meeting."

The busy restaurant hummed around them, servers rushing to and fro while a multitude of noisy conversations droned like lazy bees.

"That's okay. I just arrived a couple minutes ago myself." Madelyn sent her a smile and sipped her lemonade.

The waitress appeared and took Brie's drink order—the same as Madelyn's. The girl zipped off again.

Brie and Madelyn consulted their menus for a moment, then set them aside.

"What are you having?" Madelyn asked.

"Probably the same as you, soup and a half sandwich."

At this restaurant, which had a quick turnaround and wasn't located too far from either of their office buildings, they generally ended up ordering the same thing whenever they ate there.

"Yes, but are you having chicken salad or oven-roasted turkey breast?"

Brie laughed. "I think I'm going to live dangerously today and try the grilled cheese."

"With tomato soup?"

"Of course."

They shared another grin.

The waitress arrived with Brie's drink, then took their order. She disappeared again with quiet efficiency.

"What's new since the last time we talked?" Madelyn unfolded her napkin and laid it across her lap.

"Not too much. You know the routine. Work, eat, sleep."

*Have sex.*

She was getting plenty of that lately too—hot, passionate, wildly inventive sex that left her exquisitely satiated and ready to drop off into a heavy sleep afterward.

Maddox came over to her apartment nearly every night. And each time, in spite of giving herself pep talks during the daylight hours about keeping boundaries and maintaining a bit of healthy space between them, she could never seem to turn him away.

To her annoyed chagrin, all he had to do was crook his little finger at her and smile his sexy smile and she ended up in bed with him.

Or else having sex with him in the living room . . .

Or the kitchen . . .

Or in the shower . . .

Or even one time on top of the washing machine while the spin cycle was set to high . . .

"You sure nothing's up?" Madelyn eyed her shrewdly. "You look kind of funny all of a sudden."

Even though she shared most things with Madelyn, she still hadn't told her that she was seeing Maddox. For one thing, she wasn't sure how her older sister would react to the news. For another, she kind of wanted to keep the relationship a secret. Although it looked as if that wasn't going to last for too much longer, not if Madelyn-the-bloodhound was on the trail.

"I'm good," Brie hedged. "Just thinking about something at work. Any word from the newlyweds?"

Ivy and James were still away on their honeymoon. Last she'd heard, they had left Isle Ivy. Ivy loved the Twilight series and had named her new tropical island as an homage to Isle Esme from the books.

Madelyn nodded. "Mom got a text yesterday. They're in France. Ivy's painting and James has been taking a business call here and there. I guess they're headed for Paris and Geneva next week, more business of James's; then it's back home. So they'll be here for the Fourth."

"That'll make Mom happy."

"It will. The twins are excited about the holiday. They're already pestering Zack and me about when we're leaving to see Grammy and Grandpa. They loved last year, playing games in the garden and getting to stuff on hamburgers and watermelon and ice cream. You'll be there, of course, right?"

Every year, their parents hosted a blowout Fourth of July bash complete with food and fireworks. Friends, neighbors, and family came from near and far to join in the festivities.

Brie frowned, glad when the waitress appeared and set their meals in front of them. She busied herself opening a package of tiny oyster crackers and sprinkling them over her soup, then took a bite of her warm, gooey grilled cheese sandwich.

"What day are you coming up?" Madelyn pressed, eating a bite of her chicken salad on lightly toasted sourdough. "I think we're going to leave just before the crack of dawn on the Fourth and see if we can miss most of the traffic."

Brie spooned up some of her soup. "Actually, I'm not sure I'll be there this year."

Madelyn stopped chewing, then swallowed abruptly. "What? Why? You always come."

"No, not always. There were lots of times I didn't make it up when I was living in D.C."

"Yes, but you were in D.C., which means you had a good excuse. You're in New York now. You have to come."

"I may have other plans this year."

"What plans?" Madelyn narrowed her eyes, her nostrils flaring faintly; she was on the hunt.

Brie sighed inwardly. "Work. You know how it is."

"Work, schmirk," Madelyn said dismissively. "You've always got work. What's the real reason?"

She wished now she'd just said she'd be there. But from comments Maddox had made, she was pretty sure he expected her to spend the holiday with him. Of course, she could have explained that she needed to attend a family function, but then wouldn't he expect to come with her? She just wasn't ready for that.

Not yet.

"Fess up." Madelyn waved a finger in her direction. "It's written all over your face."

"What is?"

"Guilt. You're hiding something." She paused for a moment. "Or hiding some*one*. Who are you seeing?"

"Nobody."

*Crap, why do I have to sound so defensive?*

One would think she could do better at obscuring the truth, considering that she was a lawyer and all.

"Aha!" Madelyn pounced. "You *are* seeing someone. Tell me who he is. What he does. Is he scorching hot?"

"You know, you spend way too much time around your other friends. What are their names? Peg and Linda? They're a bad influence."

"Don't forget Suzy. And yes, they are. But quit trying to divert my attention. Tell Madelyn everything she wants to know."

"You should also refrain from referring to yourself in the third person."

"Duly noted. Now dish."

Brie's mouth tightened. She sighed and laid down her spoon. "It's Maddox."

Madelyn stared, her own spoon suspended over her soup. "What?"

"Maddox Monroe. You met him. Remember?"

"I remember. I'm just not sure I heard you right. Maybe I ought to call my ENT and schedule a hearing test in case I'm going deaf."

"Very funny."

"No, what's funny is you. I thought you despised the man and now you're involved in some hot and heavy romance with him?"

Brie looked away, slid a finger through the condensation on her glass. "It's not like that. We're just seeing each other."

"And by seeing each other, I assume you mean having sex."

"Madelyn!"

"Question asked and answered. So, when did all this start? Before or after he showed up at Ivy's wedding?"

Brie spun her glass in a tight circle. "Kind of during, if you must know."

"During?" Madelyn frowned. "What do you mean . . . *oh my God*, he was there, wasn't he? In your room? When I knocked and your door was locked. No wonder you sounded so weird."

Brie opened her mouth to deny it, but realized there wasn't much point. "All right, yes, he was with me. But we didn't actually . . . Nothing happened. . . . Well, something happened but not what you're implying."

"But enough. Wow, Maddox Monroe." Madelyn sat back, clearly mulling over the revelation. Then she started to laugh. "You are so in trouble."

"What's that supposed to mean?"

"Nothing." Madelyn laughed again. "It just reminds me of how much I once thought I hated Zack. I couldn't stand him and then, whoosh, straight to the heart."

"Your situation and mine are nothing alike. Maddox and I aren't serious about each other. We're just having a bit of fun, that's all."

Madelyn smiled. "So were Zack and I."

"Yes, but this is different. There's no real relationship, not in the 'we're dating' sense. We have sex and eat a meal together occasionally. For all I know, this fling, for lack of a better word, will be over by next week."

"Or maybe it won't." Madelyn ate a bite of her sandwich. "So he's the reason you're not coming for Fourth of July?"

Brie went back to eating her lunch too. "I'm spending the holiday here in the city with him. He said he wants to do something together, although we haven't really firmed up any plans yet."

Not that they ever really firmed up plans. Generally he just showed up at her door, or told her, as he had today, that he'd stop by her place later.

"For someone you're not really dating, it sounds pretty involved. I don't see why you don't just bring him with you to Connecticut. He's already met most of the family and Mom quite obviously adores him. I can't remember the last time she gushed over a man like that, even Dad."

"Which is exactly why I'm *not* bringing Maddox. She'll read too much into it. Knowing Mom, she'll probably starting hinting around about wedding dates and what venues we might want to reserve before all the good ones fill up. No way am I going to voluntarily submit myself to the inquisition."

Madelyn chuckled. "Yeah, on second thought, I suppose you're smart to stay away." She finished her sandwich and wiped her mouth with her napkin. "Just promise me, Brie, that you'll be careful."

"I'm always careful."

"I know. But there's something about Maddox Monroe that makes me think he's different from the other men you've been involved with."

"Oh, he's different all right. He's arrogant and opinionated and so pigheaded that he won't take no for an answer. He's like water on a rock; he just keeps dripping until he wears your resistance away. Which, I suppose, is why I've let him worm his way in despite my better judgment."

"That and the fact that he's absolutely gorgeous. From a purely investigational standpoint, how is he in the sack?"

Brie met her sister's eyes. "What do you think?"

The pair of them giggled, then broke into full-blown laughter. Some of the other diners turned their heads to stare. Rather than deter them, the looks only made them laugh harder.

# CHAPTER SEVENTEEN

Brie rolled over onto her back, her breath labored, heart pumping fast. A light sheen of perspiration glistened on her skin, the sheets twisted and forgotten beneath her naked body. Her body glowed in the aftermath, satisfaction tingling through every pore.

Maddox lay beside her, one arm pillowed beneath her head, his left leg tangled with hers. She snuggled closer, her cheek on his shoulder, and closed her eyes. For the moment, she was content to do nothing more strenuous than be quiet and let herself float.

She waited, part of her expecting him to climb out of bed soon and get dressed. It was a weekday and he usually didn't stay the night. It was easier on both their schedules if he went home so they could both catch a few uninterrupted hours of sleep.

But instead he lay there, making no move to leave.

She thought of her conversation with Madelyn, then shoved it away.

*It's just sex. Period. End of story.*

So why did every day with him seem better than the

last? And why was she starting to anticipate the hours they spent together, even when they did nothing more than sit on the couch and hold hands while they traded stories about their day?

*Crap*, was she wrong? Were they in a relationship and she didn't even know it?

Her eyes popped open; she scowled into the dark.

"I was thinking about Friday," Maddox began, his deep voice breaking the silence.

Friday was July 4.

"Some friends of mine have invited me to a beach party in the Hamptons. They're doing a clambake and later there'll be fireworks. I was wondering if you'd like to go with me."

It took her a moment to respond. "Go with? As in a date?"

*Jesus, this is worse than I thought.*

"I suppose 'date' is as good a word as any," he said, stroking an idle hand along her arm. "I've rented a house nearby as well. I thought we could spend the weekend."

*Oh, for crap's sake, we are in a relationship!*

"I—" Her voice caught, the rest of the words sticking in her throat.

"Look, it's okay if you don't want to go. Think about it and let me know one way or the other." He patted her arm, then began to move away. "It's late. I should get going."

She rolled over, reached out to stop him. "No, don't go."

"You need to sleep."

"So do you. Sleep here. We can have breakfast together."

Even though he'd stayed over and they'd shared breakfast on occasion, this was the first time she'd ever actually invited him.

He hesitated. "You sure I won't disturb you?"

*You always disturb me.*

"I'm sure. Stay."

What was she doing? She was just digging herself in deeper, making everything worse. Yet strangely enough she meant every word.

"And I don't need to think about anything," she rushed on. "Of course I'd like to go with you to the Hamptons. I haven't been to a real East Coast beach clambake in years. It'll be great."

He played his fingers over her spine, and her muscles began to relax. "You're positive? Because we could do something else, here in the city, if you'd rather."

"No, the Hamptons sound wonderful. It's where we first met, after all. Well, where we met again."

His mouth turned up at the corners. "I remember. Hopefully you won't slug me with a tennis ball this time."

"I won't. I promise. As for soccer balls or volleyballs . . ." She let her teasing words drift away.

"Very funny. Take it back."

"No way. You were mean to me and deserved it, even if I did hit you by accident."

"I'm not mean to you anymore. Now take it back or suffer the consequences."

"What consequences?"

"These."

Before she could stop him, he found a spot along her rib cage that was particularly sensitive and began to tickle her.

She squirmed, tried to get away.

He wouldn't let her go.

"Stop. Maddox, quit."

She tried again to escape, twisting and laughing. When he only redoubled his efforts, she shrieked.

"Say you take it back," he threatened, continuing his mock assault.

"I take it back." She gasped. "Aw, God, stop. Please stop."

"No soccer balls or volleyballs or any other kind of sports equipment used as weapons?"

"No, nothing." She laughed and shrieked again. "Stop. You've had your revenge. I already told you I was sorry."

"How sorry?" His fingers stopped their torment, gliding over her skin instead.

She shivered. "Very sorry." Catching her breath, she reached up and cradled his face between her hands. "Very, very sorry."

Gently, she caressed him, tracing the flesh that she'd once injured in a moment of anger and thoughtlessness. Leaning up, she kissed his cheek and temple and the corner of his eye, each touch as light as a feather, as soft as a murmur. "Very, very, very sorry."

"Three verys," he said. "That's a lot."

"It is." Her mouth whispered over his, pressing tenderly.

He rolled her over suddenly, pulling her on top of him. "I should let you get to sleep."

"Yes." She fit her lips to his again and kissed him deeply, her hands roving over his body in search of the places where she knew he most liked to be touched.

He shuddered and returned the favor.

"You need to sleep too," she said at length.

"I do." His fingers splayed across her ass, stroking her in a way that made her tremble from head to toe.

She kissed his neck and shoulders, then moved on to his chest, bending to rake her teeth across one of his flat nipples. "Surely a little while longer won't hurt," she said.

"I don't see how it can, considering how 'awake' I am already." He shifted her so she could feel his hard, straining erection.

A smile curved her lips as she met his gaze in the moonlight that was creeping in around the curtains. "Ah, and so you are. Maybe I can do something to help cure your case of insomnia."

He laughed and rolled her over again, parting her legs with his hips. "Yes, maybe you can."

"How is everything? You need more quahogs or mussels or another ear of corn?"

Brie looked over at Maddox where he sat in a beach chair next to her own. They had plates of steamed seafood and an array of accompaniments balanced on their laps; bottles of home-brewed iced tea were nestled into the sand at their feet.

She shook her head. "Thanks, but I've got plenty. It's all delicious. Your friends really know how to throw a party."

Maddox nodded in agreement, cracked open a lobster claw, and pulled out the succulent meat inside. He popped half of the tender morsel into his mouth, then gave her a closed-mouthed grin as he chewed with clear enjoyment.

She continued her meal with pleasure as well.

The sun was high and bright in the cloudless blue sky despite the lengthening evening hour. The temperature was hot, nearly ninety, but pleasant due to the refreshing breeze that blew off the gently rolling waves of the bay.

Even though she'd put on sunscreen, she was glad she'd worn her Mets cap to keep the sun off her face. David and Jana—or Janvid, as they were affectionately known—were the hosts of today's beach bash and avid

Yankees fans in spite of the fact that they lived in the Hamptons. They'd good-naturedly chided her for her choice of team attire. She'd chided them back, proudly standing her ground, even though she got absolutely no support from Maddox on the subject. At an impasse, they'd put a cold drink into her hands, pointed her toward the options of relaxing in a beach chair, playing volleyball, or swimming, and left Maddox to handle the rest of the introductions.

He seemed to know practically everyone there, all twenty-plus of them, and was happy to make the acquaintance of the few he didn't. Although Maddox was the only person she knew, the rest of the partygoers openly welcomed her and she soon felt right at home.

Rather than hang back, she and Maddox had joined in on all the activities. First, they'd played volleyball, pairing up on the same side to make sure, he told her teasingly, that she didn't get any ideas about spiking the ball in his direction. Instead, she'd shot him a narrow-eyed glare over the top of her sunglasses, which made him laugh.

Next, they'd stripped down to their bathing suits—a sleek, sexy, blue one-piece for her and a pair of black swim trunks for him—and headed into the water to cool off.

They'd frolicked in the waves until they were tired, then ran, dripping, up to the beach chairs where they'd left their clothes. They'd toweled off, then stretched out in the chairs to relax under one of the big umbrellas Janvid had thoughtfully set up for their guests.

She and Maddox sipped their drinks and idly chatted with some of the others until the call went out that they should all gather round—the food was ready.

Brie ate the rest of her clams, sausage, and buttered lobster tail, then set her fork down onto her plate. She reached for her drink and relaxed back in her chair, more than well satisfied and a little sleepy.

Overall, it had been a really great day, one of the most fun and relaxing she'd spent in a very long time. A tiny nibble of guilt went through her when she thought of her family celebrating up north without her, but she couldn't regret her decision to skip out this year.

It was nice being here with Maddox with no need to worry over any potential parental grilling about where her relationship with him might be headed.

Jana and David and their friends were polite enough not to ask any intrusive questions about her and Maddox as a couple. Then again, maybe he brought a different woman with him to Janvid's beach party every summer, so his friends weren't surprised that he was here with someone new.

Little scowl lines formed on her forehead at the thought. She took another drink of her tea and gazed out at the water.

"You finished?" Maddox gave her an inquiring look. "Did you save room for dessert? They've got a real spread set up, including a cooler with ice cream for make-your-own sundaes."

"Sounds delish, but I couldn't squeeze in another bite." She laid a hand over her shirt-clad stomach for emphasis.

After their swim, they'd rinsed off in the outdoor showers nearby, then slipped back into their clothes again. Maddox had stolen a few kisses and touches while they'd been showering. Otherwise, they'd mostly kept the PDA down to innocent hand holding.

He took her hand now. "Why don't we go for a walk, then?"

Relaxing again, she smiled and nodded.

Hand in hand, they began strolling along the beach, sea-foam and salt water swirling in rhythmic waves, rushing over the sand toward their feet, then away once again. Seagulls wheeled overhead while the white sails of small boats fluttered on the blue-gray bay beyond. The shouts and laughter of people, young and old alike, floated on the breeze. And everywhere there was an excitement that hummed like a live thing, an anticipation for darkness to descend and the fireworks to burst free so that they would fill the night sky with color and light and sound.

She walked on with Maddox at her side, strolling at a lazy pace that suited them both, her sandal-clad feet sinking quietly into the sand.

"I was thinking, when we get back to the cottage tonight, that we could—" Maddox leaned over and whispered the rest in her ear.

It was a blatantly sexual suggestion that made hot tingles whirl inside her veins and a laugh escape her lips.

"I guess I have more than tonight's fireworks show to look forward to." She stopped and wound an arm around his waist, stretched up on her toes to kiss him.

He tugged her closer and kissed her back, his tongue tangling passionately with hers. She smiled and playfully nipped his lower lip, wondering if the fireworks had started already.

One of her hands was stealing under the loose tail of his cotton shirt when something suddenly bumped against the edge of her foot.

Startled, she pulled away from Maddox and looked down. A green and white soccer ball lay on the sand near her heel. Automatically, she picked it up.

A boy of maybe ten or eleven years loped up the beach toward her, his eyes extremely green, his hair the pale color of a new moon.

He stopped, hands on his narrow hips. "That's my ball. Can I have it back?"

"Oh." She glanced down at the ball. "Sure."

But before she could toss it to him, a man jogged up, his long, thin build and light-colored hair marking him easily as the boy's father. But it was his eyes that sent a jolt through her body, her muscles suddenly frozen in place.

"Sorry about that," he said with a smile as he drew to a halt about a yard away. "The kids kicked a shot wide and . . ." His words trailed off. "Brie? Is it you?"

At her side, she sensed Maddox turn and look at her.

But she couldn't look away from the other man, her heart slamming hard inside her chest like a hammer hitting a stone.

She swallowed, her mouth gone dry. "Hello, Stephen. It's been a long time."

*Almost seven years, yet sometimes it still seems like yesterday.*

He straightened and came closer, his eyes, which were the exact shade of his son's, moving over her. "Yes, it has. You're looking good."

"You look the same."

Only he didn't, not precisely.

He was still dynamic, with Ivy League good looks and a well-mannered, innate charm that seemed to radiate from him like an expensive cologne. But there were lines on his face now that hadn't been there before and a hard, tired cynicism around his mouth and jaw that had barely been hinted at in times past.

Once, she'd been drawn to him, needing him the way a flower needs light and water, drinking in his every word, desperate for the tiniest crumbs of his attention, his affection. She'd been crazy about him, willing to ignore her whispering conscience that warned her that what she was doing was wrong.

When she thought about it all with a rational sort of logic, she'd been pathetic.

She'd believed his lies.

She'd accepted his excuses.

She'd let him use her, until the end when he'd finally shown himself for exactly what he was.

A ruthless heartbreaker and manipulator of the very worst kind.

And yet here he stood in the unlikeliest of places on the unlikeliest of days. For years she'd worried about running into him at some law conference or other professional event, but they'd never once crossed paths.

She'd always wondered how she would react if that day should ever come, playing various scenarios through her head like worn-out loops of film. But meeting him on a beach on the Fourth of July with one of his children in tow and the rest of his family no doubt enjoying themselves only a few yards away—that she had never considered.

Funny how life could sneak up on you sometimes and whap you right between the eyes.

A strong hand curved around her waist, shattering her rapid-fire musings. To her chagrin, she realized she'd completely forgotten Maddox in the past few seconds, even though he stood right by her side.

Maddox drew her closer, so that their hips and thighs touched. His possessive touch made their intimate relationship absolutely plain to anyone who cared to notice.

Stephen's eyes flickered; clearly he noticed.

"Forgive me, Maddox," she said, wanting to make her unintentional slight up to him even though he didn't necessarily know she'd made one. "Where are my manners?

This is Stephen Jeffries. Stephen, this is Maddox Monroe."

Stephen blinked at the name but gave no other evidence of recognition.

"Pleasure." He thrust out his hand.

Maddox paused for a moment, then accepted, clasping hands for a firm, quick shake. He was the first to let go.

Brie darted a glance upward out of the corner of her eye and saw that Maddox had a different opinion about meeting the other man.

Stephen blinked again, then put on his charmer's smile and moved to lay a hand on the shoulder of the boy who was still waiting to get his ball back.

"This young man is my oldest son, Jay," he said. "Jay, say hello to Mr. Monroe and Ms. Grayson. Ms. Grayson and I used to work together at the same law firm many years ago."

"Hello," the boy said, polite but without much enthusiasm.

Brie and Maddox both murmured hello back.

"Here." She held out the ball to him. "I'm sure I'm keeping you from your game."

A ghost of a smile curved his young face for the first time as he came forward to collect the soccer ball. "Thanks," he told her.

He turned to his father. "Dad, may I be excused?"

"Yes. Go on and tell your mother that I'll be there in a couple minutes. And let your sister play this time. You know how she gets when you won't let her join in."

"That's because she cries if she gets hit by the ball."

"Then don't hit her with it."

With an exaggerated eye roll, Jay tucked the ball under his arm and sprinted away.

"Kids." Stephen made a face, then laughed. He eyed them with obvious speculation. "So, do you two—"

"No," Brie said before he could go any further. "Maddox and I don't have children."

Stephen's gaze dropped to her left hand. Was he looking for a ring?

"Not married, then, either?" he said.

Her fingers curled into a fist. "Just dating."

"Now, sweetheart, don't be shy. You and I both know it's a lot more than dating." Maddox draped his arm over her shoulders and tugged her even tighter against him. Leaning down, he brushed a possessive kiss across her mouth. "After all, we spend every night together and as many days as we can. Hard to keep our hands off each other, isn't it?"

He kissed her again, then straightened. Once he had, he locked eyes with Stephen and didn't look away. It was almost as if he was warning the other man off.

As for Stephen, he looked annoyed, though he certainly had no right to be. She and Stephen had been over a long, long time ago.

She snuck another peek up at Maddox, wondering again at his mood. Surely he didn't know about her and Stephen? Even if he did, what was he worried about?

"So, are you still at Mitchell, Brown and Lovell?" she asked, hoping to relieve the tension and steer the conversation into calmer waters.

Stephen continued his staring match with Maddox for a few seconds more, then broke off and looked toward her. He folded his arms over his chest. "I am, though it's just Brown and Lovell these days. You're still missed there, you know, even after all this time."

She let out a laugh, hoping it didn't sound too strained.

"I doubt that. Associates come and associates go. I'm sure everyone moved on quite nicely without me."

"Not everyone." For a moment, he looked sad, almost regretful.

Was he sorry about what had happened between them? Did he wish now that things might have been different?

Even if he did, it changed nothing. The past, as they said, was still the past.

His expression cleared and he smiled. "Did I see that you're back in the city and working at Marshall McNeal Prescott?"

"I am."

"Impressive. They're an excellent firm."

"The best in New York," Maddox said, rejoining the conversation. "Brie was recently made partner."

Stephen nodded. "Yes, I heard that as well. Congratulations, Brie. It's a step up that is more than well deserved." His eyes moved back to Maddox. "Monroe? That name seems familiar."

Maddox shrugged. "Probably because it's so common." Maddox's arm looped around Brie's waist and he glanced down at her. "We should probably be getting back—otherwise someone may steal our beach chairs and we won't have anywhere comfortable to sit for the fireworks." He started turning her, barely affording Stephen a last glance.

"It was good seeing you, Brie," Stephen said. "Maybe we'll run into each other again sometime. Manhattan's not as large as it looks."

"Yes, maybe. Good-bye." She gave him a little halfhearted wave; then she and Maddox turned their backs and walked back the way they'd come.

Neither of them spoke at first.

"You were a bit rude, you know," she finally said. "Why didn't you tell him who you are?"

"Because I don't give a damn whether he knows who I am or not. The only reason I could possibly care is if I needed a lawyer and I don't. I've already got you and you're the best."

"Yes, well, compliment to me aside, there was no reason to be so abrupt with him. Or so outwardly possessive of me. We're dating. I think he got the picture without all the added show."

"I just wanted to make sure everything was clear so there'd be no misunderstandings." His voice was low, gruff.

"What kind of misunderstandings? What are you talking about?"

He stopped, turned her to face him. "Because he's the one, isn't he? The one who worked you over? Who put that sad, wary look in your eyes. The look you get sometimes when you think no one is watching."

She lowered her gaze. "I don't know what you mean."

"There it is. That's the look."

She blinked and forced herself to meet his eyes again, her expression wiped clear. "There is *no* look."

"You can lie to me, Brie. You can even lie to yourself, but don't think for a minute that you're fooling anyone."

"Fooling how? And about what?"

"About the fact that someone hurt you badly. I've known it for a long while, and now I know who to blame. I've sensed your pain sometimes when we're together. When I try to get past those barriers of yours and you keep me at arm's length."

"I don't have barriers and I hardly keep you at a distance." She blew out an exasperated breath. "As you took such pains to make clear back there with your chest-beating, macho-man routine, you're in my bed every night and not just to sleep. I can't remember saying no to you even once, at least not since we've been together."

Crossing the small distance between them, he drew her into his arms. "No, you never turn me away sexually. You're very generous and enthusiastic in bed. But there's more to intimacy than the physical. It's the times we're not making love that I sense the distance. You only let me get so close—then you freeze me out."

Her chest grew tight. Was he right? Did she push him away emotionally?

"And you want what?" she said. "I assumed you were satisfied with our relationship, that you just wanted to keep things easy and casual."

"I do, except . . ."

"Except what? Are you saying you want more?"

Slowly, he pulled her nearer so they touched all the way down—chest, stomach, pelvis, and thighs. "Yeah, I think I do."

Her heart gave a funny little double beat, her breathing hitching slightly with uncertainty. "How much more?"

He must have sensed her fear; obviously he was good at that. "Hey, don't have a panic attack," he said. "It's not like I'm asking for a lifetime commitment. Then again—"

"Yes?"

His hands slid along the small of her back to rock her against him. "A key to your apartment might be nice. And I'll give you one for my penthouse at the hotel. You're welcome to drop in anytime, day and night. Actually, I'd like it if you did."

Something inside her grew warm, sort of melty, like a candy bar that had been left out in the sun. But was he asking too much? Exchanging keys was serious business and she wasn't sure if she was ready.

The smile left his face. "Unless it's still too soon. You don't have feelings for what's his name back there anymore, do you?"

Automatically, she shook her head. But as she did, she realized her answer was the truth. However much she'd once loved Stephen—and at the time, it had been with her whole heart—the years seemed to have worked their magic.

Part of her had always expected it would be agony to see him again. That just a look, a few words, even a casual touch, would be enough to dredge up the old memories, the old pain.

But today, when it had actually happened, when she'd stood only a few feet away from him and spoken of ordinary things and old times, there'd been nothing.

No spark, no pull.

He was just someone she'd known once.

Someone, she realized with a sudden overwhelming certainty, that she no longer loved.

In fact, after the initial shock of meeting Stephen, it had been Maddox of whom she'd been vitally aware as he stood there beside her. Maddox who occupied her thoughts and emotions. Maddox with whom she wanted to sit tonight and watch the fireworks, then go back to his cottage, to his bed, and make love before she fell asleep in his arms.

*Holy crap, is Madelyn right? Am I falling for him?*

Her heart gave another crazy quick-time beat and her breath hitched in her chest again.

He waited, silent.

She saw him studying her expression, no doubt wondering what thoughts were tumbling through her mind while she decided on her answer.

She locked her arms around his waist and squeezed. "No, I don't have feelings for Stephen. Not anymore. You're right—he did hurt me once, but it was a long time ago. Whatever I might have felt, it's gone now. Over and done."

He eyed her, a measure of uncertainty lingering in his dark gaze. "You're sure?"

"Yes, very sure. Satisfied now?"

"Maybe." His voice was gruff.

Stretching up on her toes, she pressed her lips to his. "How about now?"

A glint of humor appeared in his eyes. "A bit better."

She laughed and kissed him again, harder and far more thoroughly, using plenty of tongue.

"Definitely better," he said on a growl when they finally came up for air.

She could feel his arousal against her stomach. Her own was sizzling in her blood as well. Maybe they should ditch the fireworks and go back to his place now. She certainly wouldn't mind.

Instead, she took his hand and began walking back, the setting sun a fiery blaze of orange and red and pink on the horizon.

They were nearly back to their beach chairs, Janvid's party going strong, when she tightened her grip on his hand.

"Okay," she said.

"Okay, what?"

"I'll give you a key."

He stopped and turned her to face him. "Really? You're sure you want to do this? You don't have to, you know. Not until you're ready."

A smile stretched across her mouth, a wonderful certainty filling her up as if the waning sun were transferring itself into her body rather than disappearing from the sky.

She felt buoyant suddenly. She felt free.

"Yes," she said, "I'm sure. Now, let's go watch us some fireworks."

Laughing, he kissed her again; then together they walked the rest of the way back, hand in hand.

# Chapter Eighteen

"...And the delegation from Indonesia arrived and everyone is all settled in? Any problems?" Maddox asked, shifting his attention away from the summary report on his computer to focus on his general manager, Oscar Johannas, who sat across from his desk.

It was Monday morning and Maddox's first day back after his holiday trip to the beach. He smothered a yawn, feeling rested despite his overall lack of sleep.

Oscar was a tidy, stocky man of thirty-five who looked like a curious mix between a brawler and a high-class fashion designer. Demanding and particular in both his dress and his habits, he enforced the rules with a tough yet fair hand. He had a sharp intellect and an ability to charm guests and staff alike. But he could be a bastard when necessary and never had trouble maintaining order. He also wasn't afraid to roll up his sleeves and do whatever tasks needed doing, no matter how menial they might appear. Whenever Maddox was away, he had no worries about leaving his flagship hotel in Oscar's capable hands.

When Maddox was in residence, however, he left his penthouse each morning and rode the elevator down to the office he kept on the first floor. Inside, he met with staff, held meetings with high-level vendors and businessmen, and kept tabs on the inner workings of his hotels, both here in New York and elsewhere. He and Oscar had a standing meeting each morning from eight thirty to nine, where the two of them reviewed that day's "hot items." Leaning back in his chair, he waited to hear what Oscar had to say.

"No, no problems to speak of," Oscar began, "although there was a bit of an incident last night."

"What kind of incident?"

Oscar paused for a moment as if considering his words. "Well, it seems that one of our Indonesian guests is a durian lover."

Maddox's eyebrows drew together. "Durian? You mean that really stinky tropical fruit? The one that smells like old gym socks?"

"And rotten onions and vomit." Oscar made a face.

"Christ. I have a good idea where you're going with this, but continue."

"Apparently, the guy had three great big durian fruits brought up to his room without our knowledge and sliced them open to share with his colleagues. The smell was so foul it drifted out into the hallway and into a couple of the rooms next door.

"Robert, my night manager, was called upstairs to find out which of the guests were ill, thinking we might have gotten hit with some sort of stomach flu. One of the maids, who'd come to do turndowns, actually did get sick to her stomach after she tried to enter the room."

Maddox rolled his eyes skyward but said nothing as he waited for Oscar to continue.

"A doctor was called before anyone knew what was really going on," Oscar said. "And because of the language barrier and a whole lot of confusion on both sides, it took a while to figure out that the damned fruit was the problem.

"Robert sent people to locate the Indonesian interpreter, who was down in the bar getting plastered. Once they got him upstairs, they had him politely but firmly explain that foods that stink like decomposing garbage are not permitted in the guest rooms. Our foreign guests apologized profusely, then offered to share the damned durian! Apparently it's a delicacy not to be missed."

At that, Maddox couldn't keep from smiling. "Did Robert accept?"

Oscar cracked a smile too. "Hell no. You ever get a whiff of that stuff? I tried it once on a dare." He shuddered. "Never again."

"Oh, it's not so bad. I had it on a trip to Southeast Asia. But I'll admit, it's an acquired taste." Maddox laughed at the expression of disgust on his GM's face. "So, how bad is the fallout?"

Oscar turned serious again. "We had to relocate the guests staying in one of the nearby rooms and offer a discount to another since we were at full capacity. We're moving Fruit Guy to another room today so we can do a deep cleaning. If the stink won't come out of the room, we may have to call in a biohazard team."

"Hopefully it won't come to that. Start with housekeeping and see how far we can get."

"Sure will. Some of the maids are refusing to go in, though. Poor Shirley, the one who tossed her cookies, had to go home to recover. I said we'd cover her lost hours."

Maddox leaned forward in his chair. "Of course. And

offer the maids who *will* go in to clean double their usual wage. I presume you're charging the Indonesians a fee for the cleaning?"

"Already on it. The head of the delegation was told this morning and said they will cover any necessary expenses."

"So, problem handled."

"Of course," Oscar agreed smoothly. "I told you it was nothing major."

"Any other small disasters I should know about?"

"One little dustup courtesy of Mrs. Russo's Pomeranian."

Mrs. Russo was a longtime guest, a seventy-year-old widow with a quirky sense of humor and an unwavering devotion to her furry little "pookie-ookie." She took the dog everywhere she went, carried inside a small shoulder tote.

"Who'd Miss Wiggles snap at this time?"

"An eight-year-old who wanted to pet her. Reached out before anyone could say a word. But the kid's okay. Didn't break the skin and Mrs. R. apologized to the parents. All's well."

"God, let's just hope that dog never actually takes a chunk out of anyone. It's a lawsuit waiting to happen."

Oscar smiled. "Which is precisely why you have all those high-priced lawyers on retainer."

Quite true.

At the reminder, his thoughts went instantly to Brie.

She'd looked like an angel this morning when he'd left her sleeping in bed, faint dawn light poking its way past the curtains, her short blond hair tousled around her face in a halo of gold.

He'd been tempted to switch off her alarm and let her sleep in for once, but knew she'd be angry at his interference. She was a professional just like him and had appointments to keep. So he'd brushed his mouth softly over hers, smiling when she'd murmured his name in her sleep. Then, he'd moved quietly through her apartment and let himself out the door.

He saw Oscar glance at his watch. Nine a.m. Time for his GM to get busy with his other duties.

"Before you go," Maddox said, "I need an extra passkey for the penthouse."

"Sure thing. Trouble with your current one?"

"No. It's for Brie Grayson. She's to have full access to my suite, the premium lounge, rooftop bar, pool, exercise and sauna facilities, and any other recreational areas I may have overlooked. Oh, and code it in so she can use my private street entrance as well."

Oscar stared for a few seconds, eyes wide with surprise, before his face rearranged itself back into its usual expression of imperturbable professionalism. In all the years Oscar had worked for him, this was the first time Maddox had ever given one of his lovers a key to his penthouse and free run of the hotel.

But Brie was different. There hadn't been anyone like her when she was twelve, and there most definitely wasn't anyone who could match her now. She was, and always had been, brilliantly and uniquely one of a kind.

Maddox smiled inside at the thought, then tapped a couple of keys on his computer. "Have security put her on the access list and also inform the kitchen to fix her anything she likes, day or night. No charge and no restrictions."

Oscar blinked again. "Of course. I'll make all the necessary arrangements right away. Anything else you need me to handle?"

"No, I'm sure your plate is full enough already. See you later."

Oscar nodded, then left the office.

As soon as he'd gone, Maddox leaned back in his chair again. With a sigh, he dragged his fingers through his hair, his mind still on Brie. Still on their holiday weekend together and everything that had transpired during those far-too-brief yet magical hours.

Honestly, it was as if he'd been put under some kind of spell. What the hell had he been thinking, blurting out a suggestion that they exchange keys? Usually it was the other way around, some latest fling asking him to take their relationship to the next level and let her start moving her stuff in—along with the expectation of a key.

But he'd never handed one out before. Whenever things got to the let's-live-together stage, he would always break it off.

So how surprised had he been when the words had come buzzing off his tongue? How strange to be the one wanting to get more intimate rather than less.

If either of them was reluctant to move things forward in this relationship, it was Brie. She'd been wounded and didn't trust easily. She guarded her heart like it was encased in titanium.

He'd felt that way himself for years. He'd tried marriage and quickly realized what a disaster that was. He wasn't cut out for a lifelong commitment and had closed himself off to the possibility ages ago.

Of course he still wasn't ready and as he'd told Brie, trading keys didn't mean forever. She was having fun and so was he. This would just make the logistics easier.

His eyes narrowed as he thought again of Stephen Jeffries—Brie's ex-lover that they'd run into on the beach. He wished he could have decked the guy, or at least kicked sand in his smug, blandly handsome face. He deserved it for whatever he'd done to hurt Brie.

She'd refused to furnish Maddox with any details and he hadn't forced the issue. Of course that didn't mean he couldn't do a little looking on his own. Just to check the prick out and see what was what.

*I shouldn't,* he thought.

Then he tapped a few keys on his computer keyboard.

Brie glanced at the clock and saw that the afternoon had zoomed past. She'd been busy-busy from the instant she'd walked off the elevator and straight into her paralegal Trish's waiting grasp.

The three-day weekend had played havoc with her workload, particularly since she hadn't checked her e-mail or logged on to her computer once while she'd been away. She'd told herself that one of the associates could handle any problems that cropped up over the holiday. And it wasn't as if she'd turned off her phone. If there'd been a real emergency, they could have reached her.

Even so, Maddox was turning out to be a bad influence—although her mother and sisters would likely feel the opposite. They were always harping on her to take a break and relax every once in a while.

Well, boy oh boy, had she ever.

The beach weekend had been nothing short of idyllic, assuming she didn't count the encounter with Stephen, and she'd decided not to.

Truly, she was over him. Now and for good.

If only she could say the same about Maddox.

Every time she saw him, she dug herself in deeper. And now she'd promised him a key to her apartment!

*What was I thinking?*

But strangely enough, she decided as she took a sip of the now lukewarm cup of English breakfast tea Gina had deposited on her desk several minutes ago, she didn't regret it.

The frightened part of her—and there most definitely was a frightened part—told her to break things off now, while she still could. To run the other way and never look back.

But another part of her, a bigger part, knew it was already too late. However long this relationship with Maddox might last and however much deeper she might get in emotionally, she had to take the chance. She'd always been a risk taker, willing to stick her neck out in hopes of achieving her goals and dreams.

Was Maddox Monroe—the boy who'd once been the bane of her existence, the man who seemed determined to keep her off-balance at every turn—was he her newest dream?

Was a life with him what she really wanted?

But it was too soon to think about anything permanent. Just because she was going to let him come and go at will from her apartment was no reason to think he wanted anything more than fun, convenient sex.

That's what she ought to want as well. What she did want, she told herself.

She wasn't in love with him yet and she planned to keep it that way.

She hoped.

It was a relief when her cell phone rang.

Then it wasn't when she saw who was calling.

Maddox.

Jitters of nervous excitement beat their tiny wings inside her stomach. Jeez, you'd think she was fifteen years old. But when it came to Maddox, she always felt a little like an overly emotional teenager rather than the mature, confident, sophisticated woman she was.

Or liked to think she was anyway.

She hit "answer." "Hello."

"Hey, it's me." His deep voice sent a fresh round of quivers through her, but of a more adult variety this time.

"Hey, *me*," she teased. "How's your day?"

"Good. Yours?"

"Busy. But then, I'm usually busy."

"Same here, but never too busy for you."

A warm sensation grew like a little sun in her chest; she only barely kept from sighing with pleasure.

"So what can I do for you, Mr. Monroe, or is this a business call?"

"No. I trust that you're working on everything for me, including the suit. I just wanted to let you know that I've got meetings lined up here at the hotel tonight."

"Oh." Some of her playful happiness fizzled. "So don't expect you for dinner—is that what you're saying? What about later? Will you be over?"

"Actually, I was thinking you could come here tonight. We can have dinner in the penthouse around seven. Then I'll have to head downstairs for a while. But I'll be all yours afterward. What do you say? I have your key ready. I only have to give it to you."

The warmth returned. "I have yours ready too. Are we really doing this, Monroe?"

"We are, Grayson." His voice was low and husky. "We most definitely are."

The flutters in her stomach turned into pinwheels, exploding ones.

"Ask for Oscar Johannas," he told her. "He's got everything arranged for you. From now on, you'll be able to just breeze in and out at will."

"Sounds good."

*Sounded great.*

"Gotta go. See you at seven," he said.

"Seven, it is."

He hung up; it took her a few extra seconds to disconnect.

With a sigh, she went back to work, a secret little smile on her lips.

"Here is your elevator passkey, key card, and entry code for the private back entrance that Mr. Monroe and senior staff use," Oscar Johannas explained. "Everything has been tested, so you should have no problems, but if you do run into trouble, just tell me or the head of security, Mr. Baxley. We'll get it straightened out right away."

"Thank you, Mr. Johannas," Brie said.

"Oscar," he corrected with a polite smile.

The pair of them were standing in the entry hall of the penthouse. Mr. Johannas, or rather *Oscar*, had insisted on escorting her upstairs to make sure she was settled in while she waited for Maddox. Apparently, he was still sequestered in one of his many meetings.

Oscar had been waiting for her to arrive, welcoming her by name only seconds after she'd walked into the elegant lobby. She remembered him from the first time she'd come to the hotel; he'd been the one to show her upstairs that time too. But whatever thoughts he might be having about the change in her relationship with Maddox, he didn't say. Too well trained, no doubt.

Oscar proceeded to rattle off a list of the hotel amenities to which she was now entitled. Her eyes widened at the extent of Maddox's generosity, including free foraging rights in his hotel kitchen. Lobster tails with drawn butter and beluga caviar at three a.m.—just ring room service.

At the end of the GM's speech, she found herself unable to decide if she felt more like a VIP guest or a pampered mistress.

One thing was for sure—she didn't feel like a girlfriend having a sleepover at her boyfriend's place. It was a peculiar sensation for a modern businesswoman to have, to say the least.

"Is there anything I've forgotten to explain or any other way I may be of service to you, Ms. Grayson?"

"Brie. And hey, if I'm supposed to call you Oscar, then I insist you call me Brie."

Oscar relaxed, a warm, genuine smile on his face. "Brie, it is. So, anything more I can do?"

"There is one thing."

"Yes?"

"Do you know how to work the coffeemaker in this place? I've got briefs to review tonight and I may need the caffeinated support to make it through."

His smile got wider. "Sure. Follow me to the kitchen and I'll get you set up."

Once the lesson was over—Maddox's ultrasophisticated stainless steel coffee/latte/cappuccino steam machine wasn't nearly as daunting as it looked—she asked the question that she just couldn't get out of her mind.

"So, do you do this often?"

"Do what?"

"Show Maddox's girlfriends around the place?"

His dark eyes gleamed; he shook his head. "No, Brie. I can truthfully say you're the first."

"Oh." A satisfied glow formed in her chest as it had earlier that day.

"We're a family here, so once again, welcome. Everyone is pleased to see Maddox so happy."

"Is he?"

"Yes, and now that we've become further acquainted, I can understand why."

She smiled, far more flattered than she wished to admit.

"Good evening, Brie. Paul will be up any minute with your meal. Maddox should be finished with his meeting and on his way up shortly."

"Good night."

Quietly, Oscar saw himself out.

It was nearly midnight when Maddox returned to his penthouse for the second time that evening.

The first time had been to enjoy a delicious but far-too-brief meal with Brie; then he'd been off for another round of discussions with some investors interested in his overseas expansion plans. Quite legitimately, he could have included Brie in the conversation, but at this early stage, he'd found that it was better to leave the lawyers out of the equation, even if Brie did happen to be more than a hired adviser.

He locked the door behind him and walked through the darkened apartment toward the main source of illumination.

He found Brie in the dining room. Her laptop screen saver displayed a picture of a herd of black-and-white striped zebras, while stacks of papers and reports were spread everywhere around her. A half-empty cappuccino in a white china cup had grown cold near her elbow and she was sound asleep, one cheek pillowed atop a lined yellow legal pad, a pen slack between the fingers of her right hand.

A low, delicately ladylike snore escaped from her lips. He grinned at the sound, knowing he would once have relished it as prime fodder for teasing. But now he thought it was one of the most adorable things he'd ever heard and luckily not something she did as a rule. He would keep it to himself, knowing better than to mention it to her when she was awake.

If she'd been resting in a more comfortable position, he would have left her to sleep. But if she stayed this way for long, she would end up with a crick in her neck. She would get a far better night's sleep in bed.

He snapped off the overhead light, leaving only a single lamp on in the adjacent living room to ward off the darkness. Bending over her, he pressed his lips ever so softly against her cheek.

"Brie-Brie," he whispered. "Sweetheart, time to go to bed."

Her eyelids fluttered slightly and she mumbled something unintelligible under her breath, then sighed and went on sleeping.

He chuckled softly. "Hey, sleepyhead, wakey, wakey."

This time she roused a little more. "Wha—Maddox? Is that you?"

"Yes. Come on. Let's get you up out of that chair so you can go to bed."

" 'S your meeting over? What time is it?"

"About midnight. I just got in."

She blinked and sat up, pushing her tousled hair out of her face. "Hmm, sorry. Guess I conked out on you."

"You were tired. Why didn't you just go ahead and go to bed?"

"I had work." She yawned widely, blinked again. "Still do. Wow, I really dropped off." She glanced sleepily around at all the papers and her notes. "Let me heat this coffee up again and I'll finish up."

"No, no more coffee and no more work. Not tonight anyway." He took the pen out of her hand, then reached out to shut off her computer.

"Hey, I was using that."

"You can use it again tomorrow. Everything will be waiting for you in the morning."

"I know, but . . ."

"You're about to drop." He urged her to her feet. "You'll function better with a solid eight hours under your belt."

"But I've got to be up by five so I can run home and change and get into the office by seven thirty."

"You're a partner now. You can go in late every once in a while and no one will say a word."

"Yes, but—"

"I already asked Oscar to pick up a few suits for you in your size. They should be hanging in the closet. And he's arranged for all your favorite bath products, toothbrush, brush, comb, and other essentials. You'll need an extra set of everything for the nights you'll be spending here, so I thought I'd get you started."

She scowled, trying to rouse the requisite outrage over his high-handed actions, but as he could see, she was just too tired. "You're . . . you're . . ."

"Yes? What am I?" Bending, he scooped her into his arms.

She gasped.

He gazed into her beautiful, sleepy blue eyes and started toward the bedroom.

"Oh, I'll tell you later when I'm not half-asleep." She snuggled her head against his shoulder and sighed wearily. "But you'd better set the alarm for six fifteen. I can't be any later than eight."

"Hmm-hmm, we'll see." He laid her on the bed.

"Maddox," she protested, her eyelids drooping again. She reached for the buttons on her blouse.

Gently, he brushed her hands aside. "Shh, let me."

With swift efficiency, he stripped her down to her bra and panties, then eased her beneath the sheets. She was sound asleep again seconds later, her head comfortably cradled on a plump pillow.

Maddox padded back out to the dining room and kitchen for a last check of lights and appliances, then returned and went into his bathroom to wash and change. He came out again less than ten minutes later, switched off his bedside lamp, and climbed in next to her. Gathering her into his arms, he closed his eyes and joined her in a world of dreams.

Brie awakened, feeling luxuriously rested and wonderfully content. She stretched against the sheets, a smile on her mouth as she bumped a hand against the warm male slumbering at her side.

She cracked open an eyelid and looked at him, lying darkly handsome against the pure white bed linens. Then her gaze drifted past, idly glancing at the luminous dial on his bedside clock.

Eight thirty, it read.

Eight thirty?

On a Tuesday?

*Oh. Good. Christ.*

She was late! And she was never late.

In a panic, she flung back the covers and leaped from the bed.

"Hey, where's the fire?" Maddox grumbled, his voice thick and groggy with sleep.

"Under my I-overslept butt." She pointed a finger at him. "*You* are so in trouble. What were you thinking, turning off the alarm? Crap, where are my clothes?"

"In the closet, as I told you last night, although I'm not surprised you don't remember, considering how sleepy you were." He sat up, ran a set of fingers through his sleep-mussed hair. "Hey, calm down. The world's not going to end because you're a little late."

"Not a little—*two hours*. And I have a conference call at nine thirty." Her stomach squeezed as the realization set in. "If I rush, maybe I can still make it."

She raced to the closet and flung open the door. Inside she found a rack of gorgeous, sophisticated feminine suits and dresses hanging on their own separate bar in the midst of his wardrobe. Her new clothes were made of luxurious materials and looked extremely expensive. She flicked a finger over one tag and rolled her eyes at the la-la designer label. A downward glance and she discovered a neat row of women's shoes in a range of complementary colors—mostly Jimmy Choos and Manolos, if she wasn't mistaken. Without taking the time to check out the styling details, she grabbed a suit in dark blue off the hanger, a shirt, and a pair of matching heels, then hurried back to fling everything on the bed.

"Your conference call isn't until eleven. So relax—you've got time."

She stopped, a light blue and white polka-dot silk shell in her hands. "What do you mean? How do you even know what's on my schedule?"

"Because I checked the calendar on your cell. I tried to wake you up at six thirty as requested, but you were really out of it. So I texted your assistant, Gina, and told her you're having a slow start this morning and could she juggle your appointments around?"

"You talked to Gina?"

"Texted, yes."

"But—"

"But nothing. She had it all rearranged and rescheduled within a half hour. You're lucky to have her. She's very efficient."

"Yes, I know that." She dropped down on the bed, the shirt forgotten. "Did she know it was you?"

His mouth tilted up in a wry half smile. "No, I used your account and kept it brief, so I presume she thinks she spoke with you. Satisfied?"

She nodded. "Sorry. It's just—"

"That you don't want word of our relationship getting around the office. I get it. Though I hate to burst your bubble, kiddo, by making the observation that we have been seen out in public together. I'm not sure how big a secret we really are."

"I know." She sighed. "But still, we don't have to advertise."

"God forbid, no. No advertising or splashy episodes of PDA." He gave a mock shudder.

She made a face at his humor. Then she turned serious again. "So I was really so asleep this morning that you couldn't wake me up?"

"Yep." He climbed out of bed, completely naked and completely comfortable with it; Maddox had very few inhibitions. "If I didn't know better, I'd think you'd taken some sleeping pills."

He arched an inquiring brow.

She shook her head.

"Exhausted. Just as I thought. I've got to quit keeping you up until all hours."

Her gaze moved over him and his long, powerful, rock-hard body. He really was quite beautiful. She sent him a slow smile. "Yes, but they've been good hours." Her eyes dropped to his shaft, which thickened and stiffened under her gaze. "Great hours."

"Hmm, so they have." He held out a hand. "Come on."

"Come where?"

"Shower. I thought we'd share."

"I'm not sure that's such a good idea."

He pulled her to her feet. "I think it's an excellent idea." Without waiting for her consent, he unsnapped her bra and pulled it off, along with her panties. "Two birds and all that."

He winked.

Her blood turned heavy and hot with anticipation. Taking his hand, she let him lead her toward the big marble-lined shower with multiple spray heads.

Reaching in, he turned them all on; steam quickly filled the space. He urged her in, under the deliciously warm spray. They were both wet in an instant.

Grabbing the soap, which smelled of fine-milled oatmeal, he worked up a lather in his large hands. He cupped them over her breasts before moving lower.

She groaned as he began soaping her everywhere, using gliding, soul-shattering strokes that nearly drove her mad. When he was finished, she took the soap and lathered him, not missing an inch.

Both of them were panting by the time she finished.

"How much longer do we have again?" she murmured as they stood together in the spray to rinse off.

Hands still slick, he slid wet fingers between her legs to discover another kind of wetness altogether. "I don't know. Long enough to run the hot water out if we want."

She convulsed with pleasure and threw her head back, her dripping hair like a sleek cap against her skull. "I want."

He crushed his mouth against hers with a demand that she returned without constraint. He walked her back until she was pressed against the slightly cool tile, then lifted one of her legs to wrap around his hip.

She twined her arms tightly around his shoulders and kissed him harder.

"I like saving time this way, don't you?" he said, nuzzling her neck.

Then he thrust into her, sure and deep.

She cried out. "God, yes!"

Shifting her hips in his capable hands, he arranged her so she could take even more of him, the pair of them slick as eels and twined around each other like vines. "We should do this every morning," he said on a low groan.

She moaned into his mouth and forgot about everything else but him.

# Chapter Nineteen

Four months later, Maddox fit his key into the lock of Brie's apartment and opened the door. He moved inside, his garment bag in one hand and a sack of groceries in the other. He dropped his luggage just inside the door, then crossed to set the groceries on the kitchen island.

He hadn't been sure what Brie might have stocked in her end-of-the-week refrigerator, so he'd stopped at the market on the way back from the airport. He'd bought a pair of thick, well-marbled rib-eye steaks; plump, golden brown baking potatoes; and a ripe, crimson-hued heirloom tomato: another quick, easy meal that he knew he would have a hard time ruining.

He'd been traveling again—Chicago this time. The trip had gone well and he'd been able to work out a few logistical kinks that had been plaguing the staff for a while. He'd interviewed and hired an exciting new executive chef as well, a James Beard Award winner who was bubbling over with fresh, cutting-edge ideas to keep the restaurant at the top of its game. Plus, he made really delicious food.

But successful as the trip had been, Maddox had been ready to head home to New York. Correction, he'd been ready to head home to Brie. *She* was the essential factor, he realized with a bit of surprise. He suspected that if she lived in Antarctica, he would have been all revved to put on a Gore-Tex parka, gloves, and boots and hike across the glaciers to reach her, wherever she might be.

The thought stopped him in his tracks as he unloaded the grocery bag, a pint of sour cream held absently in one hand.

What was he doing thinking about her that way?

He'd missed her, sure. It was only natural, after all, granted that they were intimately involved and he wasn't the sort to seek out extracurricular bed partners when he was away on business.

He wanted her, that was all. He'd been without her for days and he was looking forward to a long, satisfying night spent in her arms. There was also the fact that he just plain liked her; she was a smart, interesting woman who simultaneously intrigued and amused him.

He was never bored when he was with Brie.

As for their new living arrangement, things were going amazingly well. They alternated nights at each other's apartments depending on their schedules. To his astonishment—and he would guess hers as well—they'd slipped into the new routine as if they'd been doing it for years rather than a few short months. Being with her was easy, almost as natural as breathing. The more time they spent together, the more they learned they had in common. She liked many of the same things he did.

They both enjoyed reading political thrillers, historical biographies, and classic fiction, although he still couldn't quite bring himself to read the complete works of Jane Austen despite her assurances about how wonderful they were. He and Brie listened to the same music, discovering a mutual love for a rather obscure alternative rock band that he promised he was going to take her to see the next time they played in the city. Her favorite painters were Klimt and Monet and although he was an admirer of more contemporary artists, he also enjoyed the Art Nouveau and Impressionist periods with enthusiasm.

They even got along when it came to TV and movies, and despite their rooting for different teams, she never minded snuggling on the sofa on Sunday afternoons to watch sports.

She really was an excellent companion, both in bed and out.

There was a part of him that had half expected to be ready to break up and move on by now, but curiously he was having the opposite reaction. The more time he spent with her, the more he wanted to spend.

He'd thought this trip might be a good opportunity to enjoy some alone time. Only once he'd left, all he could think about was how soon he could be back with her again. He'd even taken to phoning her each evening before bed to talk about her day and to share the highs and lows of his. And when the chance had come today to catch an early flight back, he'd taken it without a moment's hesitation.

As for his excursion to the market so he could surprise her with dinner when she got home from work, well, he was just being considerate, perhaps a touch romantic. He was in the mood to celebrate his return, that's all.

Of course, he'd never been overly romantic with his other lovers, nothing beyond the usual trappings of flowers, candy, and elegant dinners out. Not that he couldn't be thoughtful, but generally, he did as he pleased, not the other way around.

Yet with Brie, he wanted to make her happy. Wanted to see her laugh and smile and look at him with that special light in her eyes, the one that made him feel like he'd just fought a battle and won her as the prize.

Abruptly, he set down the sour cream.

*Christ, I've got it bad, haven't I?*

He'd told her he wasn't expecting a lifetime commitment, but now he wondered. Had he asked her to exchange keys because he wanted the freedom to come and go as he chose? Or was it something far more serious? Did he wish, like today, that every time he came back from a business trip, it would be to find her waiting? Was it because he craved something more than his independent life? That he didn't want just the good times together but *all* the times—the good and bad and everything in between?

Before he had time to consider further, he heard a noise at the door. Sudden anticipation warmed his blood.

And then she was there, frozen just inside the doorway, her clear blue eyes round as they fixed on him, her pretty lips parted in a silent O. "Maddox?"

"Hey." He grinned.

"What are you doing here? I thought you weren't getting in for another four hours."

He shrugged. "The airline had an earlier flight, so I decided to surprise you."

"Well, you did." She set down her briefcase and closed the door, then glanced past him to the groceries on the counter. "What's all this?"

"Dinner."

"You're cooking dinner?"

"Just steaks and potatoes, nothing fancy."

She smiled, her teeth white and pretty. "It sounds wonderful. I thought I wouldn't see you until tomorrow, since you told me not to wait up."

"Looks like I lied." He opened his arms. "Guess I couldn't stay away."

She kicked off her heels, sprinted forward, and leaped against him. He caught her, crushing his mouth to hers, their kiss one of hot, hungry welcome.

He laughed. "Miss me?"

Her fingers tunneled into his hair, her mouth moving in ardent pecks and brushes across his cheeks, lips, chin, and jaw. "What do you think?"

"I think with greetings like that, maybe I'll have to go away more often."

"Hmm, maybe so." Her fingers went to the buttons on his shirt and began to unfasten them. "I like coming home and finding you here, waiting for me."

"I figured I ought to put that key you gave me to use." He set her feet on the floor and pulled the shirttail out of the waistband of her skirt. Reaching underneath, he sought out the warm satin of her skin.

She trembled and kissed him harder, her hands roaming over his chest. "You can put it to use anytime you'd like."

"I know something else I'd like to put to use."

Her mouth slanted over his, her tongue greedy. "Let me guess."

He sucked in a breath as she cupped him through his trousers, turning instantly hard.

"We should take a time-out if you want dinner." His voice was rough with desire.

"We can eat later. I want you first."

His eyelids grew heavy as she found the straining button on his waistband and popped it free. Scattering random kisses across his neck and shoulders and chest, she slid down his zipper with a seductive rasp.

His cock thickened even more at her touch, his blood pooling like fire as she palmed him again through his underwear. She teased him, driving him to the edge of madness.

God, he wanted her.

*Do I love her too?*

He thought he just might.

But he didn't have time to think that revelation through at the moment. Instead, he yanked off her shirt, her lacy bra along with it, and sought out the peaks of her breasts, which were pink as berries and would taste every bit as sweet. He arched her over his arm and began suckling, using his teeth and tongue in precisely the way she liked.

She let out a whimpering little cry, one he always loved to hear. He laved and suckled and nipped her other breast and was soon rewarded with another helpless, needy wail that sang from her parted lips.

"Bedroom?" she panted moments later, taking his face between her hands to kiss him wildly again.

But he didn't want to wait, not even that small fraction of time. He wanted her. Had to have her with an ache that was almost agony. Suddenly, it was as if his very life depended on their joining.

He shook his head. "No, here."

Without pause, he pushed her skirt to her waist and her panties to the floor, kicking the little bit of lace and silk aside. But rather than pick her up and put her on the counter, he spun her around and placed her hands against the edge.

"Maddox?" she said wonderingly, her voice high and quavering.

"Shh," he hushed. He kissed her neck, taking a moment to cup and caress her naked breasts until her nipples were hard points.

She arched back against him, shuddering as he eased his fingers between her legs from the front and began to stroke. He massaged her intimately, insistently, maddening her until he could tell she was trembling and on the brink.

Unable to wait another moment, he freed his heavy, throbbing erection and settled his hands on her hips. He pushed her legs wider and positioned her to accept him.

Then he slid in deep. Her tight, wet flesh closed around him like a hot, sleek velvet glove. He groaned, knowing that nothing had ever felt so good, that nothing would ever feel so good.

And he knew that, with her, he was finally home.

Hours later, they lay in her bed, the pair of them curled around each other, satiated and content, the sheets a messy tangle at their feet.

They never had gotten around to eating the food he'd brought, too wrapped up in each other to do more than stumble to her bedroom and dive onto the mattress, where they had continued on to the next bout of frenzied lovemaking.

Afterward, they'd talked, dozed a little, then roused again to make love one more time. It had been sweet and slow, that last coupling, and so wonderfully satisfying that time itself seemed to slow.

He cast a lazy glance toward her digital clock.

Nearly one a.m.

"Maddox?" Brie's voice was soft, still husky from sex and sleep.

"Hmm?"

"You awake?"

He chuckled. "Just barely. You wore me out."

"I thought it was *you* who wore me out." She slid a hand over his bare thigh. "You hungry?"

"For food, you mean? You'll have to give me a few more minutes for the other."

She giggled and snuggled closer. "I can wait. And yes, I meant for food this time."

"I could eat, I suppose."

"Me too."

But neither of them made any effort to climb out of bed.

"You know," Brie said after a moment, "when you asked me earlier if I missed you?"

"Yeah?" He stroked his hand over her arm, an odd twinge of tension suddenly running through him.

"Well, I did. I missed you a lot."

He relaxed again and kissed her. "How much?"

She stretched her arms wide. "This much."

"I missed you more."

"Really?" She rolled over, planting her forearms on his chest.

He ran a hand over her shoulders and back. "I missed you all day."

Lifting his head, he captured her lips and kissed her. "Every day."

He caressed her bottom and over the silky length of her thigh, then locked her inside his arms. "But I missed you most of all at night."

"I did too. Day and night. I couldn't sleep without you here." She pressed her open mouth to his and slid her tongue inside.

And once again, he forgot all about dinner.

* * *

Brie whistled a little tune under her breath as she walked into her office on Monday morning. The weekend with Maddox had been . . . She paused to think of an adjective or adverb superlative enough to describe the thrilling excitement and breathtaking pleasure of the past two days and three nights with him.

One might think by now that the initial heat of their relationship would be cooling off or at least starting to become ordinary, even predictable. Yet the longer she and Maddox were together, the closer and more compatible they seemed to grow.

And it wasn't just the sex—though the sex was hands down the hottest she'd ever enjoyed in her life. When it came to the erotic arts, Maddox knew his stuff. If he weren't an accomplished businessman, he could have hired out as a gigolo and made a fortune pleasuring a flock of grateful women. But luckily he was all hers.

And despite their less-than-auspicious beginnings together, she was starting to think she was very lucky indeed.

She thought again about how she'd been afraid before to let down her guard, not just with Maddox, but with any man. She'd grown a thick shell around her heart after her disastrous liaison with Stephen. But worse than the damage to her heart had been the destruction he'd wrought in her ability to trust, not just in others but even in herself.

These months with Maddox, though, were teaching her that it was safe to trust again. Safe to love.

*And do I love him?* she wondered as she sank into her office chair and swiveled around to gaze out at the bustling city street below.

A slow smile spread across her face like a dawning sunrise—warm and radiant and filled with happiness.

*Yes,* came the answer.

As impossible as it might once have seemed, a resounding yes.

Now she just needed to figure out where they went from here.

Blocks away across town, Maddox was having thoughts not so dissimilar from Brie's.

He was having trouble concentrating on the reports and schedules and contracts on his desk, his mind constantly drifting back to the weekend just past. If he closed his eyes, he imagined he could still smell and taste her, could even now feel her as she'd lain in his arms and taken him gladly into her body.

She'd left him sated and happy but wanting more, eager for the hours to pass so he could be with her again.

*Jesus*, he was worse now than he'd been in junior high. Then he'd only indulged in immature, adolescent dreams.

Now he knew the reality. Now he knew the woman.

Loved the woman?

He didn't need an answer to recognize the truth. So what was he going to do about it? Brie wasn't the sort of woman you just played around with. She would want a commitment. No, she would probably demand one, complete with vows and a ring.

His eyebrows drew into a tight line, thoughts whizzing through his mind at supersonic speed. He had one failed relationship under his belt, a marriage that hadn't worked out. What made him think a second go-round would be any more successful than the first?

*Because it's Brie. Because she and I are good together.*

They'd both been through relationship hell, but this time would be different, for him and for her. His eyes were wide-open now. He was a mature man who knew what he wanted. And he wanted Brie in spite of any past bitterness and fear. They could make this work. They *would* make this work.

Anyway, relationships were always a risk. Hell, life itself was a risk and he'd faced plenty of risks over the years. Why not one more? The most important one of all?

Suddenly, without giving himself more time to consider the whys and wherefores, he picked up his cell phone and scrolled through his contacts list in search of a number he hadn't called in years. He stared at the digits for several long moments, wondering if the number was still active.

Well, only one way to find out.

Hitting "call," he put the phone to his ear and waited for it to ring on the other end.

One ring . . . two . . . three—

"Hello."

He paused for a moment, listening to the old familiar cadence. "Ellen?"

"Yes? Who is this?"

"Hey, it's me. Maddox. I know it's been a long time, but you and I need to talk."

# CHAPTER TWENTY

"We've reviewed the discovery documents and have scheduled dates and times for most of the Mergenfeld depositions. There are a couple people on the list who we're still in the process of locating."

One of the three associates in the conference room laid a stack of hefty summary reports in front of Brie where she sat across from them at the wide, polished wood table a week later. Trish, her paralegal, was also in the meeting along with Denny, the firm's investigator, and Gina to take notes.

"Even though Mergenfeld's claim isn't as strong as it might initially appear, we still believe settlement would be a better way to go," said the second associate, who was joined by nods of agreement from his fellows.

"Maybe so, but the client doesn't want to settle." Brie opened one of the thick briefs and began to scan through, her eyes moving quickly over the words.

Everyone was silent for a minute while she read; then she looked up. "However, I will discuss the possibility of settlement with Mr. Monroe again to see if there's been any softening in that direction."

Knowing Maddox and his stubborn nature, she figured the possibility of his agreeing to pay his ex-partner a second time, for a business interest Maddox had bought the man out of years earlier, was roughly zero point zero. But greedy, dishonest types like Mergenfeld gouged money out of successful companies all the time, and if it made the most financial sense, she would urge Maddox to swallow his pride and fork out the legal equivalent of hush money just to get rid of Roger "the nuisance" Mergenfeld.

Of course she couldn't force Maddox to settle. But if it seemed prudent, she could nudge him hard in that direction. For now, though, the lawsuit was moving forward. Which meant that all the groundwork for the case needed to be laid whether it was eventually utilized or not.

"The depositions," Brie said. "I see the first ones are scheduled for next week. You three"—she waved a pen toward the trio of eager associates—"will get those started. I'll come in to observe and handle any lines of questioning that seem to need clarification. Any issues I should know about?"

Three heads shook no.

"Now, about these missing parties. Let's go over the problems you're encountering."

She took out the sheet containing the list of names of the individuals who needed to be deposed.

"Now, this first one, Alice Smith, she was a bookkeeper at the time, but she's no longer at her last known address; is that right?"

Denny, the investigator, joined the conversation. "Yes, we believe she married and changed her last name, then moved out of state. I'm tracing her, trying to locate any family or friends who might know her current whereabouts, but so far it's been mostly dead ends. I'm working on it."

Brie made a notation beside the name. "Good, keep searching."

She moved on to the next.

They were nearly to the end of the list when she read off the second to last. "Ellen Kilkenny. What's her story?"

"Rather interesting actually," Denny said, lifting his thin auburn eyebrows the way he did when he'd come across some unexpected or curious bit of information. "We located her without too much difficulty, though we had to go a few layers deep to track her current address and vital stats. She lives on some island off the coast of Washington State."

"Okay. But if you know where she is, then what's the problem? Is she refusing to cooperate? If travel is the problem, tell her we'll pay her expenses to come here to New York. Otherwise we can do the deposition via teleconferencing."

Denny exchanged a sideways look with one of the associates, who was apparently aware of whatever situation was at hand. "Well, it's not that she won't cooperate exactly. It's just—"

"Yes? Just what?"

"Well, we wanted to run it past you first to make sure you definitely want her included."

"Why wouldn't I?"

"Because she's Monroe's wife."

Brie stared, her pen frozen suddenly against her yellow legal pad. "Wife?" Inwardly, her pulse gave a weird double beat. Outwardly, she didn't react, careful not to betray the shock and confusion running through her mind. "Ex-wife, you mean."

"No, his wife." Denny thumbed through a couple of papers inside a file. "From what I could ascertain, she and Monroe have been separated for a number of years. No children, though he does provide her with a minimal level of support twice a year."

She couldn't breathe. She hurt, her chest aching as if she'd taken a punch straight through the ribs to her heart.

Married?

Maddox was married? Had been married all this time with never a word to her? No, it wasn't possible. He wouldn't do this to her. He wouldn't lie, not about something so important, so essential to them both.

It had to be a mistake.

"Are you certain?" Her voice was calm, maybe too calm, but not enough for any of the others to notice. "He's known in public circles as a bachelor. Maybe there was a divorce, but the decree got lost or misfiled somewhere?"

The words sounded ridiculous, even to her. Yet still she didn't want to accept what the others clearly already accepted as the truth.

Denny shook his head. "Definitely no divorce. They are still legally married. I double-checked at the courthouse of record. And Mrs. Monroe herself confirmed it when I spoke to her, even though she goes by her maiden name, Kilkenny. Doesn't want the press to find her apparently."

Or anyone else such as Maddox's lovers.

The room began to buzz. Had a fly gotten inside the conference room? Then again, maybe the sound was only in her head.

"So? Keep her on the deposition list?" one of the associates asked.

"What?"

"The list. You want us to leave her on it and set her up for questions?"

Brie couldn't think, her mind an odd, dark blank. And she was cold, as if she'd suddenly been tossed into a meat locker and left to freeze. Yet somehow she managed to make her muscles function.

She slammed the cover closed on her pad, reached out to gather up the binders she'd brought with her, cradling them to her chest. "I'll think about it and let you know."

Getting to her feet, she stood upright somehow, even though she could barely feel her limbs beneath her.

"But there's one more name we didn't discuss," one of the associates said, clearly confused at her abrupt departure.

"Proceed however you think best." She looked at her watch, pretending to check the time. "I've got to go. I have a call coming in any minute."

She walked out into the corridor and down the long hallway, traveling at a quick, yet even, pace. She stifled the urge to break into a run, quashed the need to scream or rant or burst into a flood of tears. She couldn't afford to let herself feel, not here, not right now. She didn't know what the associates thought of her hurrying out of the meeting the way she had, but she hadn't been able to stay another moment, fearing she might fall apart completely.

Reaching her office, she closed the door and sat down behind her desk.

Numb. Her whole body was cold, her muscles rigid with shock.

*Maddox is married?*

No, it wasn't possible. He would have told her if it was true. He wouldn't have forgotten to mention something as essential as being married! Yet Denny was an excellent investigator. He didn't get his facts wrong; he was a very careful man when it came to his profession.

So it must be true.

Oh, God, why would Maddox do something like this, lie to her like this, especially when the two of them were in love?

She sucked in a harsh breath as reality hit, the movement making her ribs ache harder.

*Maybe* we *aren't in love. Maybe it's only me.*

Because now that she thought about it, Maddox had never said he loved her, not even in their most intimate moments. He told her she was beautiful, desirable, that she made him laugh, that he enjoyed her company.

But love?

She'd put it down to the inability some men had for verbalizing their emotions. She'd known he carried around baggage from his past, even if he didn't discuss the particulars. But maybe in Maddox's case, there were no deeper emotions for her beyond sex and casual friendship. Maybe all he really wanted was the sex, even if they were practically living together these days. Perhaps she'd mistaken the closeness she'd thought he felt for something more.

She buried her face in her hands.

*Ah, God, why am I such an idiot? How can this be happening to me again?*

Because of all the things she should have asked him right off the bat, "Are you married?" seemed a straightforward enough one. But even after all of Stephen's deceptions, even as cautious around men as she'd become, it had just never occurred to her that Maddox wouldn't mention something as significant as the fact that he had a wife. The possibility that he might be married had never so much as crossed her mind.

A new chill swept through her, her skin as white and cold as ice.

When she was a kid, she'd thought Maddox was a bastard, but even then, she'd never dreamed he was a liar too.

A soft knock came at her door. "Brie?"

It was Gina.

Brie fought to get her voice working. "Yes?"

Gina cracked the door. "Your three o'clock is here. Shall I put them in the conference room?"

*Three o'clock?* Did she have a three o'clock? She couldn't even remember which client she was supposed to meet. "Yes. Conference room."

Gina paused. "Hey? You all right?"

Brie kept her gaze averted, unsure what her assistant might see in her eyes if she looked up. "Yes. It's just a headache."

*Just a heartache, actually.*

"Oh, sorry. You need some Advil or something?"

*Or something* might be nice, like a massive dose of sedatives that would put her so far under she wouldn't be able to remember much more than her name and certainly not this new nightmare she was suddenly living.

But she was going to find a way to manage; she couldn't afford a breakdown now. Somehow she would find the strength to shove her emotions off to one side and get on with her work. She would stuff them down deep inside herself where no one would see; no one would notice.

Later, she would let it all out. But only when she was

alone and had the luxury of indulging her misery where there was no one to hear.

And what about Maddox? She was supposed to go to his penthouse tonight.

Tears stung the insides of her eyelids at the reminder. No, she couldn't think about him anymore.

Not now.

She sniffed and blinked hard, forcing the moisture away. "No, I'm okay," she lied. "Tell the . . . um . . . client that I'll be with them shortly."

"Will do." Gina shut the door behind her.

If only she really were okay. Somehow she didn't think she ever would be again.

Maddox let himself into Brie's apartment. It was a little after ten at night and he'd been calling her for hours.

At first, when she hadn't shown up, he'd assumed things had gone long at work and she was running late. When another half hour had passed by with no word from her, he'd started to get antsy. He'd called her office, thinking maybe her cell was malfunctioning and she'd missed the half dozen messages he'd left. One of the associates answered and said no, that Brie had left around her usual time, and could he take a message?

Maddox had said no and hung up, genuinely worried now.

He'd decided to give her a bit more time; there had to be a good explanation for why she hadn't arrived. He'd told himself not to panic as their dinner sat untouched and congealing in the kitchen. Nothing terrible had happened to her; she would be along any minute now and tell him the whole story.

But she didn't show up, the hour growing later and later. He kept calling her cell, leaving message after message, but she didn't pick up. He considered calling her family but figured he'd just upset them if they didn't know where she was either. He tossed around the idea of calling the hospitals as well, but told himself he was overreacting.

She was fine. She had to be fine. Anything else was unthinkable.

Then it occurred to him that maybe they'd gotten their wires crossed and he was supposed to be over at her place tonight. Maybe she was there waiting and was worried just like him, wondering why he hadn't shown up. But if that were the case, then why not call him? Even if her cell wasn't working, she could still have found a landline phone to call his private number or leave a message with the hotel switchboard.

Forcing down his growing panic, he'd put on his coat to protect against the cold November wind and headed out to check out her apartment.

And so he'd let himself in, his chest knotted, heart pounding with a mixture of hopefulness and dread.

It was dark inside, so he didn't see her at first. Then he caught sight of her shape, seated in the middle of the living room sofa, her hands folded neatly in her lap.

"Brie?" he said.

She didn't move.

He snapped on the overhead light.

She flinched and squeezed her eyes closed; her face looked red, ravaged. Had she been crying? Was she ill?

"Please, turn that off," she told him, her voice strained and oddly pitched.

He complied. Making his way deeper into the room, he found a lamp to switch on instead. Soft illumination spread in a small circle through the space.

"Brie, baby, what's happened? Are you all right?"

He sat down next to her on the couch, started to put his arm around her shoulders.

She moved away, jumpy as a wet cat, practically sprinting off the sofa. She went to stand on the other side of the room, her arms crossed at her waist.

He looked across at her. "What's wrong? I've been calling you all evening. Why didn't you answer? Is your phone broken?"

For a moment, she looked as if she might not answer. Then she took a breath. "My phone's fine. I just didn't pick up."

"Why not? I must have left you at least a dozen messages. Are you sick? Something's obviously wrong—you look like you've been crying. And I've been worried."

"Have you really?"

He frowned. Her words sounded strange, hard and brittle.

"Of course I have. When you didn't show up at the penthouse, I knew something must have happened. I called your work, but they said you'd left for the evening. I called you again, several times, and when I still didn't get an answer, I naturally started imagining all sorts of awful scenarios. I was about to start calling hospitals and the police but decided to come over here first and check. Guess it's a good thing I did."

Her expression flickered for a moment at that; then the odd, remote look returned. "Yes, well, now that you know I'm not dead or under arrest, you can put your mind at ease."

He studied her, confused by her mood. He got to his feet, started toward her.

She backed away, held out her palm as if warding him off.

He stopped. "Brie, what on earth is the matter?"

"Nothing, other than the fact that I was working on the Mergenfeld suit today and my team came across some rather interesting information."

"Oh? What's that?"

"A name on the deposition list." She tightened her arms around her waist again, hands cradling her chest as if she were fighting to hold herself together. "Ellen Kilkenny. I'm sure you recognize it, seeing that she's your wife."

Maddox stared, Brie's words slamming into him like a sledgehammer.

*Shit.*

"Brie, it's not what you think—"

"Oh, really?" Her odd, cold voice grew even colder. "Then what is it? You either have a wife or you don't. Am I wrong? Is my investigator mistaken?"

"No, you and your investigator are not mistaken but—"

Her eyes went flat. "Get out."

"What?"

"I said get out. And leave your key, the one I gave you to my front door. I'll messenger over everything I have for your penthouse and the hotel tomorrow."

"Brie, you're upset and I understand, but let's talk about it. Give me a chance to explain."

"Explain? Explain what? The fact that you've been lying to me this entire time or that you conveniently forgot to mention the fact that you happen to be married? Which one of those would you like to *explain*?"

"I never lied to you. If you'd asked me if I was married, I would have told you. But you didn't ask, and frankly, it's not something I think about much, since my so-called marriage amounts to little more than a technicality."

Her hands curled into fists, her eyes like chips of blue ice.

He raked his fingers through his hair. "Look, Ellen and I have been separated for over a decade. We don't have a marriage except on paper. I don't see her; she doesn't see me. We're not married, not really."

"And yet, as far as the law is concerned, you are," she said, sounding like a prosecuting attorney. "I guess you've never heard of a little thing called a divorce. They have those now, you know, in all fifty states. Even here in New York. And Washington. Isn't that where she lives?"

"Brie, please, come and sit down." He gestured toward the sofa. "Let's talk. Let me tell you everything."

She shook her head. "No, I'm good here. And I don't need to hear everything, I've already heard more than enough."

"But you haven't."

He wanted to go to her, wrap her inside his arms, and soothe her. But he knew she wouldn't allow it, wouldn't let him so much as touch her now. His chest grew tight, his fingers bunching into fists of frustration.

"I was young and stupid when I married Ellen. We were both kids, barely into our twenties and too naive to really know what we were getting into. It wasn't even a year—hell, not even six months—before we both knew we'd made a huge mistake. She and I fought all the time, over everything, big and small. We both realized it was never going to last, that our marriage was a total disaster."

Sighing, he stuck his hands inside his pockets. "You asked about why we never divorced. I wanted to, even had the papers drawn up, but she's Catholic, very devout as it turns out, though I didn't realize how devout before we got married. Ellen doesn't believe in divorce. To her, if you make a mistake, you accept it—you don't try to run away, as she calls it.

"I'm Catholic too but more what you'd call lapsed. I don't attend Mass and religion just isn't a big part of my life. So when she asked me not to press for a divorce but to separate instead, I agreed. I was sure I was never going to want to get married again. Hell, why would I, since the first marriage was so horrible? I figured it didn't matter whether I was separated or divorced, so long as Ellen was out of the picture and I was free to do as I liked. And I have. She doesn't bother me and I don't bother her."

He paused and unclenched his hands, trying to get Brie to look at him. But she wouldn't.

"I'm sorry I didn't tell you, but when we first met, I never expected things to go all that far between us. There didn't seem any point in mentioning my situation with Ellen, not when we were just fooling around and having fun for a little while. But then things changed. Our relationship became something else. Something more."

He reached out a hand. "Please, Brie, won't you come over here? You look like you might collapse."

But she didn't move, just held her ground, still refusing to meet his eyes.

A sigh escaped him. "I don't blame you for being angry and upset with me. I was wrong and realize now that I should have told you; you should never have found out about this the way you did. Hurting you is the last thing I would ever want to do. I hope you can forgive me."

He hesitated, wondering what more to say, how to get through to her when she had so obviously shut him out. All he could do, he realized, was say what was in his heart.

"These past few months with you have been wonderful," he said. "I've never known anything like them. Or anyone like you."

She didn't acknowledge his statement by so much as an extra twitch.

Dragging his fingers through his hair again, he went on. "Look, I wanted to do this some other way, to make it romantic, exciting, but I guess this will have to do. I love you, Brie Grayson. I love you as I've never loved anyone before or will ever love anyone again. I want us to spend our lives together, to grow old and gray in each other's arms."

Briefly, she closed her eyes.

Encouraged, he continued. "I'm getting that divorce you mentioned. I've already been in touch with Ellen and told her that I'm proceeding with the divorce this time. I explained that I've met someone and that her objections no longer concern me. Brie, I realize I can't make it official yet and that this isn't the most conventional way to propose, but please, sweetheart, will you marry me?"

He waited, sure that his heartfelt words must have had some impact, that she would lower her guard again and turn back into *his* Brie again. The one who was warm and happy and whose eyes shone with what he'd come to think was love.

Instead, she didn't move, her face and body as cold and motionless as a statue. "Are you finished?" she said at last.

He looked at her, his hopes sinking when he realized she hadn't melted toward him at all. "For now."

"Then would you please go? I'm tired and have to work in the morning."

"Brie— "

"Leave the key. As I said, I'll have yours returned tomorrow."

His hands fisted at his sides. "Not until you give me an answer."

Her eyes finally lifted and met his. "To what?"

He didn't know why he was forcing the issue, since her answer was obvious, but for some peculiar reason he wanted her to say the words, to reject him out loud. "To my proposal, that's what."

"Oh, my apologies. I didn't know I needed to respond, since that wasn't a real proposal."

"Of course it was real."

"No, it wasn't. How could it be when you're not free to ask any woman to be your wife? You already *have* a wife, Mr. Monroe, unless you're going to confess to bigamy now."

"I told you—"

"Yes, I know." Her voice took on a mocking, singsong quality. "You're married in name only and your wife means nothing to you. You hate her, she's a bitch who's never understood you, and you're getting rid of her at the first opportunity. I just need to be patient and forgive you because it's me you really love. In the meantime, we can continue to shack up and have lots of hot sex while we wait for the divorce papers to come through. Then we'll run off together, maybe fly to Vegas and tie the knot at one of those quickie wedding chapels. Maybe even let Elvis officiate."

Her eyes glittered, sharp as glass. "So thank you for the proposal, but no thank you. I've had enough of your lies."

Fury burst like flames inside his chest. "I. Am. Not. Lying."

She made a disdainful sound under her breath and looked away.

"This is about him, isn't it? That bastard Jeffries, and what he did to you."

Her body turned rigid again, her arms tightening

against her waist. "How would you know what he did to me?"

"Oh, I know, because I had him checked out."

Her lips parted on a silent gasp.

"I know he was married when the two of you were involved. I know that he strung you along, and when you'd finally had enough, you dumped your red-hot career in corporate law and ran away, taking a job with the Justice Department even though it meant a huge pay cut. I know he used you and broke your heart.

"But I'm not the same as him, and however bad things might look, I am not lying when I say I love you and want you to be my wife. He and I are totally different, so do me the favor of not painting us with the same brush."

A flicker of emotion burned in her eyes, heat replacing the cold. "Oh? And why shouldn't I, when both of your brushes are dipped in the same paint? You're right. I don't trust you, not anymore. And I don't believe you. And now, I want you out. Get the hell out of my apartment and get the hell out of my life!"

His lungs heaved, frustration and anger turning into a volatile mix. He wanted to refuse, to stay right where he was and make her see that she was wrong about him, that every word he'd told her was the truth and his intentions were good. But she was set in her opinion, and right now there was nothing he could do to sway her, no way he could prove himself right.

"Fine. I'll leave." He dug into his pocket, found her key, and tossed it onto the coffee table with a metallic clink. "But don't think for a moment that this is over. I am getting a divorce and the moment the papers are signed and the judge says it's final, I'll be back. And when I do, I'm going to ask you again to marry me and you're going to say yes."

"I wouldn't count on that."

"Oh, but I am. You love me and that will make all the difference in the end."

Something shattered on her face, an expression of anguish that she couldn't quite hide. But then she pulled herself together again, the look vanishing behind the frosty facade.

She said nothing as he walked to the door.

He didn't speak again as he let himself out.

Brie crumpled the instant after he'd gone, staggering back to the sofa and falling onto the cushions.

She couldn't cry; she was in too much pain for that. Worse, she felt so torn, part of her desperately wanting to believe him, but the other part of her too cynical to think anything other than the worst.

He was right. She was painting him with Stephen's duplicitous brush. But how could she not? She'd been a fool once; she wasn't going to be a fool again.

But even if Maddox meant every word he'd said, did it really matter in the end? Because at the heart of it all was the fact that he'd lied. He'd willfully deceived her. He'd destroyed her trust, and to her, that was the most terrible crime of all.

# CHAPTER TWENTY-ONE

Never get personally involved with your client. It was the first rule of professionalism and sound business ethics.

*So why didn't I follow it?* Brie thought as she sat at her desk the next day. *Oh, right, because I'm a stupid idiot who listens to her hormones rather than her head.*

*And my heart?*

Well, it really didn't matter about her heart, regardless of how many jagged pieces it might be in at the moment. Her relationship with Maddox Monroe was over; she should have known it was too damned good to be true.

Or to last.

*Bastard. How could he do this to me?*

But he had and now she needed to find a way to move on without him.

If only she could get really angry, it would make everything so much easier. Anger would give her energy, and an inner fire of righteous indignation that would propel her forward in spite of the heartbreak and pain.

Instead all she really felt was sad, her spirits so depressed this morning she'd barely been able to drag herself into the office. Yet somehow she'd forced herself up out of bed and into the shower, then into a suit and onto the subway.

She'd let one man drive a stake through her career and chase her out of the city; she wasn't going to let it happen a second time, and, ironically, for the same reason.

At least she wasn't holding out hope this time around, waiting like some pathetic ditz for him to make good on his promises and come sweeping in like Prince Charming with a ring in one hand and a divorce decree in the other. No, this time, she knew the score. There would be no rescue and no happy ending.

If only he wasn't a client—and one of her biggest, most important clients to boot. She could always hand him over to one of the other partners, or to Barrett S., who'd recently been elevated into the ranks of partner and who'd taken to strutting around the office like a pinstriped peacock ever since. But trading Maddox's account away would be like waving a white flag. Not only would it bring unwanted attention to her affair with a client—however dead their relationship might now be—but it would make her look weak and not fully capable of performing her job.

So as much as she cringed at the idea, she was going to continue on as his lawyer and represent him to the very best of her ability. She might bleed at the sight of him and despise him for his lies, but she was a professional. Never again would she let her feelings for him show.

And Maddox?

Frankly, she no longer cared. He would get tired of her cold shoulder soon enough and move on to some other likely bedmate, some pretty chippie who didn't care whether he was "technically" married or not.

And once he'd moved on, so would she.

*Liar,* she thought, her fingernails digging into the leather blotter on her desk.

She was never going to get over him. Stephen had been a blip compared with Maddox. A calm breeze next to a hurricane. Love shouldn't hurt this much. She shouldn't ache from just the memory of his arms.

No, Maddox was going to be a scar, a wound that would heal but leave an indelible mark. Now she just needed to figure out how to survive and adapt to whatever fragments of herself and her heart remained.

Her phone rang, interrupting her wallowing. She froze, pulse speeding, half-sick, as she wondered if it was him. But he usually called her on her cell, so she was probably safe.

So much for being calm, cool, and collected when it came to doing business with Maddox.

Without giving herself more time to dither, she picked up the receiver. "Hello."

"Hey, Brie, it's Trish."

Her nerves deflated. "Oh, hey, Trish."

"Don't sound so excited. Who'd you think it was?"

"Nobody. What's up?"

Her paralegal paused briefly, then started speaking again at her usual mile-a-minute pace. "I'm doing that research on Bloomfield like you asked me to and I've hit a couple roadblocks. Wondered if you'd have time to pop by the law library where I'm set up, so we can hash things out."

Bloomfield—one of her other clients. That came as a relief.

Still, even as the tension slid out of her muscles, her low spirits returned, leaving her oddly and unexpectedly tired.

"Sure," she told the other woman, "I'll swing by. I have a few minutes. You ready now?"

"Yeah. I'll get coffee and see you in five."

"In five."

She hung up. As she did, her smartphone lit up, playing the lullaby from *Twilight*—the ringtone she'd picked for Maddox, even though he wasn't immortal or a vampire.

*Crap*, she'd forgotten about that. It would be next on her to-do list to delete.

In the meantime, the phone was still ringing.

What did he want? Hadn't they already said all there was to say last night? She stared at his name and picture—the photo something else to delete first chance she got.

Four rings.

Five.

She hit "ignore" and pushed away from her desk.

She had work to do.

Maddox disconnected.

He didn't know why he'd called Brie—just a masochist, he supposed. It wasn't like she was going to listen to anything else he had to say. She'd kicked him out last night, and exactly as promised, she'd sent the key and passes he'd given her over to him in a plain brown envelope.

If only she would believe him. If only she would see that he'd never meant to hurt or deceive her. That he loved her—so much it was driving him stark raving crazy that this issue with his separation was separating them.

But he'd meant what he'd said last night. This wasn't over between them. He was going to get her back, even if he had to move mountains to accomplish it.

And it looked like he might have to, he realized after he'd spoken with his divorce attorney. To keep it off the radar at Brie's firm, he'd gone with the top family-law guy at his old firm, meeting here at his hotel and swearing the other man to complete anonymity, unbreakable lawyer-client confidentiality.

He had already set the divorce wheels in motion before Brie and her investigator had even found out that he was still legally married. Why the guy couldn't also have discovered that he was actively pursuing a divorce, he didn't know. But he supposed it was his own fault for wanting to keep it all hush-hush, the very thing that had put him on Brie's shit list in the first place. That and the fact that he hadn't gotten a goddamned divorce eleven years ago like he should have.

But just as it had then, it looked like he was going to have a fight on his hands with Ellen. The thought put him in mind of today's call with the lawyer.

"What do you mean, she won't agree?" Maddox had said, his hand squeezing the phone. "She has to agree."

"Technically, yes, she doesn't have a choice about the divorce itself and can't stop you from filing."

Maddox was beginning to get sick of the word "technically." "But?"

"But she can greatly slow down the process. Considering the length of time you have been married—"

"We were only married in the conventional sense for a year. We've been separated for the last ten."

"Which the judge will take into account. Even so, she is entitled to an equitable distribution of assets and since you are the one with the most assets and you did not have a prenup—"

"I'm the one who's going to get screwed."

"I'll do everything I can to make sure that doesn't happen," the attorney assured him with confidence. "I know ways around these things. However, that means time. . . ."

"Which is the one thing I don't want to spend."

How ironic, after all these years when he wouldn't have cared how much time it took to pursue a divorce, now he wanted one as instantaneously as possible.

If only Brie weren't so hurt and angry. If only he didn't worry that he might lose her forever if he didn't get free in time. He couldn't risk it; he loved Brie far too much.

His fist tightened again on the phone. "See how much Ellen wants to make this go fast. I want it done and over with."

"Understood. I'll be back in touch as soon as I have news."

Now it was wait and see.

In the meantime, Brie was doing her best to cut him out of her life.

But not completely, he reminded himself. So far, he hadn't received word from her law firm advising him that she would no longer be acting as his attorney. He'd been half expecting to hear that she'd handed him off to one of the other partners.

But so far, nothing.

It could just be ice-cold pragmatism on her part. Then again, maybe she didn't really want to sever all ties with him. Maybe some part of her still loved him too much to let him go completely.

She might not take his personal calls, but she would take the ones he made for business. And that's what he would use to keep her in his life for now.

And once he got his divorce . . .

Brie Grayson had always been a challenge. He'd won her love and forgiveness once; he would win them again.

Because anything else was unthinkable.

# CHAPTER TWENTY-TWO

An icy blast of December wind struck Brie in the face, the moist heaviness in the air promising snow in the near future.

*Looks like it's going to be a white Christmas,* Brie thought as she stood on the train platform at the station near her parents' home in Connecticut. She repositioned the overnight bag on her shoulder and scanned the people moving around her in search of a familiar face.

Her brother had been tasked with picking her up again, but the redhead she spotted wasn't P.G.; it was his twin instead.

"Madelyn," she called, waving a hand to catch her sister's attention.

"Brie!" Madelyn hurried forward, a wide smile curving her lips.

They hugged, quickly but exuberantly, then broke apart again.

"Brr, it's cold," Madelyn said. "Here, give me some of that stuff you've got—then let's hightail it to the car before we freeze to death."

Grateful for the help, Brie passed her a big shopping bag full of presents wrapped in festive holiday paper, leaving her a free hand for her purse and briefcase.

Together they trudged out to the parking lot.

"Zack and the twins didn't come with you?" Brie asked.

Madelyn shook her head. "They're back at the house. Zack's on a top secret mission in the garage putting together toys, and the girls are decorating cutout cookies with Mom, though I think mostly they're just ruining their dinner and making a mess. But everyone is having fun, which is what the holidays are for."

They reached Madelyn's Volvo and took a minute to stow her belongings and the sack of presents in the trunk. She and Madelyn went around to their respective sides and climbed in. Madelyn was driving.

"So how come P.G. isn't here?" Brie buckled her seat belt. "I thought he was going to pick me up."

Madelyn started the car, then busied herself adjusting the heater. "He was, but something came up and Mom asked me to do it instead."

"What something?" She heard a note in her sister's voice that she didn't like. "Is anything wrong?"

"Look, why don't we get home and then I'll tell you about it there?"

"No," Brie said insistently, "tell me about it now."

Madelyn sighed and leaned back in the seat rather than pull out of the parking spot. "They were hoping not to put a damper on everyone's Christmas, but I suppose there's no point hiding it. Once you see her, well . . ."

"See her?" Brie's mind raced over the words, putting two and two together. "You mean Caroline, don't you?"

A look of deep sadness wiped away Madelyn's earlier smile. She nodded. "Her cancer's back."

Without thinking, Brie reached out and gripped Madelyn's hand. "Oh, God. How bad?"

Madelyn squeezed her hand back. "Bad. It's metastasized. Brie, she's riddled with it," she said, her voice cracking with anguish. "It's terminal this time."

"How long?"

"How long have I known or how long does she have?"

"Both."

"Zack and I found out this morning. P.G. stopped by for a few minutes and I could tell immediately that something was wrong. I went back with him to their house and she looks bad."

"Surely there's some kind of treatment—"

Madelyn shook her head again. "It's inoperable. They've already consulted more than one oncologist. P.G. was so desperate he even took out a second mortgage on their house so she could go to some exclusive hospital in Texas that's supposed to be doing amazing things. But after examining her, the doctors told her to go home and get her affairs in order."

"And that's it? They're just giving up?"

Madelyn gave her a direct look. "They're accepting the inevitable. Caroline says she wants to spend her final days surrounded by her family and friends, not in a hospital, hooked up to every machine imaginable. I think she has that right; it's what I'd do if I were her."

Brie fell silent, blinking back the tears that came to her eyes. "Yes, of course. It's just that she seemed to be doing so well. I thought she'd beaten it."

"We all did."

But in hindsight, she remembered her sister-in-law's tiredness at Ivy's wedding, how they'd all put it down to overwork, even P.G. How he must be suffering, watching the love of his life fade away before his eyes. And the children, to lose their mother so young.

Madelyn sniffed and dug a tissue out of her purse. She handed a second one to Brie without asking. The two of them blew their noses.

"She wants to have a nice Christmas, especially for the kids, since it'll be their last together. How she thinks she could conceal her condition from anyone, I don't know, but we're all going to pretend, to make her happy."

*Pretend she isn't dying.*

Brie couldn't speak for a minute. "Okay. Whatever Caroline needs."

Madelyn sighed and adjusted her seat belt. "We'd better be getting back. They'll be worrying about us otherwise."

Brie nodded.

But rather than put the car in reverse, Madelyn sat unmoving, clearly lost in thought.

"Is there something else?" Brie ventured.

Her sister shot her a sideways glance. "Nothing that can't wait." She reached for the gearshift.

Brie stopped her with a hand. "Well, you have to tell me *now*. Go on, whatever it is, no matter how bad, I can take it."

But could she? With the tragic news about Caroline on top of her breakup with Maddox, she honestly didn't know how many more horrible things she could stand. But her sister needed her and clearly wanted to get something else off her chest. She would deal with it for Madelyn's sake.

Inwardly, she braced herself.

Madelyn sighed, then met her eyes. "That's the trouble—it isn't bad. Actually it's the opposite, but I feel terrible being happy for myself when Caroline is . . . well, when she's . . . dying. But I've got to tell someone or I'm going to pop."

"Let's not have that. Just think of the mess," Brie said, joking to lighten the mood. "Actually, it would be great to hear something good for a change."

A secret little smile curved Madelyn's mouth. "I'm pregnant."

"What!"

Madelyn gave a half laugh, her smile widening. "Ten weeks. Besides Zack, you're the only one who knows. I haven't even told Mom. I was going to, you know, Christmas surprise, but once I found out about Caroline, I didn't have the heart. My news will keep until later."

But Brie was shaking her head. "No, no, you should tell everyone now, tonight. It's just the thing to brighten up the holiday. And Caroline won't mind—she'll be thrilled for you. I'm thrilled for you. I'm going to be an aunt again."

Crowing with pleasure, Brie reached over and pulled Madelyn into a fierce hug. Madelyn hugged her and laughed back.

"Zack is delighted, I'm sure," Brie said once they broke apart.

"Delighted is an understatement. He's already busy converting the spare room into a nursery. We're waiting on paint colors, though, until we find out the baby's sex. He says he wants another girl, but I'm kind of hoping for a boy. We'll see."

"Shall we go home and share the good news?"

Madelyn sent her a smile that was still tinged with underlying sadness. She put the car in gear. "Yes, let's."

The next evening, the constant excitement and chatter in the house was finally beginning to dissipate. Christmas dinner was long over, the dishes washed, and Zack and Madelyn's girls were snuggled into bed, dreaming about the presents Santa had left.

P.G., Caroline, and their children had come over early and spent the day, Caroline looking as gaunt and frail as Madelyn had warned she would. But Caroline was determined for this Christmas to be the best one ever and so she'd smiled and laughed with everyone else. They in turn had pretended nothing was wrong, exactly as she wished. Even P.G. did his best to be merry, playing games with the children and watching football with the adults. But he couldn't completely hide the grief and torment in his eyes, especially when he thought no one was looking.

Brie had been right about Madelyn's pregnancy, which she and Zack had shared with everyone last night over cups of eggnog—hers alcohol free. The happy news had lifted the mood in the house, a counterbalance for the inevitable sorrow ahead.

By nine, Caroline was exhausted from the long day, so P.G. had taken his family home, the trunk stuffed full of presents and leftovers. Brian and Heather, who were aware of their mother's illness, though perhaps not the true severity of it, had been unnaturally quiet now that the temporary distraction of the holiday was over.

Everyone else, including James and Ivy, who had long since returned from their honeymoon but who still acted like honeymooners, had settled in the living room around the fragrant, beautifully decorated Christmas tree. The live blue spruce, which would be planted in an already-dug hole in the front yard, rose a full eight feet toward the ceiling. Its lights twinkled, a festive reminder of the day nearly done.

Brie gazed at it for a long minute, then got to her feet. She was nearly done in too, tired after the day, bone weary after working hard to act like she was having fun when there was little fun inside her.

All day she'd thought about Maddox—or, rather, tried *not* to think of him, which was nearly the same thing. What had he done today? Whom had he been with?

But she didn't want to know. She was through with him; he was out of her life, even if he had sent her a Christmas present.

*Sneaky bastard*, he'd had it delivered here to her parents' house this morning. Her dad had signed for the box, so it had been impossible to refuse or return. She still hadn't opened it, stuffing it into her purse when no one was watching.

Back before Thanksgiving, Madelyn had asked her about Maddox: whether the two of them were still seeing each other. Brie had said no, that things hadn't worked out. To Brie's relief, Madelyn had left it alone.

For some reason that even Brie still didn't fully understand, she hadn't told Madelyn about the fact that Maddox was married. Maybe it was because she didn't want Madelyn to think badly of her for being stupid enough to get involved with not one but two married men. But the bigger reason, oddly enough, was that she didn't want Madelyn to think badly of Maddox.

Which was the stupidest reason of all.

The rest of the family was busy watching a movie on television. Brie turned her eyes to the screen and was trying to pay attention when the phone rang in the other room. Who could be calling on Christmas?

"I'll get it," she offered, getting to her feet.

The others nodded and went back to their show.

Out in the hall, she picked up the receiver. "Grayson residence."

"Hello, Brie."

Her breath caught in her throat, her grip tightening on the receiver. She didn't need to ask who was on the other end; she would know his voice anywhere. "Hello."

"Brie," her mother called from the living room. "Who is it? Do I need to come out there?"

She cupped a hand over the mouthpiece. "No. It's for me. It's . . . work."

"On Christmas night?"

"It's nothing major. Just a couple loose ends for tomorrow."

"Tell them you can't talk. You're on holiday."

"Yes, Mom. I'll be back in a couple minutes."

*That girl,* Brie heard her mother say in a quieter voice, *never can get her to relax.*

*Well, she is your daughter.*

*Yours too, Philip Grayson.*

Her father laughed; then the room grew quiet again except for the sound of the TV.

With the portable phone in hand, Brie moved away from the crowded living room, then down another hall and into a small study. She slid the pocket doors closed behind her. Only then did she put the phone back to her ear.

"You still there?"

"Yes. So, I'm work, am I?" His voice was deep and smooth, even better than she remembered.

"You'd better be, since I told you not to call me unless it has to do with business. How did you get this number anyway?"

"Your mother gave it to me a while back. Luckily I kept it in my contacts."

"Then you ought to be talking to my mother, since it's her number you called."

"I tried to call you, have been all day, but you never answer your cell."

"I switched off the ringer. It's Christmas Day, remember?"

"So it is."

She walked over to a square, well-padded ottoman upholstered in celadon geometrics and sank down. "What do you want, Maddox? Why are you calling me?"

"Do I have to have a reason? It's Christmas, remember?"

"I've already told you—"

"I know what you told me and I've been doing my best to keep my distance until the divorce comes through."

"Maddox—"

"Look, all I really wanted was to wish you Merry Christmas."

She squeezed her eyes closed, a hard lump aching in her chest. "You could have just left me a message."

"I could. But I wouldn't have gotten to talk to you, to hear you. I miss you, Brie."

*I miss you too,* she thought. *So much. Too much.*

"I know you're angry with me and I understand," he said. "But I really am getting divorced. The petition is already filed. I'll send over a copy so you can see for yourself."

"No, I don't need to see it. I believe you, but it doesn't matter. It doesn't change anything."

"Of course it does. It changes everything."

"Not the fact that you lied to me. Divorced or not, you can't take that back. How can I ever trust you again? How can I know there won't be other lies? Another convenient set of half-truths somewhere down the line?"

He was silent so long she wondered if he was still there. Then he spoke again. "You're right. You can't. I guess it comes down to you having faith in me when I tell you I'm sorry and that I will never lie to you again. I suppose it means you'll have to forgive me. Please, sweetheart. Please forgive me. I love you, Brie. Nothing is the same without you."

A tear slid over her cheek, but she backhanded it away. She couldn't let herself weaken, no matter the temptation.

"I love you too," she whispered. "But I just can't."

"Now. You can't now."

She sighed. "Maddox, don't call me anymore. And from now on, even if it's business, leave a message with my assistant first."

Another silence. "If that's what you want."

"It is. Look, I should go."

"Okay, but at least tell me you had a good day. Lots of food and presents, right? Was your whole family there?"

At the reminder, her spirits sank even lower. "Yes, everyone was here." She fought for a breezy tone. "Lots of food. Lots of presents. How about you? Did you see Daphne or your mother and stepfather and little brothers?"

"No, not this year. We Skyped. Almost the same thing."

"It's not. You should have gone out to be with them."

"Next year. Too much to do here at the hotel."

On the other end of the phone, Maddox raked his fingers through his already messy hair. He was on the sofa in his penthouse living room, the city dark and cold beyond the windows despite all the festive lights.

Or maybe he was the one who felt dark and cold without Brie's warmth beside him.

"Did you get the present I sent?" he asked.

"Yes. I'm afraid I haven't opened it yet. I don't think I should. I'm going to send it back."

"Don't." His voice turned hard. "It's nothing much. Just something I saw in a store that made me think of you. I won't take it back, so don't bother trying to return it. Give it away if you don't like it."

"I—all right."

That's when he heard it, the sadness. Yet it was something different from the tone she used when she was talking about their difficulties. He refused to call it their breakup, since in spite of her unwillingness to forgive him, to trust him, he hadn't given up hope.

Not completely.

And most definitely not after she'd admitted that she loved him, even now.

"What's wrong?" he asked.

"You mean beside the fact that I'm talking to you?"

He smiled. "Yes, besides that. Something's happened. What is it?"

She sighed. And again he could hear the underlying pain in the sound. "Nothing. Just something with the family."

"What about the family? I thought all of you got along like a house on fire."

"We do."

"So what is it?"

"Have you ever thought maybe it's none of your business?"

He didn't answer, just waited for her to go on.

"It's Caroline."

"Your sister-in-law?"

"Yes, she"—her voice cracked a bit—"she's sick. Cancer. It's inoperable. She's not going to make it."

"Ah, shit, Brie, that's awful. She's so young."

"She is. I forgot—you met her, didn't you?"

"Yes, at your sister's wedding. I liked her a lot. She seems like a kind, lovely person."

"She is. She's one of best people I know."

"And now she's sick. How's your brother doing? And their kids? They have little kids, don't they?"

"Yes, and it's taking its toll. I don't know how they're going to bear losing her, especially P.G. She's always been his rock, the very center of his world."

*Like you've become for me,* Maddox thought.

And in such a short amount of time. But then, not really, since he'd known her for decades, loved her since he was a kid, if truth be known.

He heard her crying softly. "What can I do?"

"Nothing." She sniffed, struggled to pull herself together. "There's nothing to be done."

"If you think of anything, anything at all, just tell me. Nothing is too big or small."

She sniffed again. "Thanks. Now, I really should go. I'm surprised Mom hasn't come in here to make me quit 'working.' "

He paused for a moment. "Brie."

"What?"

"I know we have our issues, but if you ever just need to talk, you know I'm always here."

"I know." But it didn't sound like she would take him up on it. "Merry Christmas, Maddox."

"Merry Christmas, Brie."

Then she was gone, the dial tone filling the empty air.

Reluctantly, he hung up too.

Upstairs in her childhood bedroom a few hours later, Brie sat on the bed, the present Maddox had given her in her hands. She traced the faint shimmer of the pretty red paper and festive gold bow, knowing she should simply return it as she'd told him she was going to.

Instead, she hesitated briefly, then reached out to tear open the paper.

Inside were two gifts, one square and boxy, the other long, narrow, and rectangular. She opened the long present first, her suspicions confirmed when she saw that it was jewelry. Light and delicate, the gold bracelet was covered in dozens of small diamonds that shimmered in the low lamplight. She lifted it free, and as she did, a tiny heart swung near the clasp. Her name was engraved on its face.

*Nothing much, huh.*

She skimmed a fingertip over the engraving, then laid the bracelet aside. She picked up the other box.

Inside was a ceramic mug with the words "World's Greatest Backswing" emblazoned on the front.

Her lips parted and a laugh escaped. He'd tucked a little note inside the cup. She opened it and read:

*In memory of the second first time we met.*

She laughed again, cradling the mug inside her hands. And then she started to cry.

# CHAPTER TWENTY-THREE

A cold December slid into a raw January with ice and winds that rattled the bones. February turned wet and snowy with a nor'easter that forced everyone inside and left the city coated in a thick blanket of white. So it was with relief that March brought glimpses of spring as the temperatures rose and the ice and snow began to melt.

But the same could not be said for Brie, who kept her distance from Maddox, determined to erase him from her mind and heart. If only she could put in a call to the IT department and have a tech clean and reboot that part of her hippocampus, it would make her days and nights so much easier to bear—especially her nights, when she ached without him next to her in her cold, lonely bed.

But people were not machines, however much she tried to function like one at work. As his attorney, she had to handle his legal work, had to see his name and be reminded of him and everything they no longer had.

To her relief, he'd done as she asked and had stopped

calling her directly, leaving messages with Gina or Trish instead. Lately, she and Maddox had taken to exchanging impersonal e-mails that focused exclusively on business, tending to avoid phone calls unless absolutely necessary, since the conversations were always awkward at best.

As for the divorce he was supposedly getting, she hadn't heard a word. A circumstance that left her feeling alternately justified in her decision to cut him out of her life as much as possible, and wallowing in a pit of misery and despair.

She'd learned through Trish that Maddox had flown to England a few days earlier; the new M Hotel London was moving along at a brisk pace. The building contracts had been settled and the permits cleared. The official ground breaking would be next week.

Even so, Maddox walked into the courtroom exactly on time. Today was the civil trial for the Mergenfeld suit. There was no jury; the case would be decided by a judge.

Maddox said a quiet hello to her and her cocounsel, then took a seat in his place at the defendant's table.

He looked wonderful. His dark hair was neatly cut and combed. His gray suit conservative but not too severe, the slim gold watch on his wrist his only adornment.

She resisted the urge to stare, her pulse beating heavily, and looked down at her notes.

It was his right to be here for the proceedings, but she wished he'd sent one of his lieutenants. Even with her second chair seated between them, having him so close was going to play havoc with her nerves.

She could even smell him, very faintly, the fresh, clean scent of his soap always better than the cologne he chose not to wear. It brought back so many memories, emotions, and cravings that had no place in a courtroom.

But she was prepared and knew the case inside out. Even with Maddox here, she felt confident about how to proceed. After all the time and effort she and her team had put in, she wasn't messing up this case because she and the client happened to have a history.

She sensed, rather than saw, Roger Mergenfeld walk in—or rather strut in. She'd met him only once at his deposition, but there was something distinctly surfer-dude about him, from his sun-bleached blond hair to his tanned, weather-roughened skin, which frankly looked a bit odd this time of year, at least in New York.

How Mergenfeld and Maddox had ever been friends, let alone business partners, was a real head-scratcher. They seemed almost nothing alike and she couldn't help but wonder if alcohol might have been involved somewhere along the line years ago, before Maddox had stopped drinking anything stronger than coffee.

Mergenfeld, she noticed, didn't look at Maddox, almost as if he was ashamed to make eye contact.

Maddox had no such problem, gazing directly, steadily at the other man, who had become a nagging, whining thorn in his side—one he planned to pull out with her help.

Mergenfeld and his lawyers conferred from their seats behind the plaintiffs' table, his lead attorney pausing once they were done to trade a moment of small talk with her. She knew him from various legal mixers and other lawsuits; she'd never liked him.

He gave her a slick, toothy smile.

She smiled back—no teeth—then laid her pen on top of her notes as if she knew every word by heart and had no doubt she would win.

The judge entered from his chambers; they all stood.

Once the judge, a practical, intelligent man who had

no patience for nonsense or grandstanding, was seated, the proceedings began.

Maddox sat respectfully in his chair and watched Brie work. He'd never heard or seen her in a courtroom and she was nothing short of magnificent. Articulate yet personable with just the right amount of friendly charm, she was able to put the witnesses at ease, even the ones who were there to represent the other side. She deftly questioned each of them, eliciting testimony that helped his side and seemed to undermine the other. Her cocounsel wasn't bad either, but to Maddox, she was the standout.

He thought they were winning; at least they seemed to be to his way of thinking. But the judge was like a sphinx. Who knew which way the old man was really leaning?

As for Mergenfeld, whom he hadn't seen in years, he hardly spared a glance. The time had not been kind to the other man, his features dissipated from hard living and drink. Probably drugs as well; Roger had never been the type to hold back on anything that fed his pleasure-driven lifestyle.

It was one of the things they'd disagreed the most over. At a time when Roger had been getting more deeply involved in the party scene, Maddox had been moving further away from it. He'd been neck-deep in the new business, his marriage had been crashing around him, and he'd started living on sleeping pills and too much booze.

Ironically, Roger had been the one to set him on the path to sobriety by offering him drugs. Just some uppers to "get him through."

But the suggestion had reminded him of his father, who'd thrown away his life and his family for money and a quick high. When his father had gone down, he'd taken the whole family with him, leaving them with nothing, their old life burned to cinders. Maddox's teen years had been hard, angry, rebellious ones, yet somehow he had managed to come through in one piece.

But in that moment when Roger had offered him drugs, he'd realized just how easy it could be to end up like his old man. He was only a lost weekend or an illegal hit away from a jail cell.

From that day forward, he hadn't had a drink or taken anything stronger than an aspirin. It had been one of the clearest and best decisions of his life.

Unlike Roger himself.

Incredible to think that he'd once partnered up with such a useless, narcissistic parasite. But Roger had been a parasite with money at a time when the banks wouldn't touch him and no one else could, or would, give him a loan. Just starting out, he believed that Roger was the answer to a prayer. Roger would put up the cash for the hotel and leave the rest to Maddox.

When Roger had said he wanted to go his own way and took a payout, Maddox had been quietly relieved. But everything came with strings. He'd just never expected to find Roger still trying to pull them all these years later.

Across the courtroom, Roger got up the nerve to look at him; he smiled nervously.

Maddox stared back, unsmiling, and refused to look away until the smile fell off Roger's face and he lowered his gaze.

Maddox listened again to the proceedings; Mergenfeld's attorney was talking.

He watched Brie, wishing she'd said more to him this morning than hello. Seeing her after all these months apart was heaven and hell combined. But he supposed they'd said everything there was to say when they'd talked at Christmas. Now it was up to him to get his divorce finalized, then convince Brie to take him back.

*Damn Ellen, and damn her foot-dragging.*

Brie told the judge she had no further questions and the witness left the stand.

The next witness was called and for a moment he couldn't believe he'd heard right. He turned his head and there she was, walking forward.

Ellen.

Brie straightened her spine and forced her emotions to go dead. She had her job to do and no matter if it killed her, she wasn't going to toss away winning this case because she didn't want to put her ex-lover's wife on the stand.

She didn't dare look at Maddox; seeing him would surely put cracks in the band of frozen steel she'd wrapped around her heart. But she had to look at his wife; she really had no choice, since she would be questioning the woman.

Ellen Kilkenny Monroe was beautiful—there was no getting around that fact. Dark-haired with skin like a magnolia petal, and deep green eyes, she could have been a model had she wished. Brie had seen her deposition video and knew the other woman was pretty, but until she came face-to-face with her, Brie hadn't realized how stunning she really was.

Brie's heart gave a painful squeeze. No wonder he'd never divorced her. What man would?

*But I have my job to do.*

After the trial was done, though, she was going to step away from work with Maddox. Today had driven home the fact that being around him, but without him, was just too hard.

*And if he and Ellen were actually divorcing?*

She had no time to think about that now.

The gold cross around Ellen's neck swung slightly as she lifted her hand from the Bible, her eyes calm as she waited.

Brie approached, doing a quick mental inventory of the things she planned to say.

"Thank you for agreeing to appear here today, Ms. Kilkenny."

Ellen Kilkenny smiled slightly and inclined her head.

"First, I believe we need to establish your relationship to the defendant, Mr. Monroe." Without really looking at him, she gestured toward Maddox. "Could you please tell us what that relationship is?"

"Yes, I am his wife."

Faint murmurs rose up from the gallery, the plaintiffs looking up in obvious surprise. Clearly their investigator wasn't as good as her investigator, Denny.

Roger Mergenfeld, however, did not look surprised. He looked angry, his brows creased with worry.

Brie drew in a breath.

Ellen, she noticed, had made no mention of a pending divorce. Brie almost asked her the question, but stopped. It wasn't germane to the case, and if the answer wasn't yes, did she really want to hear it, especially now?

"And as Mr. Monroe's . . . wife," Brie said, "you were privy to meetings and conversations between Roger Mergenfeld and Maddox Monroe at the time period under review?"

She recited the dates again for the record.

Ellen looked first at Maddox, then at Mergenfeld. "I was."

"And during this period, were you witness to any conversations between the defendant and Mr. Mergenfeld about Mr. Mergenfeld's wish to sever his partnership with Mr. Monroe in exchange for a payout amount?"

"I did, yes," Ellen said. "On more than one occasion."

*Bingo,* Brie thought, hiding a smile. With this testimony, she should just have clinched a win for Maddox. How ironic that it would be courtesy of his wife.

"Let us start with the first of those occasions. . . ."

"It is my considered opinion," the judge said later that afternoon, "that the plaintiff has failed to prove his claim of ongoing partnership. Therefore, I find for the defendant. The defendant is also entitled to compensation for any and all court costs, to be paid by the plaintiff."

Roger Mergenfeld groaned aloud, his legal team looking shell-shocked. Not only had they lost; they'd lost spectacularly.

"This case is dismissed." The judge brought down his gavel.

Talk immediately broke out.

Brie's cocounsel turned to give her a big hug. "We won! I'll let everyone at the office know. Then I'm headed out."

Brie hugged her back. "Celebrate tonight. You deserve it."

"I will." She turned and held out a hand. "Congratulations, Mr. Monroe."

"And to you."

They shook hands; then, cell phone to her ear, the other lawyer picked up her bag and left the courtroom.

Brie looked over at Maddox, who stood smiling.

They studied each other for a moment, but rather than hug, Brie stuck out her hand. His closed around hers, large and warm and so well remembered. A small tremor went through her at his touch.

"Well done, Ms. Grayson. It was a pleasure watching you work."

She shook hands quickly, then freed hers. "Winning is always good." Turning, she began packing up her briefcase.

"Brie, I was wondering—"

"Maddox?" a soft, distinctly feminine voice said from behind them.

She and Maddox looked around.

Ellen Kilkenny stood there, a hesitant smile on her pretty lips.

Brie resumed her packing.

"Sorry to interrupt, but might you have a minute, Maddox?" Ellen asked.

He frowned. "I guess, but I need to speak with Brie first."

"No, no," Brie said, not looking up from her efforts to shove the last of her files into her satchel. "You two go ahead. There will be plenty of time for postmortems once I'm back in the office." She snapped her bag closed.

He cast a glance at his wife. "Ellen, just wait for me outside."

Ellen looked from him to Brie and back again, curious interest in her expression. "Sure. See you outside."

"Brie, you must realize that I had no idea she was even in town."

"Yes, I know. We flew her in last minute when we realized what her testimony could provide. Looks like it paid off."

"It did and we've got a lot to celebrate. Let me take you to dinner tonight. Anywhere you want to go. There's that wonderful little Italian place you love. How about that?"

*Dinner? With Maddox?*

God, she was tempted, so much she could almost taste the craving on her tongue.

Instead, she shook her head. "Not tonight. I already have . . . plans," she said on a lie. "Another time perhaps."

His jaw clenched. "Why can't you forgive me? Why won't you give me another chance?"

She met his eyes. "Your wife is waiting for you."

"Soon-to-be ex-wife."

"Yes, of course. Good-bye, Maddox."

And as she turned, she felt the finality of their parting.

Was he right? Was she being too hardheaded, unwilling to forgive him and take another chance on having a future with him? Or was she doing the smart thing and walking away before she made a fool of herself yet again?

For a second, she nearly turned back, wanting to run headlong into his arms. Instead, she squared her shoulders, gripped her bag tighter, and walked toward the courtroom doors. Once through, she went faster and faster, leaving Ellen Kilkenny and her curious eyes behind, until she was free to run.

Free to run away.

Later than evening, Brie sat on her sofa, a TV drama on that she wasn't really watching as she ate Chinese takeout from the carton.

So much for a celebration dinner.

But after returning to the office, she hadn't been able to make herself stay for the party already under way. It wasn't every day the firm helped fend off a multimillion-dollar suit; one of the senior partners was already talking about an extra bonus for her.

She ought to have been thrilled. This win cemented

her place in the firm and would be a big boost for her career. Instead she felt . . . well, honestly, she didn't want to think about how she really felt or she might start crying.

Plunging the chopsticks into the carton, she ate another mouthful of noodles and shrimp.

Her phone rang.

She looked at the time, nearly ten. Then she saw who was calling.

"Hey, James."

"Hi, Brie, sorry to call so late."

"No problem. What's up?"

Silence fell. "Brie, it's Caroline. She's not doing well. If you want to see her, you'd better come. Tonight."

"I'll be right there."

"I'll send a car to drive you up."

# CHAPTER TWENTY-FOUR

The air blew icy and damp, the ground brittle with late-winter cold beneath the shoes of the mourners.

Brie listened numbly, huddled in her black wool coat as the minister recited last words over Caroline's grave.

The entire family and a few close friends were gathered to pay their final respects. P.G. looked white and half-dead; his eyes, always so lively, were blank now, as if some essential part of him was being buried with his wife. But enough of him remained that he was still there for his children—their children—his and Caroline's. He stood with a hand on each of their small shoulders, Heather's face buried against his side as she cried, a small stuffed cat clutched in her arm. Her brother, older and determined to act like a man, stood dry-eyed. But Brie had been there to watch him sob over his mother's body the morning Caroline had died, his keening a terrible thing to recall.

And then it was done, the words spoken. Each of them moved forward individually to toss a handful of cold earth into the grave on top of the casket. P.G. helped his children with the ritual, then stood unmoving as if he'd forgotten what to do next. His mother came forward to lead him gently away, the children now in the care of their grandfather.

Brie watched their sad figures walk across the cemetery toward the line of waiting cars. Then she started forward as well.

And that's when she saw him, standing at a respectful distance, tall and somber in his dark gray winter coat, silent amid the gravestones.

Madelyn looked over at Maddox as well, her own eyes damp with tears. "Shall we wait for you?"

"No," Brie said. "Go on to P.G.'s house. I'll be over soon."

Madelyn nodded, then found Zack and their children and went on their way. James and Ivy moved past, his arm around her for comfort and support as she cried quietly against his shoulder.

Brie approached Maddox, stopped a foot away. "What are you doing here?" she asked. "How did you even know about today?"

"Your assistant. I called your office and Gina told me you were at a family funeral. I knew that Caroline must have passed. Brie, I'm so sorry."

"Thank you."

"She was a lovely woman. I wish I'd had the chance to know her better."

"I wish you had too," Brie whispered. "She was . . . she was—"

Her throat tightened, grief rising inside her in a sudden rush. She'd held herself together during the service, determined to be strong for her brother, her family. But his words unleashed something and she trembled, tears pooling in her eyes, obscuring her sight.

She began to sob.

His arms wrapped around her, drawing her to his chest. He let her cry, silent and infinitely patient, waiting without expectation until she finally began to quiet. He pressed a couple of clean tissues into her hand, then held her against him again, stroking her hair and back as she slowly pulled herself together.

At length, she sniffed and raised her head. “Sorry.” Her voice was low and hoarse. “I didn’t mean to fall apart on you like that.”

Idly, he continued running a hand over her back. “Don’t apologize. You needed to get it out. Grief can do terrible things when it’s kept locked inside. Feel free to cry some more if you need to.”

She gave him a watery smile and sniffed again. “I think I’m okay now.”

But he didn’t release her and she didn’t try to move away. Instead, she leaned against him, savoring his warmth and strength, his clean familiar scent, and how good it felt to be in his arms again.

But she had to let him go, didn’t she? It would be wrong to give in to this weakness, this awful, aching longing to just let herself be his.

But as she struggled to make herself step away, a crushing grief swept through her again, even worse than before. If she let him go now, she feared it might well be forever. Suddenly she didn’t know if she could bear it. In spite of everything he’d done, everything that had gone on between them, she wasn’t sure she could live without him anymore.

“Kiss me,” she said, tipping back her head.

His dark eyes widened. “Brie?”

“Kiss me. Please. I need you.”

A light flared in his gaze; then his mouth was on hers,

searching softly, slowly, before turning increasingly more demanding, hungry, and heated.

And for Brie, it was like coming home. As if the earth had been out of orbit these past few months and had suddenly slipped back into its proper alignment.

She slid her arms around Maddox and burrowed closer, clinging to him as she met his kisses with a passionate fire that made the cold breezes ruffling their clothes seem balmy.

She wanted him.

She loved him.

Suddenly nothing else seemed to matter but him.

Gradually, they managed to stop, breath as fast and shallow in his lungs as hers.

"Brie." He brushed kisses over her forehead and across her cheeks, his eyes alive with hope. "Does this mean . . . have you decided to forgive me? To believe me?"

She considered his question. "I'm not sure, but I suppose it must."

Briefly, he closed his eyes, hugged her tighter. "I swear I'll never give you reason to doubt me again. The divorce . . . I've ironed things out with Ellen and it really is— "

She put her fingers against his lips, silencing him. "Shh, I don't care anymore. I just want to be with you." Curving her fingers, she stroked them across his cheek. "Do you love me?"

Emotion filled his eyes. "More than my life."

"Then that's all I care about now. I love you. You love me. That's enough."

He caught her hand, pressed it to his mouth. "Why the change? The other day, you were so . . . distant. I was afraid I might have lost you for good."

"You might have, but Caroline's death . . . I've suddenly realized that I've just been wasting time, making both of us miserable with my fear and my stubborn pride. I've remembered something that my brother said a few months ago before he even knew she was dying. He said that every day with her was a blessing, that he cherished each and every moment they had. Suddenly, today, because of her, I've realized that I've been squandering our moments. Our precious time."

He kissed her again, taking her mouth with a sweet, satisfying reverence that told her, in ways no words could express, the truth of his love. "I'll never deceive you or keep anything from you again," he murmured. "And despite any lingering reservations you may have, I'm going to marry you, Ms. Grayson."

"You don't have to, you know."

He scowled and made a noise that sounded a bit like a growl under his breath. "Of course I do. I can't wait to get a ring on your finger. I want to make sure the whole world knows you're off-limits to anyone but me."

"I already am. I'm done pushing you away." She smoothed her fingers over the narrow lapel on his wool coat. "You know, if you do get that divorce, you might not want to jump right back into another marriage so quickly."

"*When* I get my divorce—and it shouldn't be too much longer now—I'll be there the day the judge signs the divorce decree with a marriage license in one hand and you in the other so we can tie the knot the very same day. As for jumping back in, I've had a decade of feeling divorced, so remarrying is no rush at all." He pressed his lips to hers. "Our wedding day will be the best day of my life."

Her heart warmed, the last bits of doubt melting away. She wasn't worried anymore.

Catching his hand, she threaded her fingers with his. “Everyone will be wondering where I am. We’d better go.”

“Are you sure you want me to come along? I don’t want to intrude.”

“You’re not intruding. You’re going to be part of the family soon, so you should be with us, today of all days. Besides, I need you there with me.”

“I’ll be right by your side. Always.”

Leaning up on her toes, she crushed her lips to his, suddenly sure that he would be.

# Chapter Twenty-Five

"Can I take the blindfold off yet?" Brie asked three months later as Maddox led her carefully through the airport.

He'd waited until they'd gotten past the last security checkpoint, then stopped to insist that she put on a thick, padded sleep mask, which was unnervingly dark. She'd balked at first, but eventually agreed rather than continue to argue. She worried that otherwise they might miss their flight to wherever it was they were going.

Maddox had refused to tell her their destination; it was a secret. She hadn't even been able to pick up clues from her luggage, since Maddox had been the one to pack her bags.

Actually, he'd pretty much kidnapped her from the office this afternoon with the help of Gina and Trish, who had turned into despicable traitors since she'd gotten back together with Maddox. He had the two other women firmly in his pocket, so they were always happy to aid and abet whatever secret, romantic schemes he dreamed up to delight her with.

And delight her he did, each and every day.

Brie had to admit that in spite of her lingering grief over Caroline's death, which still had the power to hit her hard and without warning, the past few months with Maddox had been some of the best of her life.

She felt guilty at times; she was so happy. There was only one thing that could make her happier, but she knew Maddox and his lawyer were working diligently to finalize his divorce, so she never asked for details. She loved Maddox and trusted him and she vowed to be patient, however long it took.

In the meantime, they were together.

She knew she must look absolutely ridiculous at the moment, shuffling along with a mask over her eyes. On the other hand, it took a lot to surprise New Yorkers, so hopefully that cut the number of curious onlookers down to reasonably acceptable levels.

"Just a little farther." Maddox kept his arm locked securely around her waist so there was no chance of her falling.

The two of them walked on; then finally he drew her to a stop.

"Are we here?" she asked, her curiosity spiking higher.

"Almost. Just another minute."

"You've been saying that for the last *ten* minutes."

"Five. It only feels like it's been ten." Hands on her shoulders, he turned her, arranging her in the direction he wanted. "Close your eyes."

"I'm already blind."

"Close them. Please."

She huffed out a breath. "Well, since you said 'please.' "

He removed the mask. "Okay. Look."

She opened her eyes, blinking to let them adjust to

the light. The gate area came into focus; then the sign behind the check-in desk with the flight information.

"Las Vegas? We're going to Vegas?"

"We are."

"That sounds fun."

"But why all the buildup, right?" he said, repeating aloud what she'd been thinking.

"Well, it isn't like you're flying me to Tahiti. Or even Hawaii."

"Those'll come later. First, I wanted us to celebrate this." Reaching into his jacket, he withdrew a document, folded into thirds. "Read it."

She took it, recognizing the familiar feel of quality bond paper.

Official paper. *Could it be?*

She opened the pages.

"The judge signed the decree only this morning," Maddox said, his words rich and deep with obvious satisfaction. "I am finally a free man."

Her eyes widened, seeing the proof of his words before her, complete with notary stamp and judicial seal. "You're divorced."

"I'm divorced!"

With her heart about to burst from her chest, she let out a war whoop and jumped into his arms. He hugged her tightly, his arms like steel bands as he lifted her off her feet. And then they were kissing with a raw, passionate exuberance and a kind of unfettered joy, oblivious to the eyes of the other passengers around them.

Long before she was ready to stop kissing him, he set her back down. With her head still swimming from an excess of excitement and juiced-up hormones, she saw him take a pair of steps backward.

Then to her astonishment, he dropped onto one knee,

an open velvet-covered ring box in his hand. "Gabriella Felicity Grayson, I love you. Will you be my wife?"

All around her, people watched, but the only person she could see was Maddox. The man she loved, and would always love.

"Yes." She smiled, a tear running down her cheek. "Of course yes!"

He slid the large, beautiful square-cut diamond, which had to be three carats at least, onto her ring finger. Then she was in his arms again, his mouth moving with a blissful sizzle over hers while cheers and claps erupted around them.

The sound of their flight being called broke them apart.

Brie blushed and laughed as they boarded, their fellow passengers continuing to wish them well, a few cracking naughty jokes.

The first-class stewardess brought them glasses of sparkling champagne after they settled into their seats, a wide smile on her face. "Many happy wishes on your engagement. Compliments of the captain and the flight crew."

They thanked her, waiting as she moved away to kiss again.

"Vegas, huh?" Brie met his eyes, which were gleaming with unvarnished adoration. She was sure her own were twinkling with equal amounts of love, brilliant as her new diamond ring.

"So who would you rather have officiate? Regular minister, Elvis impersonator, or should we just drive through the Little White Chapel?"

"You mean you want to get married tonight?"

"Of course. I told you I was going to make you my

wife the minute I legally could. Why else do you think we're flying to Vegas?"

"But the family—no one will be there. Not to mention my mother, who will have ten shades of purple cow over us not having a proper wedding."

"Do you want a proper wedding?"

She thought about it for a moment, then shook her head. "No, not really. But I don't want to disappoint them. Everyone's been through so much lately."

"Don't worry. I already told your mother that I planned to whisk you off to the altar."

"Maddox!"

"She was sad for a minute, then told me to tell you to have the best elopement ever. We'll have a more traditional ceremony in front of our families once we get back. She's already been on the phone to my mother."

"Good Lord, did everyone know but me?"

"Pretty much." He grinned, pressed his lips to hers again. "So, what's your pick? Minister, Elvis, or Chapel?"

The engines rumbled beneath them, their seat belts fastened securely as the plane began to taxi.

Brie reached out and stroked her hand over his cheek. "The King, obviously. After all, you're my hunk-a hunk-a burnin' love."

Maddox laughed and crushed his mouth to hers, claiming her again, heart and soul.

Hours later, he and Brie lay tangled together in the sheets, their naked bodies warm and slightly damp with perspiration.

He filled his lungs and worked to slow his rapid breathing. Brie seemed to be having the same difficulty, panting from their most recent bout of wild lovemaking. Taking her left hand, he threaded her fingers through his, enjoying the way the low lamplight glinted off both of their wedding rings.

Rolling her toward him, he settled her on top of his chest, their bare legs tangling, her breasts pressing against him in the most delicious way. He ran a palm over her spine, leaning up to claim her mouth in a series of slow, sultry kisses.

"Happy?" he asked.

She smiled, her lips curving in a way that never failed to enthrall him. "Ecstatic," she said.

She slid her tongue along his lower lip. "And you? No regrets? It's not everybody who gets divorced and remarried on the same day."

"Not the same day. It was after midnight before the King pronounced us"—he lowered his voice, put on his best Elvis impression—"husband a-a-a-nd wife." He kissed her again. "No regrets. I've been waiting for this day since the moment I knew I loved you."

"Oh?" She ran a finger along his chest, tangling the tip in the short curls there. "And when was that?"

"The first time or the second time?"

Her eyes turned even bluer. "There's more than one?"

"Definitely."

"Well, then, what are they?"

"The second time I knew I loved you was last Fourth of July on the beach. I tried to tell myself later that I didn't feel that way, but from that moment on, deep down, I knew I was a goner."

"And the first time?" she said, her voice so soft it sent shivers through him.

He stroked his palm over her back and hips. She arched beneath his touch like a contented cat. "The first time was when we were kids. The minute I looked at you, the very first time we met, my tongue rolled right back toward my throat and I all but swallowed it, you were so pretty."

She leaned up, elbows braced against him. "But you were so awful to me. So rude. You hardly said two words."

"Tongue rolled up—couldn't swallow, remember?"

"Boys. Jeez." She shook her head, marveling.

Taking her hips in his hands, he rearranged her so he could slide back inside her, his erection having gotten a sudden second wind. "Girls," he said. "Good thing girls and boys fit together so well when they grow up."

She quivered around him, inside and out, her eyelids lowering to half-staff. "Yes, a very good thing indeed."

Cradling her face between his hands, he kissed her. "I loved you then, Brie-Brie. I love you now. You're mine forever."

"Forever," she vowed. "As your attorney, I would never allow you to accept anything less."

Then they sealed their promises in the most pleasurable of ways.

Read on for an excerpt from
Tracy Anne Warren's next novel,

*HAPPILY BEDDED BLISS*

Coming soon from Signet Select

*September 1818*
*Gloucestershire, England*

Lady Esme Byron hiked her sky blue muslin skirts up past her stocking-clad calves and climbed onto the wooden stile that divided Braebourne land from that of their nearest neighbor to the east, Mr. Cray.

Cray, a widower near her eldest brother, Edward's, age of forty, was rarely in residence and never complained about her trespassing on his land, so she was free to use it as if it were quite her own. Not that Braebourne didn't provide plenty of beautiful acreage to explore—it did, especially considering that her brother owned nearly half the county and more besides. But Cray possessed a lovely natural freshwater lake that sat a perfect walking distance from her family's house. The lake attracted a rich variety of wildlife, so there was always something fascinating to sketch. Plus, no one ever bothered her there; it was quite her favorite secret place.

She jumped down onto the other side of the stile, taking

far more care for the satchel of drawing supplies slung over her shoulder than she did for her fine leather half boots. She wobbled slightly as she sank ankle-deep into the mud. She stared at her boots for a few seconds, knowing her maid would give her a scold for sure. But she was always able to talk dear Grumbly around, so she wasn't worried.

Grabbing hold of the fence, she unstuck herself one boot at a time. She scraped the worst of the mess off into the nearby grass; then, with a swirl of her skirts, she continued on to her destination.

She sighed blissfully and turned her face up to the sun.

How good it was to be home again after weeks in the city.

How wonderful to be out in the open again, free to roam wherever she liked, whenever she liked.

A tiny, guilty frown wrinkled her brow, since technically she was supposed to be back at the estate helping entertain the houseguests visiting Braebourne. But all seven of her siblings and their families were in residence, even Leo and his new bride, Thalia, who had just returned with celebratory fanfare from their honeymoon tour of Italy. With so many Byrons available to make merry, she would hardly be missed.

Besides, her family was used to her penchant for disappearing by herself for hours at a time as she roamed the nearby woods and hills and fields. She would be back in time for dinner; that would have to be enough.

An exuberant bark sounded behind her and she glanced around in time to watch her dog, Burr, leap the stile and race toward her. She bent down and gave his shaggy head a scratch. "So, you're back, are you? Done chasing rabbits?"

He waved his golden flag of a tail in a wide arc, his

pink tongue lolling out in a happy grin, clearly unapologetic for having deserted her a couple of minutes earlier to hunt game in the bushes.

"Well, come along," she told him before starting off toward a stand of trees in the distance.

Burr trotted enthusiastically at her side.

Several minutes later, she reached the copse of trees that led to the lake. She was just about to step out of their protective shelter when she heard a splash.

She stopped and motioned Burr to do the same.

Someone, she realized, was swimming in the lake. Was it Mr. Cray? Was he back in residence?

A man emerged from the water—a man who most definitely was not Mr. Cray.

And who was most definitely *naked.*

Her eyes widened as she drank in the sight of his long, powerfully graceful form, his skin glistening with wet in the sunlight.

A quiet sigh of wonder slid from between her parted lips, her senses awash with the same kind of reverent awe she felt whenever she beheld something of pure, unadorned beauty.

Not that his face was the handsomest she had ever glimpsed—his features were far too strong and angular for ordinary attractiveness. Yet there was something majestic about him, his tall body exquisitely proportioned, even the unmentionable male part of him that hung impressively between his muscled thighs.

Clearly unaware that he was being observed, he casually slicked the water from his hair with his fingers, then walked deeper into the surrounding area of short grass that was kept periodically trimmed by the groundskeepers.

She shivered, her heart pounding wildly as she watched him settle onto the soft green canopy of grass and stretch out on his back. With a hand, she motioned again to Burr to remain quiet. She did the same, knowing if she moved now, the beautiful stranger would surely hear her.

One minute melted into two, then three.

Quite unexpectedly, she heard the soft yet unmistakable sound of a snore.

*Is he asleep?*

She smiled, realizing that's exactly what he was.

She knew she ought to leave; this was the perfect chance. But then he shifted, his face turning toward her, one hand resting at his waist, his knee bent at an elegant angle.

And she couldn't leave.

Not now.

Not when she was in the presence of such artistic majesty—as if the universe itself had given her a gift. How could she refuse the opportunity? She simply had to draw him.

Without giving the impulse so much as another moment's consideration, she sank quietly onto a nearby rock that provided her with an excellent view of her subject. Burr settled down next to her and laid his chin on his paws as she extracted her pencil and sketchbook from her bag and set to work.

Gabriel Landsdowne came abruptly awake, the late afternoon sun strong in his eyes. He blinked and sat up, giving his head a slight shake to clear out the last of the drowsy cobwebs.

He'd fallen asleep without even realizing it. Apparently, he was more tired than he'd thought. Then again, that's why he'd come here to Cray's, so he could spend a little time alone, doing nothing more strenuous than taking a leisurely swim and lazing away the day. He could have done the same at his own estate, of course, but the place always put him in a foul mood.

Too many bad memories.

Too many unwanted responsibilities to ignore.

His usual crowd would laugh to see him doing something as prosaic as taking a solitary afternoon nap. On the other hand, he was out of doors naked, so they would most certainly approve of that.

Smirking, he stood up, brushing an errant blade of grass from his bare butt. He was about to cross to the stand of bushes where he'd left his clothes when he heard a faint rustling sound behind him. He turned and stared into the foliage.

"Who is it? Is someone there?" he demanded.

The only answer was silence.

He looked again, but nothing moved; no one spoke.

Maybe it had been the wind?

Or an animal foraging in the woods?

Suddenly a dog burst from the concealment of the trees, its shaggy wheaten coat gleaming warmly in the sun. The animal stopped and looked at him, eyes bright and inquiring but not unfriendly. He seemed well fed but was of no particular breed, a medium-sized mix of some sort. Part hound and part something else.

"Who might you be, fellow?" Gabriel asked.

The dog wagged his tail and barked twice, then spun around and disappeared into the trees once more.

Just then, Gabriel thought he spied a flash of blue in the woods.

A bird?

The dog must have sensed it too and had gone off to chase whatever it was.

Shrugging in dismissal, Gabriel turned and went to retrieve his clothes.

"It's high time you were home, my lady," Grumbly scolded as Esme hurried into her bedroom a couple of minutes after the dressing gong rang. "I was on the verge of sending one of the footmen out after you. Och, and look at those boots. What new mischief have you been about this afternoon? Tromping in the mud."

"Oh, don't carry on, Grumbly," Esme said, using the maid's old nickname given to her when Esme was still in apron strings. "I went for a walk, then stopped at the stables afterward to check on Andromeda. Her wing is still healing and she needs food and exercise twice a day."

Andromeda was a hawk Esme had found in the woods last month, shot with an arrow. She'd nursed her through the worst and hoped the bird might be able to fly again with enough time and care.

Mrs. Grumblethorpe *tsk*ed and turned Esme around, her fingers moving quickly to unfasten the buttons on Esme's dress. "You and your animals. Always worrying over some poor, misbegotten creature. Rabbits and birds, hedgehogs and box turtles. You're forever dragging something back, to say nothing of all the cats and dogs and horses."

Three of Esme's cats—all strays she'd rescued—lay snoozing in various locations around her room, including a big orange male, Tobias, who was curled up on a cozy spot in the middle of her bed. Her maid didn't approve, but she'd given up that battle long ago.

Burr, who had trailed in with Esme when she'd returned, lay stretched out in front of the unlit fireplace hearth. He snored gently, clearly tired after their recent adventures.

Esme thought again of the splendid naked man at the

lake and the drawings of him that were now inside her sketchbook.

A flush rose on her skin.

She thought too of how he'd almost caught her as she'd been leaving. Good thing he'd assumed the noise she'd inadvertently made was Burr.

Good old Burr.

Who was the stranger? she wondered not for the first time. Certainly no one who lived in the neighborhood. She would have remembered a man like him. Peculiar, though, that he seemed oddly familiar, as if she had seen him somewhere before. She'd thought and thought and just couldn't place him.

Oh, well, it would come to her—or not. She wouldn't concern herself. After all, it wasn't as if she were likely to see him again, let alone be introduced.

She didn't have time to ruminate further as Grumbly removed her dress and half boots and sent her over to the washbasin to tidy herself for dinner.

In far less time than one might have imagined, Esme stood clean, elegantly coiffed and attired in an evening gown of demure white silk—presentable for company once again.

She'd hoped with the Season over, she might be able to put all the entertaining behind her for the year. But then Claire had decided to host one of her autumn country parties, inviting the usual gathering of friends and family, in addition to a few new acquaintances from London.

Esme sighed inwardly, wishing she could spend a quiet evening with just the family, then retire early with a good book.

Instead, she straightened her shoulders, fixed a smile on her lips, and headed downstairs.

* * *

"Might I procure a beverage for you, Lady Esme?"

Esme glanced up from where she sat on the end of the long drawing room sofa and looked into the eager gray eyes of Lord Eversley.

Only minutes before, the gentlemen had rejoined the ladies after dinner, strolling in on a wave of companionable talk, the faint lingering aromas of cigar smoke and port wine drifting in as well.

Esme had been listening with only partial attention to the other women's discussion of fashion when the men entered and Lord Eversley approached to make her a very elegant bow.

He'd been seated next to her at dinner, his conversation both pleasant and interesting. He was attractive, personable, well-mannered, and intelligent—in short, everything any sane young woman could want in a husband. Plus, he was heir to an earldom and a fortune that was impressive even by her family's standards.

Eversley had been one of her most attentive suitors this past Season and his presence here obviously amounted to Claire and Mallory's rather badly disguised attempt to further the relationship. A little nudge in the right direction, she could hear them saying, and wedding bells would ring.

She ought to be cross with them. Really, she should. But she knew they only meant well. They just wanted her to be as happily married as they were. If only they would believe her when she said that she wasn't interested in a husband.

Not right now.

Not for a good long while if she had any say in the matter.

Luckily, her oldest brother, Edward, was in no hurry

to get her off his hands, content to let her remain here at home for as many years as she liked.

The time would come when she needed to marry. Until then, she would have to find ways to avoid the overtures of interested young men, even ones as thoroughly eligible as Lord Eversley.

"Thank you," she said in answer to his question, "but I already had tea."

"Ah," he said, linking his hands at his back. "A stroll, then, perhaps? The gardens here at Braebourne are quite splendid, even by lantern light."

"Indeed they are. Again, I am afraid I must refuse. Another time perhaps? I have walked a great deal today, you understand, and my feet are far too weary for another outing at present."

Her feet were never weary—everyone in the family knew she could beat paths through the fields like a seasoned foot soldier—but Lord Eversley didn't need to be apprised of that fact. Hopefully none of the others were listening and would give her away.

Yet apparently someone else *was* listening. Lettice Waxhaven—another of the London guests, who happened to have made her debut along with Esme this past spring—leaned forward at just that moment, a fierce gleam in her pale blue eyes. "Yes, where were you this afternoon, Lady Esme? We were all of us wondering, what could be so fascinating that you would vanish for the entirety of the afternoon?"

Esme hid her dislike for the other young woman behind a tight smile. Why her mother and Lettice's mother had to be old childhood friends who had been unexpectedly reacquainted this Season, she didn't know. It was because of the renewal of that friendship that Esme found herself far too often in Lettice's company.

"I was just out," Esme said. "Walking and sketching."

"Really? Pray tell, what is it you sketch?" Lettice asked as if she were actually interested—which she was clearly not.

But Esme wasn't thinking about Lettice's false sincerity. Instead, she was caught up in memories of the beautiful naked man by the lake and the drawings of him that she'd done while he slept. Suddenly she was grateful for the room's warmth, since it disguised the flush that crept over her neck and cheeks.

"Nature," she answered with a seemingly careless shrug. "Plants and animals. Anything that takes my fancy at the time."

And oh my, had the glorious stranger taken her fancy.

"Lady Esme is quite the accomplished artist," Lord Eversley said with enthusiasm. "I had the great good fortune to view a few of her watercolors when we were last in Town." He smiled at her, clearly admiring. "She is a marvel."

Lettice's mouth tightened, her eyes narrowing. It was no secret—at least not to Esme—that Lettice had long ago set her cap at Lord Eversley and that so far he had failed to take notice of her. Esme would have felt sorry for her were Lettice a nicer person.

Lettice blinked and rearranged her features into a sweet smile, as if realizing that she'd let slip the well-practiced air of kind innocence she wore like a mask. "Oh, I should so like to see your sketches. Perhaps you might show them to us?"

"Yes, Lady Esme," Eversley agreed. "I too would greatly enjoy a chance to view your newest work."

"Oh, that is most kind," Esme said, hedging. "But I suspect you would find my efforts disappointing."

"Impossible," Eversley disagreed. "You are too good

an artist to ever draw anything that could be deemed disappointing."

"You give me far too much credit, Lord Eversley. What I drew today amounts to nothing of importance. Just a few random studies, that's all."

Nude studies of an unforgettable male.

Sleek limbs corded with muscle.

A powerful, hair-roughened chest.

Narrow hips.

Taut buttocks.

Impressive genitalia—at least *she* found it impressive, considering it was the first real, flesh-and-blood set she'd ever seen.

And his face . . .

Planes and angles that begged for an artist's attention, rugged yet refined, bold and unabashed.

Captivating.

"Truly, they're mostly rubbish and I have no wish to offend anyone's eyes with the viewing," she said, hoping Eversley would take the hint and let that be the end of it.

Instead, he persisted. "You are too modest, Lady Esme. Why do you not let me be the judge?"

"Who is modest?" her brother Lawrence said, joining the conversation. A few others turned their heads to listen as well.

"Lady Esme," Eversley explained. "Miss Waxhaven and I are trying to persuade her to show off the sketches she did today, but she is too shy."

Leo, Lawrence's twin, laughed from where he sat next to his wife, Thalia. "Our Esme? Shy about her art? That doesn't sound likely."

"Yes, she's usually raring to share," Lord Drake Byron agreed.

"That's because even her bad drawings are better than anything the rest of us can do," Mallory said before she shot a glance over at Grace. "Except for Grace, of course. No offense, Grace, since you are a brilliant artist too."

Her sister-in-law smiled. "None taken." Grace looked at Esme. "Do let us see, dear. I know we would all enjoy a glimpse or two of your latest efforts. I particularly love the landscapes you do."

Cheers of agreement and encouragement rose from those gathered.

Esme's chest tightened. "No, I couldn't. Not tonight. Besides, my sketchbook is upstairs. There's no need for all this bother."

"It's no bother," Edward said. "We'll have one of the servants fetch it." He glanced over at the butler. "Please ask one of the maids to collect Lady Esme's sketchbook and have it brought here to the drawing room."

"Right away, Your Grace." The servant bowed and exited the room.

*No!* Esme wanted to shout.

But it was too late. Any further protestations on her part would look odd, causing speculation about why she was so adamant that no one see her sketches. When her siblings said that she had never before shown a great deal of modesty concerning her work, they were right.

This could still work out fine, so long as she didn't panic. For the most part, her sketchbook contained renderings of birds and animals, field flowers, trees in leaf and the landscapes for which Grace had shown a partiality. The sketches of the man were at the back of the book. So long as she was careful, she could show the innocent drawings in the front—and only those.

All too soon one of the footmen walked in, her blue clothbound sketchbook in hand.

She leapt to her feet and hurried across to take it before anyone else could. "Thank you, Jones."

Quickly, she clutched the sketchbook against her chest, collecting herself. Then she turned to face the waiting company.

"Here we are," she said brightly as she crossed to resume her seat. "Since you all wish to see, why don't I just hold up the drawings rather than passing the book around?"

Slowly she cracked open the book, careful to go nowhere near the back pages. She thumbed through, looking quickly for something she hadn't already shown her family.

"Ah, here we are," she said, relieved to have found a new sketch. "I drew this of the hills toward the village earlier today."

Actually, she'd drawn it last week.

She held up the book, fingers tight on the pages.

Murmurs of appreciation went around the room.

"Lovely," Lady Waxhaven said.

"Astounding," Lord Eversley pronounced. "As I said before, you are a marvel, Lady Esme. Show us another."

"All right."

Bending over the book again, she found a new sketch. This one of her dog Burr lying under a tree.

She held it up, eliciting more positive remarks and smiles from everyone—everyone, that is, except Lettice Waxhaven, who looked as if she wished she'd never started this.

That made two of them.

She showed one more of farmers in the field, then closed the book, holding it on her lap. "There. You have all had your art exhibition for the evening. Now, enough. Please go back to what you were doing before, talking and drinking and enjoying the evening."

"Esme is quite right," Claire said with a broad smile. "Let us make merry. Perhaps a game of cards or some dancing? I should dearly love to hear a tune."

"That sounds wonderful, Duchess," Lettice declared, openly enthusiastic. Her gaze went to Eversley. "Do you dance, my lord?"

"Indeed," he said. "Mayhap you could play for us, Miss Waxhaven? You're quite accomplished on the pianoforte, as I recall."

Then he turned to Esme. "Lady Esme, what about you? Would you care to take to the floor?"

Lettice Waxhaven's face drained of color.

Esme actually felt sorry for her—and rather cross with Lord Eversley for being so obtuse. She stood, intending to refuse him. But before she could, Lettice stalked forward and deliberately bumped her shoulder, though Lettice did a good job making it look unintentional.

The sketchbook flew out of Esme's grasp, pages fluttering wide before the book spun and landed on the floor.

She moved quickly to retrieve it, but Lettice Waxhaven's loud gasp let her know it was already too late. Everyone else was turning and looking, the page with the beautiful naked man lying open for them all to see.

Breath froze in Esme's chest and she couldn't seem to get enough air, her thoughts spinning as she tried to think of an explanation for what she'd drawn.

"What in Hades' name is that?" Lawrence said, his voice loud enough that she jumped.

"I believe we can all see *what* it is," Leo answered, his face wearing the identical look of shock and outrage as his identical twin's. "The only thing I want to know is how we're going to kill him."

"Kill who?" Esme squeaked, suddenly finding her voice.

Leo's and Lawrence's gazes shot to hers, while the rest of their family and friends looked on.

*"Northcote,"* Leo said, spitting out the name as if it were a curse.

"Our neighbor from Cavendish Square," Lawrence finished.

ALSO AVAILABLE FROM
*NEW YORK TIMES* BESTSELLING AUTHOR

# Tracy Anne Warren

# THE LAST MAN ON EARTH

When two rival ad executives clash over business and power, they find out that sometimes heated rivals in the office make for scorching bed partners behind closed doors...

**"Few things are more fun than an enemies-to-lovers romance, and Warren delivers with *The Last Man on Earth.*"**
**—*The New York Times Book Review***

**"Zippy yet soulful...deeply relatable characters and strong writing make this a good start to a connected series."**
**—*Publishers Weekly***

**tracyannewarren.com**

Available wherever books are sold or at penguin.com

facebook.com/LoveAlwaysBooks

s0569

ALSO AVAILABLE FROM
*NEW YORK TIMES* BESTSELLING AUTHOR

# Tracy Anne Warren

# THE MAN PLAN

Ivy Grayson is coming to Manhattan to pursue her dreams. First stop: the luxury apartment of a long-time family friend—billionaire financier James Jordon. The last time James saw Ivy she was just a girl—one he'd always thought of as his "little sister." Now she's a dynamic woman who knows what she wants, and how to get it. And what she wants is James.

**"Fans of feel good contemporary romances will adore *The Man Plan*."**
**—Caffeinated Book Reviewer**

**tracyannewarren.com**

Available wherever books are sold or at
penguin.com

facebook.com/LoveAlwaysBooks

s0568

ALSO AVAILABLE FROM
*NEW YORK TIMES* BESTSELLING AUTHOR

# Tracy Anne Warren

# THE BEDDING PROPOSAL

*The Rakes of Cavendish Square*

Lord Leo Byron is bored with the aristocratic company he keeps; he needs a distraction, preferably in the form of a beautiful new female companion. So when he sets eyes on fascinating and scandalous divorcée Lady Thalia Lennox, he's determined to make her intimate acquaintance. But the spirited woman seems to have no intention of accepting his advances no matter how much he chases....

Once a darling of Society, Thalia Lennox now lives on its fringes. The cruel lies that gave her a notoriously wild reputation have also left her with a broken heart and led to a solemn vow to swear off men. Still, Leo Byron's bold overtures are deliciously tempting....

**"Splendidly emotional and delicously sensual."**
**—Romance Junkies**





s0608